WAR

THE TRUE REIGN SERIES, BOOK 3

JENNIFER ANNE DAVIS

REIGN PUBLISHING

Published by Reign Publishing

Cover Design by KimG-Design
Editing by Mary C. Weller

ISBN (paperback): 978-0-9992395-6-8
eISBN: 978-0-9992395-5-1
Library of Congress Registration Number: TX 7-965-222

~

Addison

~

The third in my own personal trilogy.
You are my inspiration for Rema.
May your spunkiness and love for life never cease.

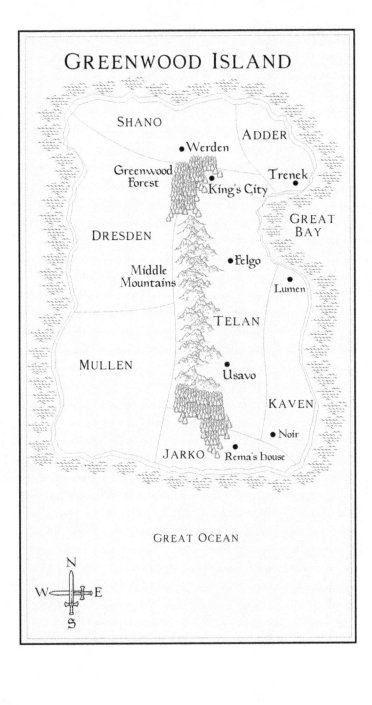

GREENWOOD ISLAND

SHANO

ADDER

• Werden

Greenwood
Forest

Trenek

• King's City

GREAT
BAY

DRESDEN

• Felgo

Middle
Mountains

Lumen

TELAN

MULLEN

Usavo

KAVEN

• Noir

JARKO   Rema's house

GREAT OCEAN

N
W   E
S

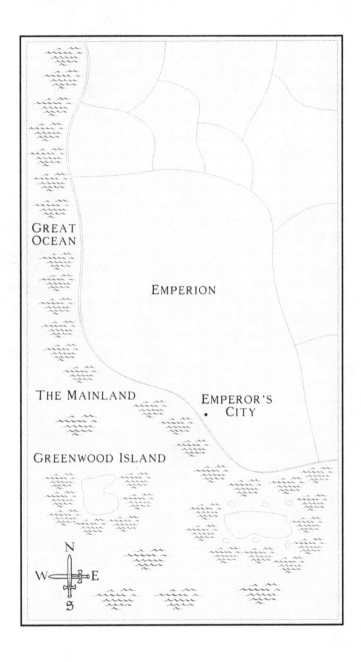

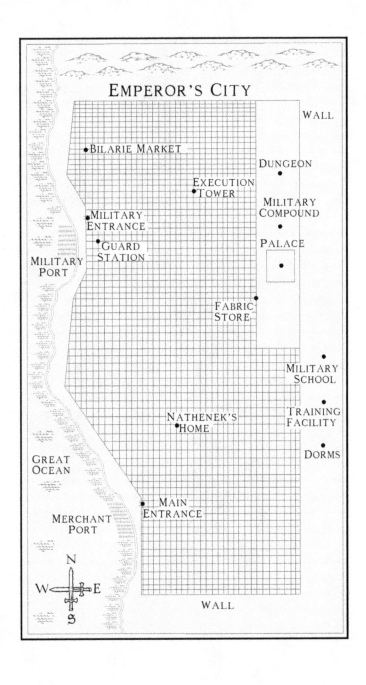

PROLOGUE

Mako

*M*ako knelt next to the wooden shack, observing the Emperion ship. It was difficult to see the details of the vessel since it was the dead of night and a thick, heavy fog concealed the moon and stars. "No one's about," he mumbled to Darmik and Savenek. Even though a few men roamed the pier, he didn't see a single person aboard the large ship.

"Maybe we beat Captain here?" Savenek suggested.

It was possible. They had taken the east tunnel down the Middle Mountains, traveling nonstop for three days to reach the town of Plarek, located at the Great Bay. If Captain had gone a different way, it could take him another two days to arrive.

Darmik shook his head. "Something's wrong. I can feel it."

"There's only one way to find out," Mako said. They had to sneak closer to the ship and investigate. Besides himself, there were only six others in their group. They would be far outnumbered if Emperion soldiers were lying in wait for them.

"I'll go," Darmik offered.

Mako hesitated. They couldn't afford to lose Darmik—he was

their best bet at rescuing Rema. However, if Emperion soldiers were indeed aboard the ship, they most likely wouldn't harm Darmik since he was the prince of Greenwood Island. Mako nodded. "If it's safe for the rest of us, signal with your left hand."

Wasting no time, Darmik slid into the shadows, making his way toward the ship.

Mako whispered to Savenek, "Go and tell the others to hold their positions by the storefronts. Tell them to be prepared to attack if necessary."

Savenek nodded and crept away.

Mako watched as Darmik approached the ship, crouching low, withdrawing his sword, and ascending the ramp. When he reached the top, he jumped over the railing, landing on the deck. Mako could no longer see him. No shouts rang out, no warning cries arose, and no sounds of fighting ensued.

A few moments later, Savenek rejoined Mako. "Audek, Neco, Ellie, and Vesha are ready when you are."

Mako nodded, continuing to watch the ship for any movement.

"Is something the matter?" Savenek asked.

"No."

"You seem tense."

"Because I am. Be quiet and keep your eyes open."

Savenek unsheathed his sword, clutching it in his right hand as he sat alongside Mako as he watched the ship.

Darmik appeared at the bow of the ship, giving the all-clear signal.

"Let's go," Mako ordered. The two of them joined Darmik aboard the vessel.

"They're not here," Darmik said, punching the mast.

Dread, as thick as the night fog, covered Mako. "Savenek, go and check the marina's log. See if another ship has recently left."

He nodded and hurried away. Mako observed the pier. The majority of business was conducted during the daylight hours so

2

very few people were about. A few sailors tended to a boat, while others slept just off the wharf.

"There are two Emperion soldiers below deck. I knocked them out and tied them up," Darmik said, pacing like a caged animal.

"We can question them when they wake," Mako said. Darmik's eyes narrowed, seemingly aware of the mistake he'd made in rendering the men unconscious. "In the meantime, let's go and ask the people on the pier if they've seen anything." They descended the ramp. Mako was glad to be back on solid ground.

"They left!" Savenek shouted as he ran over to them. "The ledger states that a merchant vessel set sail for Emperion an hour ago."

Darmik's hands shook. "Everyone on the Emperion ship, now!" he shouted. "We're leaving!"

"Calm down and think like a commander," Mako scolded. "We need to talk about this."

"There's nothing to discuss." Darmik leaned toward him. "Every minute we stand here arguing adds to the distance growing between Rema and us. If we want to save her, we have to leave immediately." His eyes shone bright with a mixture of fury and fear.

Mako understood his reaction; however, in order to have a solid plan in place, they had to think and act rationally. "Why did Captain take a merchant vessel instead of his own military ship?"

"The merchant vessel was slated to leave in the morning," Savenek said. "It was fully stocked with the crew nearby."

"What about the Emperion crew?" Mako asked. "Where are they if they're not on board?"

"The crew and soldiers are inland," Darmik muttered. "They've infiltrated the army at King's City, a two-day's ride from here."

Since Captain's military ship wasn't ready to sail, he'd chartered a regular merchant vessel. Mako glanced at the Emperion ship. "So we need supplies and a crew to sail that thing?"

Darmik nodded, pacing on the dock.

"Savenek—find a crew for hire. Check the local taverns. Darmik—tell Neco and Ellie to acquire food and water. Have Audek and Vesha obtain any other provisions you deem necessary. As soon as we have everything, you can set sail."

"What about you?" Darmik asked. "Aren't you coming with us?"

"No," Mako said. "I can't leave the rebel army. We need to go forward with our plans and prepare for battle. We'll be ready when you get back from Emperion."

Darmik gave a curt nod and took off running.

Mako handed the sailor a large burlap bag of coins.

"This will only be enough to get them there," he said.

Glancing at the ship, Mako watched Savenek sprint up the ramp, carrying a crate of food. "I understand." He pulled out another bag of coins, handing it to him.

The sailor took the money and slipped it under his weathered jacket. "Once the food and water are loaded, we'll set sail." He turned and boarded the ship with his crew.

These sailors came highly recommended by the local tavern owner—a man who had worked with Mako's men on more than one occasion. He promised that they were good, hardworking, and loyal sailors.

Savenek ran down the ramp, stopping before Mako. "Everything's on board."

"What about the items Darmik requested?"

He rolled his eyes. "It's all there—the weapons, uniforms, everything."

"Good." Mako didn't know what else to say to Savenek. The boy was like a son to him, and this could very well be the last time he saw him.

"Stop," Savenek said, putting his hands on Mako's shoulders. "I'll be fine. You trained me to be a competent soldier."

He nodded. "Be careful. Emperion people are very different from us."

"Let's go!" Darmik shouted over the ship's railing. Neco, Audek, Ellie, and Vesha were already on board.

"We'll be back with Rema, I promise."

"Don't make promises you can't keep."

Savenek smiled. "I'll return with Queen Amer. Then we'll invade King's City and retake the throne. I promise." Excitement shone on the boy's face. He spun around and sprinted up the ramp, joining Darmik.

Mako hated having to place his trust in someone he'd once considered his enemy; nevertheless, Darmik had been to Emperion before. If anyone could sneak into the hostile kingdom and rescue Rema, it was him.

The sails went up into the dark night, the fog slithering around them. Water slapped against the ship as it slowly moved away from the dock, disappearing into the thick, ocean mist.

CHAPTER ONE

Rema

*R*ema peeled her heavy eyelids open. Everything swayed before her. Rolling onto her side, she vomited. When she went to wipe her mouth, she discovered her wrists were tied together with thick rope.

Where am I? What is going on? The last thing she remembered was standing in her bedchamber, an arm snaking around her chest, and a cloth being shoved over her mouth and nose. Then everything had gone black.

She pushed herself up, her arms shaking and head pounding. Sitting on the wooden floor, it felt as if everything around her was moving. Vomit rose in the back of her throat. She took several deep breaths, trying to calm her queasy stomach. This was probably from whatever toxin with which she'd been dosed. The feeling would go away once it was out of her system.

Glancing around, several crates of food and barrels lined the walls. Most likely, this was a storage room. A few beams of light filtered in between the wood plank walls. She tried to stand, but her ankles were also bound together. The smell from her own vomit made her stomach heave. She crawled to the corner farthest from where she had thrown up.

Leaning against a barrel, she closed her eyes, waiting for the nausea to pass. Was she somewhere in the fortress? Who would have done this to her and why? It felt as if she was moving up and down. Another side effect from the toxin no doubt.

Several voices shouted from somewhere above her. Several feet pounded by, the ceiling vibrating. All the floors in the castle were stone. The only wooden one was in the barn, and that was only one level. Cold fear prickled through her. Where was she?

More yelling and feet stomping came from above. A loud groan vibrated around her as the floor shifted. Rema was thrown sideways, and a couple of the crates toppled over beside her. She used them to push herself into a standing position. It felt as if the floor moved. How much toxin had she inhaled? Since her ankles were bound, she hopped toward the door. The walls around her creaked, and the floor shifted again. She lost her balance, falling to the floor.

The door flew open and light burst into the small storage room. A figure dressed in black strolled in. "You're finally awake." The man towered above her.

His voice had a soft drawl to it, very different from the way people on Greenwood Island spoke. "You're the Emperion assassin," she whispered, her heart racing.

The man crouched before her. "I am," he said, his voice low and hypnotic. "Welcome aboard *The Scorpion*."

Everything made sense—the vomiting, the feeling that the floor was moving, the food in the storage room. Rema was on a ship.

"I'm taking you to Emperion. The emperor wants to see you beheaded." He grabbed her arm, yanking her to her feet. "I can't have you die before we get there." He tossed her over his shoulder and exited the room.

She squinted against the bright sunlight as the assassin

plopped her on her feet. Her fear vanished as she beheld the magnificent sight before her. Enormous, ivory sails vigorously flapped against the wind as the ship cut through the ocean. She hopped to the railing, looking over the side in amazement. Water surrounded the ship in all directions.

Rema wanted to scream with joy and hug someone—she was sailing across the ocean! Granted, she was on her way to be executed, but she had faced a similar situation before and lived. It would do no good to dwell on that. She had always wanted to see the world, and this might be her only chance to do so. Besides, an opportunity to escape could present itself.

"Why are you smiling?" the assassin asked in his odd accent.

Now that she was outside, she could see her kidnapper better. He appeared to be in his early thirties and had a tall, stocky build, blond hair cut close to his head, and freckles covering his face. She'd never met anyone else who had blond hair like hers before. His blue eyes narrowed, studying her. She glanced away, not answering him. Taking a deep breath, she smelled the cool, salty air as the sun warmed her skin.

The assassin grabbed her hands. She tried jerking them away, but his grip was too strong. His deft fingers untied the knot, and her bindings fell to the floor. He knelt and fumbled at the rope around her ankles.

"You understand you're going to be executed?" he asked as he stood before her.

"Yes." The water went on as far as she could see.

"Then why aren't you crying?" He scratched his head, observing her as if she was a complicated puzzle he couldn't solve.

Rema laughed. "I'm on a ship, sailing across the ocean." *The ocean!* She'd never left Greenwood Island and had never been on a ship before. Even though her circumstances were far from ideal, she planned to make the most of this experience. And right now, she felt a sense of freedom.

The man shook his head.

"Why did you undo my bindings?" she asked, curious. She flung her arms out, taking advantage of not being tied up, and let the wind rush around her, whipping her hair and clothes every which way.

He smirked, leaning against the railing next to her. "Something tells me you aren't going anywhere."

Which was true—she couldn't swim her way to land. She'd have to wait until the ship docked to try and get away.

"If you try to escape, I'll gut you and take the pieces to the emperor." Something sharp dug into her side. Glancing down, the assassin held a small knife just below her ribs. She blinked, unable to believe how fast he moved. If he wanted her dead, she'd be dead. He withdrew the knife and stood with his arms crossed, studying her. "You seem far too content to be aboard this ship."

Rema closed her eyes and tipped her head back, swaying with the ship's steady rhythm. Opening her eyes, she laughed. "This is magnificent!" Never in her wildest dreams had she envisioned being aboard a ship.

The assassin shook his head again. "Since you've found your sea legs, I'm going to put you to work instead of keeping you in the storage room."

Her shoulders relaxed. He wasn't going to lock her back up. Interesting.

He furrowed his eyebrows. "Follow me." Turning, he headed toward a narrow staircase leading from the lower deck to the upper one.

"What's your name?" she asked, hurrying after him.

"Captain." He climbed the steps two at a time. "However, the man in charge of this ship is also bestowed the same title, so you may call me by my real name—Nathenek."

"Where are we going?" She wanted the opportunity to explore the ship.

He abruptly stopped and faced her. "Aren't you the queen of Greenwood Island's rebel forces?"

She didn't know why he asked such a ridiculous question. *He* kidnapped *her*. He should know very well who he'd taken. "Yes." She placed her hands on her hips.

Nathenek leaned toward her. She refused to back away and show fear, even though she desperately wanted to put some space between them.

"You don't cry when I inform you of your pending execution, you haven't barked out orders, and you haven't made crazy demands. You are unlike any noble woman I have ever met."

She laughed. Didn't he know she was raised on a horse farm as a commoner? "Do you usually converse with the people you intend to kill? Does it make it more fun to get to know them before murdering them?"

"No." His eyes darkened. "When I'm given a target, I hunt that person down and kill him quickly. This is the first time I've . . . traveled with my assignment."

"Well, you're not what I'd imagined an assassin would be."

Nathenek remained in her personal space, his hair so short it didn't move in the wind. His uniform reminded her of Darmik's— black pants and a simple tunic bearing the emperor's crest. Instead of blue accents, the crest was interwoven with emerald green.

"Have you met many assassins?" he asked. "Do you employ them in your rebel army?" He cocked his head to the side, awaiting her response.

She squinted against the bright sun. "You're the first one I've met."

"You can be sure I'll be the last."

A rope came loose and a sailor scrambled to catch it. Nathenek whipped out a knife, throwing it. The knife sailed through the air, piercing the rope to the mast. At least if he decided to kill her, he'd be quick. She swallowed the lump in her throat.

Once they arrived at Emperion, Rema would make every attempt to escape. For now, she would do her best to try and get to know this strange man. Perhaps he had a weakness or soft spot she could uncover and use to her advantage.

Nathenek spun on his heel and headed inside. Rema followed him through a doorway. It took a moment for her eyes to adjust to the dark room.

"This is the galley. You can help the cook." He nodded toward the young man holding a large knife in one hand with several potatoes piled before him on the counter.

"The kitchen?" she asked in disbelief. "Because I'm a woman, you assume I want to work in the kitchen? Cooking?" Without meaning to, she pointed her finger at Nathenek's chest. "You may not be like other assassins, but you *are* a typical man."

The cook stopped chopping the potatoes and stared at Rema. "Ain't no girlie working in here with me."

"I need to do something with her," Nathenek mumbled. "There has to be a job for her here."

"Can I please work outside on the deck instead of in the galley?" She wanted the sun on her face and the ocean around her, not to be cooped up in this small, windowless room.

"You need to talk to the ship's captain about the girlie," the cook said. "He won't want her messin' up stuff or gittin' in trouble. Ships ain't meant to have girlies on board."

"Fine." Nathenek grabbed her arm, taking her out to the upper deck.

Rema walked with a wide gait to maintain her balance as Nathenek dragged her to where a man dressed in a crisp, blue uniform stood, peering through a long tube. This man must be the captain in charge of *The Scorpion*.

He put the tube down and turned to glare at her. "What's she doing above deck?"

"I plan to put her to work," Nathenek said. "What job can she do?" He still had a tight grip on her arm. She wanted to pull free, but something about the ship's captain made her stand still.

"She can't be up here."

"I don't want her down in the storage room during our voyage. Emperor Hamen expects her delivered alive."

"She's not going to die from being tied up down there. On the other hand, she will have problems if she remains out here. I won't vouch for her safety. Some of my men haven't been with a woman in a long time."

It felt as if she'd jumped into the icy water of the Somer River. The thought never crossed her mind that the sailors on board would violate her. What if Nathenek didn't care what these men did to her? What if he allowed them to abuse her, so long as they didn't kill her? She glanced over the railing. The drop was high, but nothing she couldn't handle. Yet, once she was in the water, how far could she swim? How long would she last? Was death by drowning better? Probably.

Nathenek's hand squeezed her arm, and she let out a small cry.

"Very well," he snapped. "I will keep her with me." He dragged her back down the stairs and through another doorway.

"Please not the storage room." Not only had she vomited in there, but there weren't any windows. "If I'm going to die soon, can't you grant me this one small mercy?"

Inside the dark hallway, the rise and fall of the ship worsened, making her stomach roll. The assassin hauled her past several doors. He pulled out a key, about to unlock one of them, when a man stepped into the hallway behind her. She spun around and came face to face with Trell.

"What are you doing here?" she asked. Had Nathenek kidnapped him, too? He didn't answer.

The old man glanced at Nathenek. "What are you doing with her?"

Nathenek unlocked the door and shoved Rema inside, slamming it closed behind her. On the other side of the door, the two men spoke in hushed whispers, too soft for her to hear. What was Trell doing here? If Nathenek hadn't kidnapped the old man, then were they in league with one another? After all, Trell was from Emperion.

Groaning in frustration, she examined the tiny room. There was a single bed with a footlocker at the end of it and a small desk under the round window.

Nathenek came in, locking the door behind him. He grabbed the chair from the desk and shoved it under the handle. Rema froze, having no idea what to do. Did this man intend to violate her? She quickly thought of everything Savenek taught her. But then what? Even if she managed to get free from the assassin, where would she go? Could she jump to her death?

"Why do you suddenly look so frightened?" he asked.

Biting her lip, she glanced at the door.

"That's to keep you safe. So no one can get in. I always secure my bedchamber. It's habit." He walked over and plopped on the bed. "This is my berth. You can stay here until we arrive at Emperion. It's not much, but at least it has a window."

"Why is Trell here?" she demanded.

"I'm not going to discuss him with you."

She let the issue drop, for now. If she pushed too hard, he'd probably throw her in the storage room.

Finding it difficult to stand, she slid down to the floor and leaned against the footlocker. "How long?" she asked, holding her head against her hands. She would not vomit in this room.

"What?" Nathenek kicked off his boots and stretched out on his back.

"Until we get there."

"Two weeks." He crossed his ankles and put his hands under his head.

The boat lurched to the side, but nothing in the room moved. Curious, she looked at the bed and desk. Both had been nailed to the floor.

"Since I can't work, what are we going to do all day?"

He sighed. "Unfortunately, there's not much to do. This is my first assignment off the mainland. On the journey to Greenwood Island, I studied maps memorizing the terrain and city placement. I reviewed Darmik's history at Emperion's military school. I thought he'd be assisting me. Things obviously didn't turn out the way I planned." He let out a deep breath. "I also exercised daily. That's about it."

Rema needed to do some form of exercise to maintain her strength; otherwise, she'd have no chance to escape. "For the next two weeks, am I just going to sit here?"

Nathenek didn't respond.

If she couldn't be on the top deck, this journey was going to be miserable. Her stomach felt queasy again.

"What did you think of Greenwood Island?" she asked, trying to focus on something other than feeling so awful.

"It was cold, wet, and green."

"Is it very different from Emperion?"

"Does it matter?" His head tilted to the side so he could see her.

"I guess not. I'm just trying to pass the time."

He grunted. "I didn't particularly care for it."

"Because it's so different from what you're used to?"

"Yes and no." He focused on the low ceiling above him. "I grew up in the military. My family sent me into service when I was eight years old."

"So young?"

"That's typical. Families are required to send a certain number of children to the emperor's service."

Aunt Maya had taught her a few things about Emperion. It wasn't much, but she wished she'd paid more attention. She never thought there would be a reason to know the details of the empire.

"I excelled in stealth warfare so I was put on track to be part of an elite team. When I was fifteen, I saw my first battle." Nathenek remained quiet for several minutes. Rema wondered if he was done talking, or simply mulling over thoughts from his past.

"I won't go into details, but when the battle was over, I was a changed man." Rema thought she heard a hint of sadness and regret in his voice.

"I was recruited to the emperor's personal guard. On duty one day, the emperor approached and asked if I wanted to serve as one of his assassins. To be chosen is a great honor, and I accepted. I am one of only three dozen that do his bidding."

"How many people have you killed?" she asked, not really wanting to know, but thankful he was talking to her.

He shook his head. "Up until this trip, eighty-two."

His answer seemed strange. Realization dawned on her. It was as if a cold bucket of water was tossed on her head. How had she forgotten about the massacre in Jarko? Her arms shook and breathing became difficult. This person was responsible for the deaths of hundreds.

Rema sprang to her feet, rushed to the bed, and jumped on top of Nathenek—her hands wrapping around his neck. Consumed with an intense desire to watch the life drain from him, she squeezed harder. Tears streamed down her face. "How could you kill all those innocent people?"

His blue eyes looked steadily at hers.

He wasn't fighting back.

What was she doing? Letting go, she stared at her hands. Had she really just tried to kill him?

Nathenek reached up and took hold of her shoulders. In one swift motion, he flipped her over and onto the bed. Now he straddled her.

"How could you?" Rema choked out. "All those innocent people in Jarko. You killed them." She couldn't stop crying.

"I told you, I'm a soldier. I grew up in the military. It's ingrained in us to follow every command." His voice was soft, yet there was a dangerous edge to it.

"Let me go."

He released her and stood next to the bed. "Don't ever touch me again. Otherwise, I'll kill you."

"Why didn't you fight back? Why did you let me strangle you?" She sat up on his bed.

"Why did you try to kill me?" he countered.

"I don't know," she whispered. "I wasn't thinking."

"Exactly." His face scrunched with some emotion she didn't understand. "It was done from passion—hate. It wasn't consciously or purposely done."

She slid her feet to the floor but didn't stand.

"I'm not sure how to say this so I make sense and you understand. But in Jarko, it's not what you think." Nathenek sat on the floor before her. "I'm a soldier. I am given an order, and I always carry it out. In Jarko, no one would speak about you. I was convinced you were hiding somewhere in the region. Normally, I am hidden in the shadows when I kill with my dagger. But in Jarko, everyone saw me. When we couldn't discover your location, Prince Lennek gave the order to burn everyone's homes. When people ran out screaming, he ordered them to be shot with arrows. I obeyed." He bowed his head. "It reminded me of battle. Something I loathe."

"Lennek gave the order? Not you?" The prince had always appeared disinterested when it came to the army.

"Yes. I was sent for you, and only you. I had no business killing anyone else. Especially women and children. Prince Lennek gave the command, and we carried it out. No one questioned the order. That's when I left him and started hunting you on my own."

"Why are you confiding in me?" Did it make him feel better to confess his crimes? Especially to someone who was going to die? "You're an assassin. You should be used to it."

Nathenek knelt before her. "You asked why I *allowed* you to strangle me. I was trying to explain myself. My *crimes* are orders I follow. Not an act of passion." He stood and glanced out the window. It was too high for her to see anything but blue sky. "I want to remind you to *never* touch me again." His voice was hard, cold, and lifeless. He gestured toward the bed, indicating it was time for her to move. She slid back to the floor, leaning against the wall.

"You are my eighty-third assignment. I have completed eighty-two in the time allotted and without a single issue. You are the first to present a complication. Luckily, Darmik led me right to you. He was so injured that he never noticed me following him." The corners of his lips rose in a faint smile.

Nathenek sat on his bed. "I will hand you over to the emperor, and my eighty-third assignment will be complete."

Rema tried with all her might not to think about Darmik. However, she couldn't keep the images of him away. What did he think happened to her? Did he know the assassin had kidnapped her? Or did he think she ran away? Or was she presumed dead?

Closing her eyes, she felt Darmik's soft lips against hers. His strong hands caressing her back.

Oh Darmik, she thought, *I'm so sorry for being captured. I love you.*

CHAPTER TWO

Darmik

*D*armik clutched the railing, digging his nails into the wood. *This can't be happening,* he thought. His worst nightmare had come true—Rema was taken from him. He would kill anyone who harmed her. Bile rose in the back of his throat just thinking about her alone with Captain. He punched the railing and let out a ragged scream. The thought of her stepping foot on Emperion soil was almost too much for him to bear. If there was any chance of saving her, it was up to him. And he was running out of time.

Glancing at the stars, he tried not to let his imagination get the better of him. It would do no good thinking about what was happening to Rema at this very moment. Was she scared and alone? Injured? Balling his hands into fists, he tried to contain his rage. He knew exactly what Emperion did to their prisoners.

"Standing at the bow of the ship in the dead of night won't get us there any faster," Savenek said as he came and stood next to him.

The sails of the ship were fully extended, the boat traveling at high speed. Still, it wasn't fast enough. "What are you doing out here?" This man had no right to worry about Rema—that was Darmik's job.

"I couldn't sleep. Between vomiting and my head pounding, this journey isn't off to a very good start."

"It'll pass," Darmik said, unable to suppress a small smile. He crossed his arms and leaned against the railing, staring at the man before him. "Why do you think Captain took her alive? Why not kill her and take evidence to Emperor Hamen?"

Savenek leaned over the railing and vomited. The motion of the ship wasn't pleasant, yet Darmik felt no compulsion to expel the contents of his stomach. He hoped Savenek was tougher than this in battle; otherwise, they'd never make it out of Emperion alive.

Savenek wiped his mouth with the back of his hand. "I've been wondering about that. It's almost as if he wants you to follow him."

"For what purpose?" The chilly wind whipped around Darmik's body.

Savenek slid to the floor, leaning against the side of the ship. "I don't know. I can't think straight when I feel this awful." His face turned pasty white.

Pacing on the deck, Darmik tried to figure out what Captain's plan was. If he intended to take Rema to the emperor to be executed, he'd have to keep it quiet so no one knew of the threat she posed to the throne.

"How can you even walk?" Savenek moaned. "My legs can barely hold me up."

Neco came out from below decks, carrying a bucket. He dumped it over the side of the ship.

"Not you, too," Darmik said, exasperated.

His friend glared at him. "Everyone below is vomiting." He turned and went back inside.

Darmik resumed pacing. "Captain left me a calling card. It said,

Thank you for the hunt. Although it was a little tedious, you led me right to her. —C—." Clasping his hands behind his back, he stopped in front of Savenek, looking down at him. "Maybe it's a clue and not a calling card?" There had to be a reason for Captain's actions. This was a highly skilled, professional assassin.

"You're overthinking it. He's taunting you to make you feel guilty. After all, it's your fault Captain found her in the first place."

"I want to know if your theory is correct. If Captain wants us to follow, then are we walking into a trap?"

"Why would he care about us?" He rubbed his face.

Darmik squatted so he was eye level with Savenek. "That is precisely what I'm trying to figure out."

Savenek abruptly jumped to his feet, vomiting over the side of the ship again.

Darmik shook his head. There was a lot to do before they arrived on the mainland. "I'm going to bed. When you feel better and can strategize and plan with me, let me know."

Still bent over the side, Savenek raised his hand in acknowledgment.

After tossing and turning for several hours, worrying about Rema, Darmik finally gave up trying to sleep. He shoved his feet into his boots and left his room. A foul stench assaulted him in the hallway. Covering his nose, he ran to the ladder, quickly climbing it. As he stepped onto the deck, the fresh sea air cleared his nostrils.

However, Darmik was not prepared for the sight before him. "You have to be kidding me."

Neco scowled at him while rubbing Ellie's back as she vomited over the side of the boat, Savenek was sprawled on the floor with a green-faced Vesha kneeling next to him, and Audek hung over the railing moaning.

"Is every single one of you sick?" Darmik asked. "How are we going to plan to rescue Rema when none of you can even walk? I wanted to go alone, but all of you insisted on coming. I told you this wasn't going to be easy." He looked at the sky, trying to clear his impatience before he snapped. "You have until the end of the day, and then I expect everyone to start strategizing with me. Is that clear?"

They all groaned which he assumed meant yes. He turned on his heel and went to speak with the helmsman.

The elderly gentleman smiled as he approached. "I take it it's their first time at sea?"

"Yes, the whole lot of them." Darmik folded his arms. "Any news?"

The helmsman shook his head. "I have a man posted on the main mast whose sole purpose is to search for the merchant vessel."

"It had a head start of several hours. If we can't catch it, is it possible to arrive before it does?"

"If the map you gave me is accurate, and Captain is headed to the main port like you suspect, then I believe we will be able to dock before him. This ship is smaller and faster. If the weather holds, we can do it."

"Excellent."

"There is one additional matter that needs to be addressed," the helmsman said, ducking his head. "I need someone to clean up the mess in the sleeping quarters. I don't have any men to spare."

"I'll do it," Darmik growled. "Just get us there as fast as you can."

~

Darmik was sick to his stomach—not from cleaning below deck or the motion of the boat—but because of what he'd seen. He knew this was a military ship built for speed. Apparently, it was also designed to transport prisoners. The first level consisted of the sleeping quarters and kitchen. Under that level was the armory, storage facility, and human cages. Each cage contained a trough for food and water, chains for the prisoner's wrists and ankles, and a bucket for bodily functions. Next to the cages was a long table lined with several instruments used for torturing people. More terrifying than that sight, was seeing blood and bones in the cages and on the table.

After making the gruesome discovery, Darmik went to get some fresh air. What if he was too late and couldn't save Rema? Or the emperor—his uncle—refused to release her? Someone could be torturing her right now.

He rubbed his hands over his face. He knew, better than anyone that he couldn't allow himself to think about the worst-case scenarios. Emperion loved to use psychological intimidation to torture their prisoners. Darmik couldn't let them succeed. He had to focus on the task at hand—saving Rema. He would be no good to her if he started thinking about the *what-ifs*. He'd sworn to devise a plan to save her, and he would. No matter what.

"Don't tell me you're getting sick now," Savenek said, coming to join him at the bow of the ship. "Serves you right."

Darmik shook his head. It was hard to convey the ruthlessness of Emperion to someone who had never been there—someone as egotistical and arrogant as Savenek.

"I assume you have a plan," Savenek said, leaning on the rail next to him.

"No, I don't. There are too many variables. I have a couple of ideas, but nothing set in stone."

Savenek smiled. "Then I'll just have to come up with something myself." His mood had much improved. He'd obviously found his balance aboard the ship.

"If you're ready to start strategizing, then go inside and get everyone. We'll meet in the room at the end of the hallway. There's a table with several chairs in there."

Savenek didn't move. "I know this is a near impossible mission; that it's unlikely we'll all survive. But I feel like there's something I'm missing. Something you're not telling me." He leaned over the railing, watching the rough ocean below.

Darmik propped his elbows on the railing. "What you're missing is an understanding of your enemy." Trell's words came back to him. *Most battles are won by those who understand their enemy. I've always found one only has to look to the arts. Sculptures, books, paintings. They reveal the true identity of a culture. If you understand that, then you know your enemy. You can find their weakness and attack.*

"I fear we are a step behind Captain—that he is playing some sort of game we don't even understand much less know we're playing." If Darmik failed to save Rema, his companions were doomed. He wished they'd stayed behind.

"Tell me about the emperor so I have an idea of what we'll face."

"There are no words to describe him." Darmik closed his eyes, trying to banish the memories. "I will say this—he always knows his enemy. The emperor figures out what his enemy wants most, loves the most, and uses it against him."

"But he's your uncle so that has to help."

That strained relationship was their only hope of saving Rema at this point. "Emperor Hamen is worse than my father."

Savenek raised his eyebrows. "I find that hard to believe."

"Go below deck. See what's on the bottom level. That will give you a small glimpse of what we're about to walk into."

"Okay."

After he left, Darmik stared out at the great ocean before him. He never thought he'd return to Emperion—the war-driven, land-hungry, empire. Unwanted images flashed through his mind—standing before his entire military class, naked, being whipped; being submerged underwater, held down, unable to breathe;

having to take the new cadets, only ten years old, and beat them with a stick for crying out in the middle of the night because they missed their parents; and a completely lethal, obedient army that carried out any order the emperor gave, without question.

What was this savage kingdom going to do to Rema? Simply execute her? Or would the emperor destroy her mind and body before killing her? Darmik's uncle held little regard for family. Hamen never showed any kindness toward him when he was there for his training.

"I figured you were up here making yourself go mad," Neco said, patting him on his back.

Darmik rubbed his eyes. This was probably what Captain wanted—to mentally torture him.

"You need to get inside," Neco said. "Let's focus on a plan."

He nodded, unable to speak.

"Savenek's in there making a big old fuss. Let's go put that pup in his place, yeah?"

Darmik looked at his friend.

"Don't even say it." Neco held up his hands. "We all *chose* to be here. You're not responsible for us. All we ask is that you lead us."

He couldn't be an effective leader if he didn't pull himself together. Rema needed him, and he had to be strong for her. "All right. Let's go devise a plan to get Rema back."

The two friends ducked inside the ship. As Darmik descended the ladder, Savenek's angry voice echoed from down the hall. Maybe it hadn't been the best idea to send him to where prisoners were kept, but he needed to have a clear picture of what they were going to face.

"I can't believe you let him come," Neco mumbled.

Darmik had been thinking the same thing. At the end of the hallway, he entered the room where Audek, Vesha, and Ellie were sitting around the table while Savenek stood, waving his arms, ranting about something regarding Rema.

When Savenek saw him, he said, "Your uncle is one sick and

twisted bastard. I hope you don't take after him." His chest heaved up and down. "Well? What's your plan?"

In order to save Rema, he needed Savenek on his side; he needed his trust and loyalty. And right now, he had neither. He clenched his hands into fists, fed up with his attitude and lack of respect.

Neco shook his head. "Not in here. If you insist on doing what I think you're going to do, please go to the top deck were there's more room."

"I'm afraid I'll throw him overboard," Darmik replied.

"So?" Neco chuckled.

"What's going on?" Vesha asked.

Darmik pointed at Savenek. "You, top deck. Now."

Savenek jerked back. "Why?"

This was exactly why Darmik needed to do this. He turned and left, knowing Neco would explain to Savenek that he was being challenged. It was something Darmik did with the men from his army—if they wanted to move up in rank, they had to fight him to prove their skills. The exercise established understanding and respect among his men.

Out in the open air, he swung his arms, stretching. Several of his wounds were still healing, but they wouldn't impede him. Hearing voices approach, he went to the middle of the deck and stood with his feet shoulder-width apart, waiting.

His mind drifted back to his first challenge. He'd only been at Emperion's military school for three days. The officer leading his squad was showing them how to do a flying sidekick while unsheathing a longsword at the same time. Darmik asked a simple question—why not use a dagger instead? Since he questioned authority and showed insubordination, the officer assigned five cadets to attack him.

At the time, he was seventeen and served in the King's Army on Greenwood Island, so he wasn't a novice. When the five cadets came at him, he was shocked by the determination and brutality they exhibited. Since they weren't allowed to use any weapons, one cadet went to punch him in the stomach. Darmik blocked the blow, but another cadet kicked him from behind, sending him to his knees. Before he could recover, another cadet grabbed his hair, yanking his head up. One punched his jaw, while another kicked his side.

Sprawled on the ground, the cadets had repeatedly kicked him until he passed out. When he woke up, he was still on the ground, covered in blood. Since there wasn't a medical ward at the campus, and no one would help him, Darmik was forced to crawl to the room he shared with the cadets who had done this to him.

His torso was purple, his face black and blue, one eye swollen shut, and he could barely move his jaw. From that point on, Darmik never questioned his commanding officers out loud—ever.

Savenek stood before Darmik. "You want to fight me?" He smiled, confidence leaching from him.

"No. I'm challenging you. No weapons. Hand to hand only. First one to pin the other down, unharmed, wins. Understand?"

Savenek nodded. "What's the point?"

"To show you that you have a lot to learn. I'm in charge of this mission, and you will give me the respect I deserve—no more snide comments."

Savenek stood, staring at him.

"Do you want to rescue Rema?" Darmik asked.

"Of course I do."

"Then I need your loyalty."

Neco folded his arms, standing next to Ellie, watching. It looked like he was trying not to laugh.

"I don't need to fight you to prove anything," Savenek said.

Darmik grabbed Savenek's shoulder, digging his fingers in. "You're arrogant and don't understand how to follow authority. I am challenging you. Once I win, you will swear allegiance to me."

He whacked Darmik's arm away. "My loyalty is to Rema, not you."

"If you want to save her, you need me. And I want you focused and doing exactly what I say. Otherwise, I'll throw you overboard."

Savenek snickered. "What happens when I win?" His fist flew toward Darmik's face.

Darmik ducked and shoved Savenek's right leg, throwing him off balance. Straightening, he kicked Savenek's chest, causing him to tumble to the floor. Savenek quickly rolled to the side and sprang to his feet. Hunching slightly forward, he came at Darmik, trying to tackle him to the floor. Darmik twisted and broke free, shoving him backward. It was time to end this. He ran and jumped on Savenek, wrapping his legs around his neck, knocking him to the floor. He twisted and sat on top of him, victorious. Savenek tried to squirm free, but Darmik had him pinned down.

"Swear loyalty to me, or I'll throw you overboard."

Savenek growled, still trying to break Darmik's hold. Darmik leaned his elbow on Savenek's neck, applying pressure.

Savenek banged his hand against the floor. "Fine," he said, seething with rage. "I concede."

Darmik loosened his hold ever so slightly. "And?" he prompted.

"I swear loyalty to you."

"No more disrespect. No more inappropriate comments. I want you on your best behavior. Understand?"

"Yes." His face was turning bright red.

Darmik released him and jumped to his feet. He reached down. Savenek clasped his forearm and stood.

"I've never been beaten before," he said, wiggling his jaw and placing his palm to his face.

"I know," Darmik said. "Emperion is going to change that."

He smiled grimly. "I'm starting to understand."

"You two done?" Neco asked.

Savenek nodded.

Excellent, Darmik thought, *he is already keeping his mouth shut.*

Vesha rushed to Savenek's side, but he waved her away. Audek pouted, handing Neco a few coins.

Neco smiled. "Never bet against Darmik. He wins every time."

Darmik surveyed all five faces. They had a lot of work to do before they set foot on the mainland. The hot sun beat overhead. "Everyone below deck. It's time to formalize our plans and prepare. You're all going to play a vital role in recovering Rema."

CHAPTER THREE

Rema

*R*ema's head smacked the corner of the footlocker, waking her up. Pushing herself to a sitting position, her back ached and her hip throbbed with pain from sleeping on the hard floor. She'd spent most of the night thinking about Darmik. They had finally figured things out and a relationship was blooming between them. They'd even said that they loved each other. Now, she'd never see him again. And her Aunt Maya and Uncle Kar. She wished she could hug them one last time. They'd done so much for her over the years.

She rubbed the sleep from her eyes. Even if she managed to escape from the assassin, how would she get back to Greenwood Island? There had to be a way out of this mess. Could she feasibly fake her own death? Make everyone think she jumped overboard, while secretly hiding on the ship somewhere?

"I'll tie you up," Nathenek said, making her jump. He was still in bed, his blue eyes carefully watching her. Throwing off the covers, his legs slid to the floor. "If you give me any trouble at all, I'll put you back in the storage room."

"I understand," she said, trying to placate him.

"I don't think you do." He stood, wearing only his cotton sleep pants and undershirt. "I'm very good at reading people and understanding their intentions. If I see you plotting or thinking about escaping, that's it. There won't be a second chance."

She nodded, mentally kicking herself for being so transparent.

He pulled on his tunic, making himself presentable. "Excuse me," he said, coming to stand before her. She moved out of the way. Nathenek opened the footlocker, removing some clothes. "Here." He handed them to her. "They'll be big on you, but better than that thin nightdress you're wearing."

After spending time in the frigid Middle Mountains, the cold air didn't bother her like it used to. Regardless, she took the items, thankful for the practical clothing.

"I'll be back in a few moments." He left, closing and locking the door behind him.

Rema yanked on the rough, wool pants. Taking off her nightdress, she tossed it to the floor and put on the undershirt and tunic. The clothes were huge, so she rolled up the sleeves and pants.

Her stomach no longer felt queasy. Now she was ravenous. Hopefully Nathenek would feed her. He claimed he needed her alive and well for the execution, so he should be willing to bring her some food.

Glancing around the tiny room, she wondered what she would do all day. If she was going to be stuck in this small berth, then she needed to find a way to maintain her strength. When the opportunity presented itself, she wanted to be fully prepared and able to escape. She started doing jumping jacks. After one hundred, she stretched her arms and legs. It felt great to move her body.

The door latch rattled and Nathenek entered. Rema quickly plopped on the floor, hoping he wouldn't question what she'd been up to. He squatted, handing her a loaf of bread and a small water pouch.

"That's all you get until tonight." His eyes scanned her body, assessing her.

Rema tore the bread in two, saving half for later. "Thank you."

He stood. "I'll be back."

"Where are you going?" She shoved a piece of bread in her mouth, wondering how long it had been since the last time she had eaten.

"The top deck." He smiled, mocking her. "I don't want to be cooped up in this room all day."

"Good," she said, feigning pleasure. "I'd rather be alone. I'm much more interesting and make a far better conversationalist than you do."

Shaking his head ever so slightly, he turned and left, locking her inside. Sighing, she finished eating and then took a few small sips of water. Once finished, she stood, ready to get back to work. Closing her eyes, she envisioned Savenek and everything he'd shown her. She started running through the various drills he'd taught her.

After several hours, exhausted and out of breath, Rema sat and devoured the last of her bread. She took a gulp of water and stretched out on her back, staring up at the ceiling. Thoughts of Darmik invaded her mind and tears filled her eyes, blurring her vision. After her almost execution, she thought she had been handed a second chance at life. When Darmik arrived in the Middle Mountains, *for her*, she was elated. He gave up everything for her—his father, brother, crown, and army. Even the hideous "L" Lennek had carved on Darmik's chest was proof of everything he had suffered for her. When they kissed, she felt loved and complete.

Now, here she was, stuck on a ship headed to Emperion. She reached for her key necklace and noticed it was gone. Panicking, she sat up and shoved the collar of her shirt aside, frantically searching for it. Either Nathenek had taken it, or the necklace had fallen off when he carried her down the mountain.

Glancing at the footlocker, she wondered if her necklace was hidden in there. Standing before it, she tried lifting the lid. It was locked and wouldn't budge. Frustrated, she kicked it. Placing her hands on her hips, she paced around the room, searching for something she could use to break open the lock. She didn't see anything that would work.

What would Darmik do if he were in her position? He certainly wouldn't give up. Closing her eyes, she pictured him before her. *Stay focused and maintain your strength. When you get a chance to escape, take it. Even though your mother gave you the necklace, it is just a necklace. Your life is far more valuable than the heirloom.* Rema opened her eyes, a fierce determination taking over. She would not sit around wallowing in her situation. Squaring her shoulders, she prepared to go through her drills again.

She vowed to get away from Nathenek.

She would not be executed.

And she would most definitely find her way back to Darmik.

Voices came from the other side of the door. Rema hurried and sat on the floor, trying to calm her heavy breathing. She wiped her forehead, removing the dripping sweat. The door opened and Nathenek stepped inside, his eyes sweeping over the room and settling on her. Without saying a word, he handed her a loaf of bread and a cup of water. After removing his tunic, he climbed into bed, facing the wall.

Starving from exercising all day, she quickly inhaled the food. "Is bread the only thing I'm going to eat for the duration of our voyage?"

"I haven't decided," he mumbled.

"Do you plan to keep me in this tiny room the entire time?"

He grunted. "It's the safest place. Be quiet and go to sleep."

"You're an assassin. Wouldn't I be safe with you?" He didn't respond. "All I'm saying is that it's cruel to keep me holed up in here." She glanced around the room wishing another bed would magically appear. Sleeping on the hard, wooden floor for a second night wasn't very appealing.

Nathenek rolled onto his back. "Why?"

She needed to convince him to let her out of this room. "You're taking me to my death. Don't you think I want to feel the sun on my face and smell the ocean air before I die?"

"What difference does it make? You're going to die, regardless of being stuck in here or not. Wouldn't it be easier not experiencing those things?"

"All my life I've been sheltered, people claiming it was for my own good. In some sick twist of fate, it seems I'm destined to go to my death that way." The room turned dark as night descended. Rema could only see an outline of Nathenek's body. "Can I at least have a blanket? Or would it be better for me to be miserable and cold, since I'm going to die anyway?"

"Has anyone ever told you how infuriating you are?" Nathenek snatched his top blanket, throwing it at her.

She caught it, wrapping it around her body and shoving part of it under her head as a pillow. "Thank you." And she was not infuriating. If anything, she was rather pleasant given her circumstances.

"I didn't do it to be nice. I just want you to shut up and go to sleep." He rolled over, facing the wall again.

Rema smiled. She'd gotten what she wanted.

When Rema woke up the next morning, Nathenek was gone. She folded the blanket, placing it on his bed. She stretched her arms and legs, preparing to exercise.

The door slammed shut, causing her to jump at the sound. She spun around and came face to face with Nathenek.

"What are you doing?" he demanded, his voice barely above a whisper.

"Does it matter?"

He sat on the edge of the bed, pulling a loaf of bread out of his pocket and handing it to her. "I suppose it doesn't."

She tore into the bread, devouring it all. The downside of her exercising was her increased appetite.

"Do you plan to work out during our entire journey?" He folded his hands on his lap.

"As opposed to sitting here, crying?" she asked around a mouthful of bread.

"Yes."

"I'm sorry to disappoint you." She swallowed her food. "I have no intention of sitting here, wasting away. It's not in my nature."

He glanced up the ceiling, appearing lost in thought.

"Let me ask you a question," Rema said. "Would you sit here all day if you were in my position?"

"I suppose not." Nathenek stood and went to the window, gazing outside while she finished eating her food. "Fine," he said after several minutes. "I'll take you to the top deck."

Her eyes widened in shock. Was he serious? Or simply playing with her?

"There is one condition, though." He turned and faced her.

"What is it?" Dread replaced the excitement she felt a moment ago.

"You have to dress like a boy."

She jumped to her feet. "That's it?" He nodded. "Deal."

He knelt in front of the footlocker and opened it up. Rummaging around inside, he found a cap and handed it to her. "Pull your hair up so no one sees it."

She did as he asked, shoving her hair under the cap. He also gave her a belt which she used to cinch her pants up higher so she wouldn't trip on the material. "What about shoes?"

"I have an extra pair of boots."

They were huge on her, but after being barefoot for so long, it felt like soft blankets cushioned her feet. "How do I look?"

Nathenek stood before her. "Good." He adjusted the cap lower on her forehead. "You remind me of my sister. She's stubborn like you." He patted the top of her head. "Let's go." He led her through the dark hallway to a ladder bathed in sunlight. "Stay by my side," he ordered as he ascended.

Rema climbed right on his heels, eager to see the ocean again. When she stepped onto the deck, Nathenek waved her over to the side of the ship, near the railing. The ocean's beauty stole her breath. There was so much water in every direction it was simply astounding. One sailor was hanging on the tall center mast, while several others on the deck tended to the sails, mopped the floor, or assisted the captain with various tasks.

"What are your duties while on board?" she asked Nathenek.

"You," he said bluntly. "The emperor assigned me the task of hunting you down and bringing you before him to be executed. He gave me endless resources to do so."

A thought occurred to her—Nathenek may not know why the emperor wanted her dead. He could be unaware of who she was— the one person Emperor Hamen feared—the legitimate heir to the Emperion throne. If Nathenek knew, would that change anything?

She needed to tread carefully. Casually leaning against the railing, she said, "You mentioned I'm the first prisoner you've ever dealt with?"

"Yes. Usually I assassinate my target immediately. You're the first one that I've had to bring to the emperor for termination."

Even with the warm sun beating down on her, Nathenek's cold words made her shiver. "Can I ask you a question?"

"You can ask," he said, leaning on the railing next to her. "It doesn't mean I'll answer."

Playing with the end of her rolled sleeve, she tried to decide how to phrase what she wanted to say. "Why does the emperor want to see me executed? Why can't you kill me like all the others?"

With his head still facing forward, his eyes sliced over to her, sly and calculating. For a brief second, she thought he knew the real reason. He looked back at the ocean. "I'm sure you know King Barjon is the empress's brother."

"I do."

"And you plan to kill him and crown yourself as queen."

"That is correct. But do you know why I want the throne?" She twisted to face him.

"The rebels claim you are the true heir." He peered down at her.

"I am," she said. "King Barjon slaughtered my family to gain control of Greenwood Island."

"Yes, I already know this." He crossed his arms. "What are you getting at?"

Taking a deep breath, she said, "I'm just wondering how well you know your history."

"My knowledge of Emperion is impeccable."

They stood facing one another. Rema wondered how receptive he would be to learn of her true lineage. Would he embrace it? Or kill her on the spot?

He leaned toward her, lowering his voice. "How well do you know your history? Because I doubt you know anything about Emperion, our customs, or how intimately your suitor, Darmik, is connected to the ruling family."

"I know the emperor is Darmik's uncle." That was common knowledge. So why did Nathenek bring it up? What was she missing? What didn't she understand? Clutching the railing, she gazed out at the water again. He probably didn't know that Darmik had denounced his family and was no longer loyal to them.

His head turned at something behind her. She glanced over her shoulder and saw a hooded figure go below deck. "Why is Trell here?" she asked.

"Why do you care about the old man?"

"Because he's a good man. And he's elderly. Aren't you concerned about him making this journey across the ocean? Especially with his failing health. I can't imagine what the emperor wants with him."

Nathenek rubbed his face. "You aren't supposed to know he's here."

"Why? Are you going to kill him? Or is he selling us out? Giving the emperor information about the rebels?"

He nodded toward the water. "There's a group of dolphins."

Scanning the ocean, she searched for them. A second later, one jumped out of the water. She kept watching. The beautiful, dark gray creatures zipped along, not far from the ship, occasionally jumping as if playing with one another. "They're magnificent! I never knew creatures such as these existed." She'd been sheltered for far too long. There was so much of the world she wanted to see and experience.

He smiled.

This was a side of the assassin she hadn't expected to see. "Are we here for any particular purpose? Or are we just enjoying the sun and view?"

"Nothing with me is ever for enjoyment or pleasure," he replied. "We're here to practice." He pushed away from the railing and went to the center of the deck, motioning her to join him. "Since you've been exercising in the room, I assume you did some training while at the rebel camp?"

"A little," she replied, standing before him.

"Good. I want you to get me to the floor."

Rema came at him, trying to knock him off balance. She shoved him, tried bumping him, and even attempted to trip him. Nothing worked.

"I'm glad you're not afraid to get your hands dirty." He chuckled.

She growled in frustration. How could she beat an opponent who was not only taller but weighed considerably more?

"Stand about five feet away from me," he ordered. "You want to walk toward me. While my eyes are focused on your face, quickly move your right leg and hook it around my left leg." He demonstrated the technique for her. "Place your hands on my shoulders, jerk my body toward you, and then shove me back while using your leg to pull mine in."

She did as instructed, and Nathenek went down.

"Good, now punch me."

She lightly hit him.

"Then run away." He jumped onto his feet. "Let's run through the drill a few more times."

"Why?" she asked, adjusting her cap.

"What do you mean?"

"I want to know why you're bothering to train me when you're taking me to be executed."

"Since you insist on exercising in the berth, I figure you might as well do it out here where you can help me. I prefer to train on a daily basis with an opponent. It keeps my skills honed." He gestured at the ocean surrounding them. "And I prefer to practice outside."

His reason seemed weak, but she didn't care. At least she was outside in the fresh air with the sun shining down on her, learning skills used by an assassin. They repeated the drill several more times until she had it down.

By the time they finished, she was exhausted and covered with sweat. The ocean water looked cool and inviting. "I wish I could take a swim."

"You could if we weren't out in open water."

"Oh," she said, dumbfounded. She'd only said that in jest. She didn't realize people swam in the ocean.

"You didn't know that?"

She shook her head.

"I forgot King Barjon doesn't allow travel between regions." He reached for her hand, examining the tattoo on her wrist. "I have one, too." He tugged up his sleeve, revealing a crude, black tattoo in the shape of an X. "We get them when we enter the military. It denotes a person's rank." He pulled his sleeve down, covering it. "Let's get you inside. I'm starving."

Nathenek led her back to his room. He locked her inside while he went to eat with the crew. She was so exhausted that she grabbed the blanket from his bed, laid down on the floor, and fell asleep.

~

The next morning, Nathenek was gone. It frightened Rema how easily he could come and go without making a sound or waking her up. She supposed it was a necessary skill all assassins possessed.

A plate of boiled potatoes sat next to her. The food was cold, but she quickly devoured it. After eating, she began stretching. Her muscles ached from working with Nathenek yesterday.

"Good, you're awake," he said from the doorway, startling her. "Here's your breakfast." He tossed her a loaf of bread. "Let's go."

She caught it and hurried after him, eating along the way. "Do you have any water?"

He pulled out a small waterskin and handed it to her. She took a few gulps before attaching it to her belt. They were about to step onto the top deck when he said, "Fix your cap."

It had slipped back, exposing some of her hair. She quickly adjusted it, making sure all signs of her womanhood were hidden. It was silly—certainly the crew knew she was a woman. After all, she was on the top deck the first day wearing her nightdress. Perhaps being clothed like a man was simply to limit curiosity and attention? Whatever the reason, she trusted Nathenek had her best interests at heart—he would ensure her safety in order to deliver her to his emperor.

Out in the fresh air, she took a deep breath and smiled, enjoying the sun's warmth on her body.

"Today we're going to work with these." Nathenek pulled out two small knives. "Have you ever thrown one before?"

"No." Savenek had taught her some basic sword work, and she knew how to shoot a bow. But those were the only weapons she was familiar with.

"Why are you smiling?"

"This sounds like fun." And it was something that could come in handy.

He shook his head. "You should have been born in Emperion. You would've made an excellent soldier." He stood with his feet shoulder-width apart, a knife in each hand.

"Emperion blood runs through my veins," she whispered.

"I figured it did. Your blonde hair and blue eyes give you away. Everyone from the lower class has your coloring." Bending his arms, he quickly threw one knife and then the other, embedding each one in the wooden door fifteen feet away.

"Your turn." He motioned for her to join him. "Stand like me."

She stood two feet from him, imitating his stance.

"Good, now stand like that and face the door over there." He pointed to where his knives were embedded.

She did as he said while he retrieved his weapons, yanking them from the door.

He came and stood next to her. "When you throw, there are a couple things to keep in mind." Rema nodded, trying to commit all he said to memory. "You need to relax, clear your head, and put heat behind it."

She raised an eyebrow. "That seems contradictory."

"It's not. I need you to trust me."

Yeah, right, Rema thought. She couldn't trust the man taking her to her death.

"Shake your arms, loosening them." She did as he said. "Excellent. Now, when you hold the knife, you need to keep it secure in your hand, but you don't want a death grip." He flipped a knife in the air, caught it, and handed it hilt first to her.

She hesitated and then took the weapon. Nathenek reached up with his other hand, dangling her waterskin. "How did you do that?"

"Just remember what I do for a living," he said, handing it back to her. "And don't try anything." She nodded. "Now lift your throwing arm back," he instructed. "Reach forward, lightly flick your wrist, and release." He threw his knife. It landed in the door, the hilt shaking from the impact. "Your turn."

She pulled her arm back. When she reached forward, she flicked and released the knife. Only it didn't strike the wood—it bounced off.

"Again." He retrieved the weapons.

Rema spent the remainder of the day and into the early evening practicing. Nathenek drew a round target on the door to help her aim. She could strike the door, her weapon sticking almost every time, but she wasn't able to hit the target consistently yet. Her hands ached—blisters formed and popped on her fingers, bleeding in a few places.

Nathenek finally made her quit for the night. When he locked her in the berth, she grabbed the blanket and collapsed on the floor, exhausted. Her eyelids became unbearably heavy, but she forced herself to stay awake so she could eat. Luckily she didn't have to wait long. Nathenek returned a few minutes later carrying two bowls of soup. He'd never eaten in the room with her before. Sitting cross-legged on the floor, across from one another, Rema wondered why he decided to join her tonight.

He placed the bowl in front of her. She stared at the wooden spoon. The thought of holding it in her hand made her blisters sting in pain. Removing the spoon, she picked up the bowl and brought it to her lips, drinking the warm broth.

"I can put something on your hands to help with the pain."

Setting the bowl down, she nodded.

He went to the footlocker, pulling out a small jar and a strip of fabric. "Do you want me to do it for you?"

"Yes, please." She didn't know how to put the medicine on her own hands.

He opened the jar and used two fingers to scoop out some of the pungent-smelling goo, rubbing it onto her raw skin. She bit her lip to keep herself from screaming in pain. Then he deftly wrapped the fabric around her hands. "They'll be healed by tomorrow."

"Thank you." A tingly sensation spread over her hands, taking the pain away. She picked up her bowl and sipped some more soup. "You could've let me suffer. You know, since I'm going to die anyway."

He chuckled. "I could have." He ate a spoonful of soup. "I didn't do it to be nice. I simply didn't want you to drop the bowl and make a mess." He took another bite.

She suspected he was lying. As much as he tried to hide it, he was a good man. "Do you have a family?" she asked, wanting to understand him better.

"My parents and sister live in Emperor's City. My brothers, all seven of them, are serving the emperor, like me."

"You're not married?"

"No. When I took the oath to serve Emperor Hamen, I vowed not to marry. Only the assassins in his elite guard are required to make this promise."

That was a harsh requirement when he was already devoting his life to the emperor's service. "Seven brothers and one sister. You must've had an interesting childhood."

"My brothers are older than I am. They enlisted in the military at age twelve. I grew up playing with my sister."

She recalled him saying that he went into the military at age eight. "Why did you enlist younger than most?"

Nathenek sighed, putting his bowl down. "It's obvious you know nothing of Emperion and our ways." He leaned back against the wall, stretching his legs out before him. "I don't want to go into details, but know that Emperor Hamen rules over the largest empire. The entire place is centered on conquering other kingdoms and maintaining its current holdings. In other words, it is solely focused on war. If the emperor wants more soldiers, he gets them, no matter their age."

Eight children from one family—all forced into the army. She couldn't bring herself to ask if they were all still alive. "Your sister managed to avoid enlisting?"

"Technically."

"I don't understand." She finished her soup and set the bowl down.

"I went in her place. While she may not be serving in the military, her life is defined by it."

"Did she marry a man in the military?"

He chuckled. "No, most certainly not. She married a baker. But her oldest child is ten. In two years, he'll be required to enlist." He stood and removed his tunic.

"I'm sorry."

He reached for the oil lamp, turning it off and sending the room into darkness. "Good night." He climbed into bed.

"King Barjon is an oppressive ruler. Not in the same way Emperor Hamen is, but he's ruthless nonetheless. I'm tired of one person controlling the lives of many—especially when the good of ordinary citizens is overlooked. A ruler should listen to and lead his subjects."

Nathenek didn't respond.

Not wanting to bother him with her chatter, she pulled off her tunic, using it as a pillow. Wrapping the blanket around her body, exhaustion overtook her and she fell into a deep sleep.

CHAPTER FOUR

Darmik

$\mathcal{T}$he only one without any training was Ellie. Neco offered to teach her some basics, but this concerned Darmik. He needed his friend focused on rescuing Rema, not protecting Ellie.

Sitting around the table, he outlined his plan. Their ship was headed to Emperion's military port, located north of the main merchant port, where he believed Captain was headed. Since the military ship was smaller and faster, he estimated they would dock a few hours before Captain did. Once in port, he would announce that he was there on a diplomatic mission. He intended to be escorted to the palace where he would speak with the emperor before Rema arrived.

"What do you plan to tell your uncle?" Ellie asked.

"This is where it gets tricky. Emperor Hamen will perceive Rema as a threat. The only way he'll let her live is if she's not the true heir."

"What are you saying?" Ellie asked.

"I want to convince him he has the wrong person, and Rema is simply a commoner whom I'm engaged to."

"How do you plan to do that?" Neco asked, raising his eyebrows, looking skeptical.

It surprised him that no one questioned him using the term *engaged*. He stood and began pacing around the small room. "As you know, Rema bears the royal mark on her shoulder."

"You want to remove it?" Savenek asked.

"Or I could cover it with makeup," Ellie suggested.

Darmik nodded. "Something along those lines. What do you think?"

"I can cut the mark off and stitch her up," Vesha said. "Rema will have a scar, though."

"Makeup will be easier," Ellie said.

"Don't you think the emperor will check?" Neco asked. "He'll see the scar or the makeup."

"And that's assuming we can remove the tattoo or cover it with makeup before the emperor checks," Savenek added.

Darmik stopped pacing and sat on the empty chair, facing everyone. "I'm open to ideas."

"Why don't we try to intercept Rema before she makes it to Emperion?" Savenek offered.

He'd already considered the possibility, but they were headed slightly north of the merchant ship. "If we're lucky enough to catch her boat, we will certainly grab her."

"Can't we arrive at the merchant port first and wait for her there?" Vesha asked.

Darmik shook his head. "A military ship can't arrive at the merchant port—especially undetected. The moment the ship arrived, the army would swarm aboard and we'd be unable to rescue her. We have no choice but to dock at the military port, north of there."

"Once we dock, can't we get off the ship and travel to the merchant port?" Savenek asked.

Darmik leaned back on his chair, looking at the five faces around him, all staring at him with hope. "All of you need to understand something," he said. "We're entering another kingdom. They have different rules and customs. While I appreciate your suggestions, they're unrealistic. When our ship arrives, we will need to state our names and purpose for being on the mainland. We won't be able to slip away unnoticed."

"Very well," Savenek said. "We'll stick with your plan."

"I'll work on mixing some things together to make skin-colored makeup to cover her tattoo," Ellie said.

"I'll check medical supplies for a needle and thread," Vesha added.

"I want everyone to get a good night's rest," Darmik said. "Tomorrow, we'll train and I'll teach you Emperion etiquette."

Audek scrunched his nose. "Etiquette?"

"Yes," Darmik mused. "You need to know how to greet the emperor. I can't have you do something to offend him. Otherwise, he'll have you beheaded."

Audek shivered. "Etiquette it is."

Darmik's back hurt from standing so straight and stiff in the courtyard among hundreds of other soldiers. The hot sun beat down on his exposed neck, causing him to sweat in his full military uniform. The two prisoners stood on the raised platform. The first one, a boy about twelve years old, was crying. The executioner shoved the boy onto his knees and pulled his wrists forward, locking his forearms into metal cuffs.

The warden read the charge. "This boy has been caught stealing food from the Bilarie Market. Six tangerines. The penalty is loss of both hands so he will never be able to steal again."

The executioner raised his axe. Darmik's stomach twisted in pain. Surely stealing food didn't deserve such a severe punishment. The axe came down, and the boy screamed, a bloodcurdling sound. The axe went up.

Darmik wanted to close his eyes; however, if he did, he'd be the one up there receiving a punishment for disobedience. The crude weapon flew down, and the boy's second hand fell off. Blood squirted everywhere. The boy lay on the ground, his arms still locked in place. He must've passed out. A soldier removed the metal cuffs and pulled him roughly from the platform.

Darmik's legs shook and his hands tingled. He couldn't pass out. He'd be beaten to the brink of death if he did. His vision swam.

The warden moved to the second prisoner with a bag covering his head, concealing his identity. "This one is found guilty of treason. The punishment is death."

The executioner shoved the prisoner onto his knees, locking his head and arms into the equipment. The executioner grabbed his axe with one hand, removing the bag covering the prisoner's head with the other.

It was Rema.

Darmik screamed.

He sat up in bed, breathing hard, covered in sweat. It was only a dream. Memories of his time in Emperion infused with his greatest fear of losing the woman he loved. Ever since boarding the ship, he'd been having these nightmares.

Even though it was still dark outside, he slid out of bed and dressed. He went up to the top deck to practice sword drills until everyone else woke up. Hopefully, the physical exertion would focus his mind. He unsheathed his sword and started running through various drills.

Barjon's angry face appeared before him. "You're doing it wrong!" he snarled. "Can't you do anything right? You're eight years old and can barely lift the sword."

"I can do it," Darmik insisted. "I just need a little more practice."

Barjon swung and hit his arm. The sword dropped to the ground with a loud clank. "I don't know why I waste my time with you. Lennek's the only worthy one." He stormed away.

Darmik bent down and retrieved the sword. Standing, he tried the maneuver again, perfecting it. He smiled, but no one was around to see his accomplishment. Determined not to fail his father, he did it again and again, until the sword became an extension of his arm, and he didn't have to even think about the movements.

The following days fell into a routine. After breakfast, everyone went to the top deck where they spent the morning doing physical training. Darmik led the drills. One afternoon, Savenek offered to show him some of the rebels' exercises. They were rather impressive, so Darmik incorporated them into their daily routine.

Ellie caught on quickly. Often times, she and Vesha practiced together and sparred with one another. Darmik enjoyed working with Savenek and Audek—they knew moves he was unfamiliar with and posed a greater challenge than he was used to. Neco even made a comment that he was impressed with everyone's skill.

The afternoons were focused on Emperion protocol. Darmik explained how everything was centered on the army and war— from the structure of the city to the way the people behaved. Those who served in the military were honored while those who did not were the lowest members in their society. The higher-ranking officers were Emperion's elite noble class.

Darmik showed them how to greet one another by respectfully bowing one's head. He also told them to remain quiet at all times. Emperions discouraged individual thought and questions weren't tolerated. Everyone needed to keep his or her emotions hidden at all times. Emperions were known for using a person's feelings as a weapon. Darmik wanted them to present themselves as a respectful envoy from Greenwood Island, and he planned to speak on their behalf.

The brothers stood side by side, bows raised.

"Closest shot wins," Lennek said. "You go first."

Darmik focused on the target thirty feet away. He'd been practicing every day since Trell gave him the bow for his tenth birthday. Pulling back the bowstring, he released it. The arrow sailed through the air and landed with a thunk, dead center on the target. He smiled.

Lennek grunted and released his arrow. It arched through the air, missing the target completely, and landing in a tree.

"I win."

Lennek threw his bow on the ground. "What did you do?" he demanded. "You sabotaged my weapon, didn't you?"

"Of course not, brother." He never cheated. It hurt his feelings that his brother would accuse him of such a thing.

"I take lessons every day. You don't. How did you beat me?"

Darmik looked at the ground, no idea what to say to appease his brother.

"Guards!" Lennek shouted, turning to face the soldiers responsible for the princes' safety. "Take Darmik to the king. Now."

"I'll go," Darmik mumbled. "You don't need to drag me there." He was escorted to Barjon's office.

"Father," Lennek said. "Darmik needs to be taught a lesson." He proceeded to tell him his version of the story.

King Barjon's eyes narrowed. "Darmik won?"

"Only because he cheated," Lennek whined.

"Leave us," the king demanded.

Once alone with his father, Darmik said, "I didn't cheat. It was a fair win."

The king smiled. "Nothing is ever fair." He pulled out a leather whip. "Remove your tunic."

When Darmik wasn't having a nightmare about his father and brother, he was haunted by his time at Emperion. He always dreamed about some traumatic experience he'd tried to forget—like the time he was forced to fight a fellow cadet to the death.

"Only my ten best men from this unit can go on," Officer Gaverek announced. "That means one of you fails."

Darmik stood straight and tall at attention. He'd done well on all his tests and challenges. Several of his fellow cadets were slower, not as qualified as he was. He should be safe from being sent home in disgrace.

"I've decided to take the two worst cadets and have them fight until one of them dies. Winner stays. I won't have to waste time sending the loser home." No one spoke. *"I've chosen Jimek—who is consistently coming in last for our runs."* Officer Gaverek stopped before Darmik. *"And I've chosen the soft prince, since no one likes him."*

Panic swelled inside of Darmik. This wasn't fair. He shouldn't be forced to fight a fellow cadet to the death. His hands became sweaty as he stepped forward, everyone forming a circle around him and Jimek. When Darmik went to throw the first punch, Jimek morphed into Rema right as his fist struck her nose.

Awakening in a cold sweat, Darmik shook his head, trying to banish the visions of Rema screaming in pain. With shaking hands, he got dressed and went to the top deck. The air was hot and muggy even though the sun hadn't come up. They had to be close to Emperion. He estimated they'd been aboard the ship for two weeks. Any hope of intercepting Rema's vessel had vanished. He was going to have to become the person he didn't want to be— the king's son, Prince Darmik. It was the only way he could save Rema.

"Land ho!" a voice rang through the gray sky of dawn.

Darmik scanned the horizon, not seeing anything.

Several sailors ran to the sails. One approached him. "We'll be in port soon. I suggest you tell the others to prepare."

Darmik's heartbeat quickened—this was it. He ran to Neco's quarters, pounding on the door.

"Yes?" Neco asked, pulling open the door and squinting.

"Land has been spotted. Wake everyone. It's time."

Without waiting for a response, Darmik rushed to his berth. Emperions were all about rank. He needed to show that he outranked everyone except the emperor. Opening the footlocker, he pulled out his black pants and commander's tunic. After dressing, he strapped his sword belt around his waist and sheathed his blade. Bending down, he retrieved his crown from the footlocker. He stood, staring at it. He never thought he'd wear it again. The sapphires looked almost black. Placing the crown atop his head, he felt as if he was betraying Rema just by wearing it. He had to remind himself that he was doing this for her. He knew the task before him wouldn't be easy.

Taking a deep breath, he went to the top deck to make sure everyone was ready. Much to his satisfaction, they all wore the uniform of the King's Army.

"Excellent," Darmik said, coming to stand before them.

Savenek tugged at his collar. "We could have worn our uniform," he mumbled.

"No," Darmik replied. "Your uniform has Rema's crest. The emperor would have recognized it. We must bear King Barjon's colors."

Ellie fidgeted with her tunic.

"What is it?" Darmik asked, knowing she had a question.

"It's just that . . . well . . . we're women."

Audek laughed. "I most certainly am not a woman."

"Not you!" Ellie said, exasperated. "Vesha and I. Won't they know something's wrong since women aren't allowed to join the army?"

"In Emperion, the emperor allows women in his army. He even allows them to fight. No one will think twice about the two of you."

"You're positive the emperor doesn't know you've defected?" Ellie asked.

"There's no way for him to know—unless Captain arrived before us." He clasped his hands behind his back. "I want everyone to remember what we discussed. You are all members of the King's Army. I handpicked each of you to accompany me here. You are all highly trained soldiers." Everyone nodded. "And remember, my positions as commander and prince are equally important as me being the emperor's nephew."

Land shone on the horizon. The sky lightened, welcoming day.

"Places everyone!" Neco shouted. Audek, Savenek, Ellie, Vesha, and Neco all stood at attention along the railing on the port side of the ship.

Darmik remained near the center of the deck, feet shoulder-width apart. Taking a deep breath, he exhaled and put on his game face—no emotion, only his bland expression giving nothing away, as he'd been taught to do by the very people he was about to face.

The ship neared the military port. Hundreds of ships were docked there. Neco glanced at Darmik, his lips tight with concern. Neco knew they were entering a hostile kingdom with the largest army, but to see it firsthand was another matter. Darmik gave a curt nod, trying to get his friend to focus. Neco faced forward again.

The crew brought the sails down as the boat entered the port. Darmik instructed the helmsman to steer the ship directly to an open slip. As the vessel made its way through the harbor, several soldiers from nearby ships stared at them. When they neared an open slip, shouts rang through the air. Emperion soldiers swarmed the dock.

As the anchor dropped, Darmik glanced over the side of the ship and said, "Welcome to Emperion." More than a hundred soldiers stood below, swords drawn. While he suspected this would happen, his companions did not. They fidgeted nervously on the deck, hands lingering near scabbards.

"Relax," Darmik said, "all of you. That's an order."

"But you still want us at attention, right?" Audek asked.

Darmik rolled his eyes. "Yes, at attention, but don't look so bloody scared!"

A ramp was shoved up against the ship. Holding his head high, Darmik kept his face blank and went to the top of the ramp, prepared to face the Emperion Army.

Before the soldiers could question him, he shouted, "I am Prince Darmik, son of King Barjon of Greenwood Island. I am here on a peaceful, diplomatic mission. I want to speak to my uncle, Emperor Hamen."

The soldiers stood frozen, swords pointed in his direction. One man, dressed in the uniform of a lieutenant, walked forward to the bottom of the ramp. "Prince Darmik," he said in his thick Emperion accent. "Welcome. I was not informed of your visit."

"That is because my visit was not planned in advance. I have a message of the utmost importance from King Barjon for Emperor Hamen. Please escort me to my uncle. Immediately."

The lieutenant smiled. "Prince Darmik, or should I call you Commander?" His eyes narrowed, giving him a shrewd look. "Please forgive our inhospitality, but surely you, of all people, know I will not escort you to the emperor, unless the emperor so orders."

Darmik had feared this would happen. It was the absolute worst-case scenario.

"Arrest them all," the lieutenant ordered. "I want to know how they managed to get one of our military ships."

The Emperion soldiers rushed on board. Several came at Darmik. He kept his hands clasped behind his back, knowing any sudden movement would get a sword in his side. When he offered no resistance, a soldier pulled Darmik's arms forward and fastened metal rings around his wrists, cinching them together. His crown, sword, and daggers were removed. Glancing at his friends, he saw them being similarly bound and disarmed.

"Take them to the main dungeon via the military route," the lieutenant ordered. Thankfully, they were being kept together. If they were sent to separate locations, Darmik knew he'd never see them again. This was the one, and only, thing working in their favor right now.

Someone roughly shoved Darmik down the ramp. At the bottom, a dozen soldiers surrounded him. No one spoke as they escorted him along the dock. Stepping onto solid ground, his legs wobbled. It would take some time to acclimate to being on solid ground. Focusing on his surroundings, the enormous wall enclosing the city loomed ahead, just as he remembered. It was tan stone, matching the sandy ground. The wind kicked up, tossing small pieces of sand against his exposed flesh. Even though the sun had just come up, the air was already stifling hot.

"Move it." A soldier slammed the hilt of a sword into Darmik's back. It almost sent him to his knees. Gritting his teeth, he remained upright, knowing the games these soldiers liked to play. In order to survive, he had to be strong and not show an ounce of weakness or fear.

Since this was the military's port, there was an entrance in the wall used strictly by soldiers entering or exiting Emperor's City. When they reached it, the guards stationed there opened the gate.

Darmik followed the soldiers through the wall and into the city. Streets crowded with merchants and people stretched in every direction. Sand colored structures lined the streets. In the distance were low rolling hills. Not much had changed in the ugly and inhospitable city since the last time he'd been here.

The soldiers led him to one of the larger buildings across the street. The emperor's crest had been carved above the door. The lieutenant pushed past his men and went inside while everyone else remained outside, waiting in the hot sun. Darmik wanted to turn to make sure his friends were still with him, but he knew better than to appear concerned.

After several minutes, the door opened and a soldier stepped out. "Will the foreigners please come forward?"

Darmik did as asked, hoping his companions all followed suit.

"First-rank officers only, escort the prisoners inside. Everyone else, return to your stations at once."

Two soldiers approached Darmik, each grabbing one of his arms and bringing him inside.

"Use the second door," the soldier instructed as they entered the building.

They stopped at a door with the number two engraved on it. One of the soldiers unlocked and opened it. Darmik pretended to stumble so he could glance back, checking on his companions. They were close behind, a soldier guarding each one. The man escorting him shoved him through the doorway. Another soldier stepped next to him, holding a torch that revealed a narrow set of stairs leading downward. Not wanting to show any fear, he quickly descended, the soldiers right behind him. At the bottom, a long tunnel stretched out before him, no end in sight.

He recalled his studies about Emperion. There was an entire network of tunnels under the city. It allowed for not only prisoner transportation, but also evacuation of the city if need be.

No one spoke as they traveled at a brisk pace for about five miles. Darmik took mental note of each turn they made. When he came to a set of stairs leading upward, he quickly calculated the route in reverse, memorizing it in case they needed to escape. He went up the stairs noting there were only half as many as he'd descended. They were still underground. He started to go down another hallway when a black iron door to his left opened. Someone shoved him inside a small room, slamming the door shut behind him.

He was alone.

Another door opened revealing two soldiers dressed in solid black. This was the dungeon.

"Where are the members of my guard being taken?" Darmik demanded. He needed to stay with his companions. Neither soldier responded.

A third soldier, dressed in the uniform of a prison warden, stepped into the room. "The members of your guard are going to be interrogated."

Intense panic filled him, but he willed it away. "They are my escorts and companions. If it's information you want, interrogate me, for they know nothing of value."

The warden smiled. "We are going to interrogate you, too." He spun on his heels. "Bring the prisoner with me," he ordered.

The two soldiers seized Darmik's arms, dragging him forward. "I am the emperor's nephew. I am also a prince. I demand to be treated accordingly. Take me to speak with Emperor Hamen. Now."

A putrid smell wafted through the dark, stone hallway. Darmik knew what awaited him and feared Vesha and Ellie would not survive. "If any harm comes to my companions, you will answer for it." How had he not foreseen this as a possible outcome? He figured they might be taken into custody, but not interrogated. What purpose would it serve? He would not die in this dungeon without his uncle even being aware of his presence. It was time to change the plan.

The warden stopped before another iron door. "Put him in there," he ordered. "Prepare him for a standard interrogation. I'll be back after I've seen to the others."

The soldiers shoved Darmik into the room and he fell on his side. A single table stood in the middle of the room, chains attached to both ends. The two soldiers came in, closing the door. One dragged Darmik to his feet. When he turned Darmik around, about to push him onto the table, Darmik shifted his weight, slamming his elbow into the man's face and knocking him over.

The other soldier rushed at him. Fighting with his wrists bound together was difficult, but he'd done it before. The man threw a punch, and Darmik ducked. They circled one another, sizing each other up. The soldier on the floor started to stand. Darmik didn't have much time if he wanted to win this fight. He faked a swing toward the man's head. When the soldier lifted his arms to block the strike, Darmik side-kicked him in his stomach. The soldier hunched forward and Darmik smashed his bound fists against the man's back, sending him to the floor. Darmik knew the other guard was behind him, about to strike. He spun and kicked the soldier's face, knocking him over. Darmik quickly grabbed one of the soldier's swords and hit each man on the head with the hilt, rendering both unconscious.

Standing next to the door, he placed his body flat against the wall, waiting for the warden to return. Sweat dripped down his forehead. A high-pitched female scream laced with pain echoed through the dungeon. Steeling his resolve, he didn't let it affect him. If anyone discovered his weak spot, the interrogator would hurt his friends, trying to get him to cooperate. He couldn't let that happen.

Several minutes later, the door swung open and the warden entered. Darmik grabbed the man's tunic, yanking his body forward. He slammed the warden's head against the stone wall. The man fell to the floor, unconscious.

Time was of the essence. Darmik pulled the warden's limp body up, using it as a shield. Stepping into the hallway, all was quiet. Emperions tended to keep people they arrested near one another for interrogation purposes. His friends should be close by. Going to the next door, he listened. Voices came from the other side. Darmik lowered the unconscious warden to the floor. Searching the man's pockets, he found a set of keys. He fumbled with them until he located the one for his manacles. Once his wrists were free, he stood, pulling the warden up with him. Taking a deep breath, he reached for the handle, flung the door open, and rushed inside, once again using the warden as a shield.

One soldier held Savenek in an arm lock while the other opened manacles attached to the table with a chain. Darmik shoved the warden's body at the soldier near Savenek. Then he jumped over the table, landing next to the startled soldier. A jab, reverse, and a roundhouse kick sent the man to the floor. Darmik grabbed one of the chains and swung it at the man's head, knocking him out. He turned to help Savenek.

Savenek stood over the body of the other soldier, smiling.

"Is he unconscious or dead?"

"Unconscious," Savenek mused. "I thought you told us to do whatever they said."

"Well," Darmik answered, "there's been a slight change in plans." He peered into the hallway.

"What's the new plan?" Savenek whispered, coming to stand next to him.

"Not sure. But things are too quiet. Something's not right."

The soldiers started to stir. "Want to lock these guys in here?"

Darmik nodded. "Grab the keys in the warden's right pocket. There should be one that unlocks your manacles."

Once Savenek's wrists were free, they stepped into the hallway, locking the door behind them. Darmik pointed at the next door, and Savenek nodded. As before, Darmik grabbed the handle, throwing the door open. They rushed inside. Savenek took one soldier down while Darmik incapacitated the other.

Audek lay on the table. Savenek quickly shuffled through the keys until he found one that unlocked the manacles encasing Audek's arms and legs.

"I take it things aren't going as planned," Audek said, sitting up.

"No," Darmik snapped, pacing about the room.

"Well, what are we waiting for?" Audek asked. "Let's go rescue everyone else."

Darmik shook his head "We'll never make it out of the dungeon."

"So far, it's been fairly easy," Savenek said.

"We have two options. We can stick together and try to rescue the rest of our group. If we do so, we run the risk of being recaptured. If they catch us, we could all be killed." He glanced into the hallway—no one was about. "Or, we can assume capture is imminent and split up, hoping one of us makes it out alive."

"Which plan has a higher likelihood of success?" Savenek asked.

Darmik calculated the risks of each option. Their chance of escape was slim. However, he believed one person could evade capture more easily than all six could.

"I suggest we skedaddle," Audek said.

"What do you want to do?" Savenek asked.

"I hate to ask this of you," Darmik said, "but I think we need to split up. The two of us will stay together and we'll leave everyone else here as a distraction."

"All righty." Audek hopped back up on the table. "Lock me in."

Savenek rushed over and reattached the manacles. "For Rema."

"Yes," Audek said. "For our queen."

Darmik heard voices. "Let's go."

He and Savenek ran from the room. When they reached the end of the hallway, they slid against the wall, listening. Voices came from around the corner. Darmik was about to head in the other direction when he heard voices coming from that side as well. They were boxed in.

"I'm sorry."

"For what?" Savenek asked.

"This." He punched him in the stomach. Savenek doubled over in pain just as Emperion soldiers rushed into the corridor, surrounding them.

"It's about time," Darmik snapped. "Detain him and take me to see my uncle."

CHAPTER FIVE

Rema

*R*ema held on for dear life, sweat dripping down her face and back. She couldn't believe how humid it was. The closer they got to Emperion, the hotter it became.

"Excellent!" Nathenek yelled up to her. "Now slide down carefully so you don't burn your hands."

She'd just reached the top and wanted a moment to look at the view before she attempted to make her way down the rope. For some reason, Nathenek had decided to have her climb one of the ropes attached to the mizzenmast. He said it would be good for her. She wasn't so sure about that, but it did remind her of her cliff back home. The wind whipped around her body, making her feel as if she was flying.

For the past two weeks, Nathenek had been pushing her harder and harder each day. The result—her muscles were toned and far stronger than before. Keeping her legs hooked around the rope, she began lowering herself. Four feet from the bottom, she let go, jumping onto the deck.

"Did you hurt your hands?"

"Nope." She held them up to show him. They were red and calloused, but unharmed.

"Good, let's practice the sword work I taught you yesterday."

For the next two hours, they ran through various drills, side by side, mimicking one another, moving in perfect unison. Rema thoroughly enjoyed working with Nathenek. He was an excellent, patient instructor, and she learned a great deal from him. His cold exterior had melted away and he was pleasant to be around.

When they stopped for a water break, the captain of the ship came over. "Land has been spotted," he informed them. "We should arrive at sunset."

Fear coursed through her. She'd managed to forget about her execution by focusing on training. Everything was about to change.

"Thank you," Nathenek said to the ship's captain. "We'll be in my room preparing. Let me know when we're about to dock."

The captain nodded and left. Rema kept her mouth shut as she followed Nathenek to his berth. The second she stepped foot on land, she would escape. She would need to be fully aware of her surroundings and ready to run or hide when the opportunity presented itself.

Nathenek closed and locked his door. "We need to talk." He went over to the footlocker and opened it. He dug around inside and pulled out her key necklace. "When I first kidnapped you, this was around your neck."

She went to grab the chain but he stood, raising it out of her reach.

"Where did you get it?" he asked.

"It's a family heirloom. Give it back."

"Do you have any idea what this means?"

"Yes, I do." She folded her arms across her chest. "I know exactly what it means. Do you?"

He lowered the necklace, placing the key on his palm. "Tell me what it means."

"Not that it's any of your business, but that necklace has been handed down from generation to generation in my family. It symbolizes the true heir to the throne."

His eyes narrowed. "For Greenwood Island?"

"Yes, now give it to me." If Nathenek showed it to the emperor, he would know she was the rightful heir of Greenwood Island, thus making her the true heir of Emperion. He would kill her at once. However, if he knew about the secret tattoo on her shoulder, all he had to do was look at it and she'd be condemned to death.

Nathenek's fingers curled around the key.

Running out of options, she tried a different approach. "Is your loyalty to the Emperion line? Or is your loyalty to the emperor?"

His head jerked up. He took a step toward her, coming too close for comfort. "They are one in the same."

"Are you sure about that?"

Nathenek cursed under his breath. Was he finally starting to understand her true heritage?

"I want my necklace back."

"I'm sorry," he said, putting it in his pocket. "I can't give this to you right now." He took a step back, rubbing his face with his hands.

"Why not?" she demanded. "It's mine."

Nathenek clutched her upper arms, startling her. "Listen to me," he said, his voice cold and hard, sending chills through her body. "Keep your mouth shut about the key, or I'll kill you."

Something pierced her side. Glancing down, Nathenek had let go of her arm, unsheathed his dagger, and dug it into her skin just below her ribs. She'd never even seen him move. She nodded, afraid to say anything at all.

He let go, putting his dagger away. "Now listen closely. When we arrive, we'll be disguised as merchants as we travel through the city to the palace. Then I will take you in through the servants' entrance and inform the emperor you're here."

Why did he bother to tell her his plan? "And then I'll be executed?"

"Yes."

"By you?"

His eyes darkened. "I'm an assassin, not an executioner. He'll either have me kill you immediately and, if that's the case, I promise to do it swiftly and as painlessly as possible. Or, he'll have you publicly executed in the city. That occurs the first day of every new week."

Someone knocked on the door. "Captain told me to tell you we're coming into port."

"Thank you," Nathenek called out. Then to Rema, he said softly, "We don't have much time."

She was aware how little time she had to escape. Could she jump off the boat and swim to shore? Or should she wait until they were on the dock to get away?

He pulled a brown cape from his footlocker. "Put this on."

The air was hot and sticky—unlike anything she'd ever experienced before. The last thing she felt like doing was putting on a heavy cape. Besides, it would make it impossible for her to swim.

"Trust me. Not only is the sun hot, burning exposed skin, but the sand is severe. You'll need the cape for your protection."

She reluctantly took it, draping it over her shoulders. There was extra fabric around her shoulders and she pulled it out, thinking it was a hood, but the material was too long.

"That's for your face," he said, putting on his own cape. "If a sandstorm hits us, wrap the fabric around your head to protect your ears, nose, and eyes."

A sandstorm? As frightened as she was, she was equally intrigued by the fact that she was about to step foot on foreign soil.

"Fix your cap so your hair is completely concealed."

While she adjusted her cap, Nathenek closed and locked his footlocker. He picked it up, lifting it above his head. "Let's go."

Rema followed him to the top deck where there was a flurry of activity going on. The sails were being lowered and men ran around, yelling commands she didn't understand.

"Wait here," Nathenek instructed, placing her out of everyone's way. He hurried over to a man dressed in a long, brown cape, his head concealed by a large hood. She wondered if it was Trell, and if so, what the assassin planned to do with him.

Nathenek set his footlocker down and handed the man a small bag and some papers. The man nodded, briefly glancing her way. Nathenek returned to her, leading her toward the front of the ship, away from the mysterious man.

"What's going to happen to Trell?" she asked.

"That is none of your concern." His harsh tone made her flinch.

They stopped next to the railing on the starboard side of the ship. Several docks jetted out from one main pier, all filled with ships of various sizes. Beyond the bay, a massive wall lined the beach in each direction. There was only one gateway in the tan wall, and a horde of traffic accumulated in that area.

On the other side of the wall, rows upon rows of buildings could be seen, going on for miles. In the far distance were bare, rolling hills. The sun beat down, sizzling hot, and the air felt heavy. Rema swayed, lightheaded.

Nathenek grabbed her arm, keeping her upright. "Are you ill?"

"No." She yanked her arm away from him. "Just nervous about my death."

The ship came into an empty slip. Sailors heaved the massive anchor over the side and into the water. Nathenek drew her away from the railing. "I know you want to see, but I can't risk anyone recognizing me." He wrapped a strip of fabric around his face, leaving only his blue eyes exposed. "When we descend the ramp, keep your face down and don't speak to anyone."

She nodded. "Where's the emperor's palace located?" Once

she escaped, she needed to make sure she didn't head in that direction.

"We must travel through the city a couple of miles. It's on the backside."

That would give her plenty of time to escape. The thought of being in a foreign country, especially one as hostile as Emperion, was terrifying. Still, she knew she could get away and survive on her own.

"Let's go." Nathenek took Rema's elbow, guiding her toward the ramp. Several of the crew members were already carrying crates down the ramp, stacking them on the dock. "Grab one," he murmured to her. "Put it on top of your head. Be careful to keep your balance when you descend."

Her heart pounded. Now was not the time to make a run for it. She needed to wait until she was around more people and could easily blend in and disappear among them. She wondered what was inside the crates. Food? Supplies? Whatever it was, King Barjon had no right to export products while so many in the kingdom suffered from a lack of food. Grabbing a crate, she hoisted it up and on her head. It wasn't too heavy, and she made it off the ship and down the ramp with ease.

After setting the crate on top of another one, an atrocious odor made her gag. It smelled like a dead, rotting animal. She pulled her wrap around her face, trying to block the foul stench. The dozens of people unloading the merchant ship seemed unfazed by the odor. Before she had a chance to get lost amidst the chaos, Nathenek snatched her arm, pulling her away from the dock and toward the entrance in the wall.

"Keep your head down." He held onto her arm with an iron grip.

They stepped off the pier and onto solid ground. Rema swayed, her legs feeling like mushy oatmeal. Nathenek held her upright.

"Walk fast and with purpose. Whatever you do, don't leave my side."

A small laugh escaped her.

"You think this is funny?" He leaned down, his face only inches from hers.

"You act like you're trying to protect me."

"I am."

"By taking me to the emperor to be executed? I don't think so. I'll take my chances here if afforded the opportunity."

He shook his head. "Death by execution is a mercy compared to what will happen if the army gets ahold of you."

"After spending two weeks with me, I thought you knew me better than that." If he expected her to cooperate and be led to her death like some animal, he was sorely mistaken. She would fight, and she would get away.

Nathenek stopped, dozens of people moving past him as if he wasn't even there. Everyone wore capes that covered their entire bodies, including their heads, leaving only their faces exposed. No one glanced Rema's way as she stood before Nathenek. It was almost as if they were afraid to look or linger.

"The army is ruthless," Nathenek whispered in her ear, still holding onto her. "They beat you down in order to break you— make you obedient. Yes, I know you well enough to know you would survive. But you wouldn't be *you* anymore. And I can't let that happen." He pulled back slightly, looking at her. He raised his eyebrows, waiting for her to respond.

Words escaped her. Why did he care what happened to her now? He was taking her to her death, why show her mercy? It didn't make any sense.

He nodded toward the wall's entrance. "Let's go." He released her, taking a step back.

If she ran, would he catch her? Could she get lost in this crowd? Her foot inched its way back, putting her out of arm's reach.

"If you run, they'll shoot you." He pointed to the top of the wall, where archers stood with bows at the ready. "Only someone guilty of a crime runs. No questions asked."

She had absolutely no intention of dying or letting the army get their hands on her. Her best bet would be to enter the city and find an elderly person or a mother—someone who would be sympathetic and aid in her escape. Then she could hide, acquire supplies, and board a merchant ship voyaging to Greenwood Island. She would return to *her* kingdom, to *her* people, and to *her* Darmik. Destiny couldn't be so cruel as to take everything from her—her entire family, her love, her life. She refused to allow it. She would fight with every ounce of her being.

Nathenek grinned and turned away from her, walking directly toward the wall's opening. She hurried after him, knowing he would see her safely inside. Dozens of soldiers guarded the entrance, checking the papers of everyone who entered.

Nathenek stopped before a younger-looking soldier, handing him two pieces of paper. "For me and my wife," he said in a rough voice. The soldier glanced over the documents and waved them through. Nathenek took the papers back, shoving them inside his cape. Rema kept her mouth shut, following meekly behind him. Why didn't he declare that he worked for the emperor and was transporting a prisoner? Why did he want to keep his identity concealed from everyone?

Once inside, Nathenek slipped his arm around her waist, keeping her close to him. Traveling through Emperor's City was beyond anything she had ever imagined. It was like walking through a sinister dream. Buildings lined both sides of the narrow streets. People walked shoulder to shoulder. The two-story structures, made of smooth stone blocks, were light brown, matching the sandy ground. It was ugly. No greenery, no living plants, and no color.

"Stop gawking," Nathenek hissed in her ear. "Keep your head down and walk faster."

Someone bumped against her shoulder.

"Sorry," she mumbled. The stranger hurried away, too busy to respond.

Nathenek growled and shoved her down a dark alley, pushing her up against a wall. "Stop talking." He placed his hands on either side of her head, his entire body shielding hers as he leaned in. Anyone passing by would think they were two lovers embracing in a kiss. "You have a ridiculous accent. It stands out."

"Sorry."

"We need to get through the city unnoticed." His eyes focused on hers, as if pleading with her to cooperate. "Stop looking around, walk right next to me with your head down, and act like you have a purpose."

"A purpose?"

"Yes." He rested his forehead against hers. "Like you know where you're going and what you're doing so you don't stand out."

She leaned her head back against the wall behind her, away from him. She did have a purpose—to find someone sympathetic who would help her.

He sighed. "If you don't cooperate and do *exactly* as I say, I'll drug you again."

"And drag my body to the palace?"

His eyes narrowed. "If I have to."

Shoving against his chest, she said, "Fine, let's go." She'd play along, doing as he said while keeping her eyes open for an opportunity to escape.

"My sister never does what I ask either. She always has to make things difficult, instead of trusting me." He took hold of her arm. "So obstinate."

Once again, they entered the busy street, traveling quickly among the hordes of people. Rema kept pace with Nathenek, her head down, like she'd been here a thousand times before. Half the people they passed wore brown capes similar to the one she had on. The rest of the people sported long brown pants and plain tunics, even the women. Every single person had either a scarf or fabric wrapped around his or her neck, with very little skin exposed. Another thing she noticed: there weren't any elderly people or children about.

Even though the sun was starting to set, Rema was covered with sweat. She felt like she was a lit candle, wax dripping down her sides. How could people stand this heat?

Nathenek cursed. In the distance, a wall of dark clouds was rapidly moving toward them. People started running and a *bong* sound rang throughout the city. Doors started slamming shut. People covered exposed windows with wooden boards.

"Hurry!" Nathenek ran, dragging Rema behind him.

"What's going on?" She tried keeping up with his long strides.

"A sandstorm is coming."

Darkness descended over the city. The streets became eerily void of people. A hissing sound neared, and Rema shivered. "Where are we going?" The wind kicked up, tossing her cape violently around her body. Little pieces of sand flew through the air.

"Use your scarf!" Nathenek shouted.

A loud, rumbling noise vibrated through the streets, filling her with panic. She tried covering her face, but the wind was so strong she couldn't wrap the fabric around her mouth and nose. She ended up holding it against her face with her free hand.

"Almost there!" Nathenek cried, hauling her alongside him.

If Savenek hadn't forced her to run in order to build up her stamina, she'd never have been able to keep pace with Nathenek. Sand whipped by, pounding against the walls of nearby buildings, stinging her body and even slicing through her clothing. They wouldn't last much longer. Rounding a corner, they ran down another street as fast as possible.

Nathenek threw himself against a door on the left, his fist beating on it. The door opened a couple of inches. He shoved Rema inside, slamming it closed behind him. She blinked, taking in her surroundings. A young child stood in a narrow hallway before her.

"Thank you," Nathenek said. "No one else is out there. You can go to your room." The boy nodded and left without saying a word.

"Where are we?" After the howling wind outside, her voice sounded loud in the quiet hallway.

He scowled at her. She forgot she wasn't supposed to talk. But it wasn't like there was anyone around to hear her. She mouthed *sorry* and followed him down the hallway. He stopped before a door, pulled a key out of his pocket, and unlocked it.

Rema stepped inside the pitch-black room, unable to see a single thing. She heard the door close and lock. There was a shuffling noise, and light appeared before her. Nathenek stood there, holding a small candle.

"Where are we?"

"My home." He turned and lit several more candles throughout the small room.

It reminded her of the berth aboard the ship. "You live here?" There was a cot, dresser, and a desk. No fireplace, no kitchen, and no privy.

"Yes." He sat on the edge of his bed. "I'm not home very often." He removed his boots, sand trickling out. "I'm either at the palace working, or on assignment. The only time I'm here is to sleep for a few hours."

How could he stand to live in a place that felt like a cage? There wasn't even a single window.

Rema swayed. It felt like she was moving up and down. Her stomach rolled in discomfort. "Why do I feel as if I'm still on the ship?" She sat on the floor and ripped her cap off, clutching her head in her hands. She wished the sensation would pass.

"I'm surprised you lasted this long. You'll adjust. It'll take some time, though."

"Funny coming from you—considering I have little time left."

The stone floor was cold, and she started shaking uncontrollably. Closing her eyes, she felt her body being lifted, the rocking motion increased, and then she was placed on the soft bed.

She opened her eyes. Nathenek knelt beside her, his eyebrows knit with concern. "Would you care for some water?" He covered her with a blanket.

"No," she whispered, afraid if she ate or drank, she would vomit. She closed her eyes again.

"I didn't plan on coming here," he said. "Since we have, go ahead and sleep for a couple of hours while I come up with a revised plan." With his fingers, he gently brushed her hair off her forehead.

"I don't understand," she mumbled.

"We can't go outside until the storm has passed. We're stuck here for at least a couple of hours." His hand rested on her head.

"No." She opened her eyes, staring at him. "I mean, why are you being so kind?"

He snatched his hand away from her. "I need you strong enough to walk the three miles to the palace."

"You're not going to poison me if I take a nap?"

"No, I'm not going to hurt you. There is nothing to fear."

She drifted off to sleep.

Rema felt her body rocking up and down, but the sensation was tolerable now. Peeling her eyelids open, she glanced around the candlelit room. Nathenek was sitting on a wooden chair, hunched over, staring at something on the palm of his hand. She watched him. He sighed and leaned back, a gold chain slipping through his fingers.

"Is that my necklace?" She sat up on the bed.

"You're awake." His fingers curled over the key as he stood and slipped the necklace into his pocket. "We should leave."

He blew out the candles, the smoky smell filling the tiny room. Rema stood and stretched, unable to see a single thing.

A hand encircled her upper arm. "I need you to trust me," Nathenek whispered in her ear. "From here on out, do exactly as I say."

"You want *me* to trust *you?*" Was he playing her for a fool? Trying to get her to have faith in him in order to make his job easier? She didn't understand him. One minute, he was kind and helping her; the next, he was cold and harsh. Who was the real Nathenek? The only thing she knew for sure: he was an assassin and she didn't want to die.

Nathenek exhaled, his breath blowing the stray hairs by her ear. "Never mind," he said. "Let's go."

He jerked her hands forward, wrapping something rough around her wrists. "What are you doing?" she demanded, unable to see in the dark room.

"I have to bind you. I would never deliver a prisoner to the emperor any other way." He gently pulled her forward, guiding her through the doorway, down the hall, and out into the dead of night.

The sky was clear and a sliver of moon provided enough light to see. Nathenek kept hold of her arm as they made their way along the empty city streets. Walking at a brisk pace, Rema's chest tightened. How was she going to beg someone to help her when no one was around? Her only other option was to break free from Nathenek and make a run for it.

Something moved up ahead. Two figures stepped away from one of the buildings. Nathenek's hand squeezed her arm as he roughly dragged her along.

"It's after curfew," a deep voice said. "State your business." The moonlight shone on the figures, revealing two soldiers with their swords drawn.

"I'm following orders of His Royal Majesty, Emperor Hamen. I'm transporting a prisoner of the utmost importance."

"Your name?"

"Nathenek, of the Elimination Squad, First Division."

"We'll escort you the rest of the way so you won't be stopped again." The soldiers abruptly turned and walked down the middle of the street, Nathenek pulling her along behind them.

How in the world would she escape now? She couldn't possibly outrun three armed men. Yet, her only other option was to be taken to her death. She had to try. When they turned a corner, she reached up and shoved Nathenek toward the side of the building. He released her and she spun around, running as fast as she could.

Something long and hard hit her legs, tripping her. As she fell forward, she raised her bound wrists, preventing her face from smashing against the ground. A hand grabbed the back of her cape, lifting her as if she weighed nothing. Nathenek held her suspended in air, the two soldiers right next to him. One bent down and retrieved Nathenek's longsword, handing it to him. Nathenek released her, and she dropped to her feet.

He sheathed his sword, a snarl on his face. "You do that again, and I'll throw a dagger in your back. You can rot in the street. The vultures can pick away at your body for all I care."

"It doesn't matter to me. I'm going to die anyway. Might as well try and get away instead of being taken meekly to the emperor."

The two soldiers turned and resumed walking. Nathenek grabbed her arm, tugging her forward. "Let's go."

They didn't pass a single person as they traveled to the palace. Yet, somehow Rema felt people watching her, especially when Nathenek became extra rough and pushed her. He even tripped her a couple of times.

After walking a good hour, the buildings abruptly ended, leaving nothing but open land before them. "Where are we?" Rema asked, wondering if the palace was near.

74

One of the soldiers glanced back at her. "You're not from around here, are you?"

"That is none of your concern," Nathenek answered, his fingers digging into her arm.

Rema didn't see anything but sand up ahead. They walked for another fifteen minutes in silence before stopping at massive iron doors set into a wall easily five times her height. She marveled at how well the wall blended into the landscape.

"This is as far as we go," one of the soldiers said.

Nathenek nodded. "Thank you for the escort."

After the soldiers left, he knocked on a wooden door that she hadn't noticed before. He mumbled a few words to someone on the other side. The door opened, granting them entrance.

When she stepped through the doorway, a burlap sack was shoved over her head. She reached up and tried pulling it away, but someone smacked her hands. Another person roughly felt around her body.

"She's clean," Nathenek said, a hard edge to his voice.

"Standard protocol."

"Let's go," Nathenek growled, yanking her along.

"Get this off my head," Rema demanded. Not being able to see caused her heart to beat erratically, and she started shaking.

Nathenek chuckled. "All prisoners are hooded." His cold and malicious voice sent chills down her spine. He grabbed her wrists much more roughly than before, doing something with her bindings. When he let go, she felt a rope now attached to her bound wrists, like a lead rope used on horses. He wound something around her neck, cinching the burlap bag closed.

"What are you doing?" Panic set in. Was she going to be hanged? She couldn't breathe very well. She tried tearing the bag off. Someone laughed and the rope attached to her bound wrists jerked forward, making her stumble to the ground.

"Get up," Nathenek growled.

Tears slid down her cheeks, soaking into the bag. She didn't want to cry and be weak. She needed to calm down and focus so she could fight her way out of this. She couldn't afford to lose it now. Forcing herself to stand, they walked in silence for several minutes, her breathing loud with the bag covering her head.

"Captain Nathenek," a voice said. "Good to see you."

"I assume Emperor Hamen is asleep?" Nathenek said, coming to a stop.

"He is, although I have specific instructions to wake him upon your return."

Rema was yanked forward, and she fell to her knees. Fingers dug into her right shoulder, pinching her skin, making her cry out in pain. "Then summon the emperor. Let him know his package has arrived."

CHAPTER SIX

Darmik

*T*he ring of guards surrounding Darmik and Savenek parted as a robust soldier bedecked with medals glided forward.

"Darmik," the man said, "we meet again."

Darmik pushed Savenek, hunched over and clutching his stomach, to the floor, wanting him to remain quiet. Standing tall, he faced his old mentor—the one who had ordered his beatings numerous times, trying to break him. "Gaverek, good to see you." He used every ounce of energy he had to remain composed. No one could know how much he hated and feared this man.

"Still causing trouble, I see."

Savenek moved to stand, but Darmik put his foot on his back, pushing him to the floor. "I'm trying to understand the lack of respect you Emperions are showing me. I am a prince and commander, here to see my uncle. Locking me in the dungeon is not a very wise move on your part. I suggest you inform Emperor Hamen that I'm here with vital information."

Gaverek chuckled. "The emperor already knows you're here.

While he is interested in the information you claim to have, he is also concerned by your unannounced visit." He pointed at Savenek. "Get him back into his cell."

Two soldiers grabbed Savenek, dragging him away. Darmik kept his focus on Gaverek, trying not to show any interest or concern for his companion.

Gaverek came closer. "I can't take you to the emperor until I know you'll behave."

Fear shot through Darmik. These Emperion soldiers weren't going to interrogate his friends, they were going to torture them. He would survive. He'd been through it enough times to know what to expect. But Ellie and Vesha wouldn't last more than five minutes. He swallowed, trying to keep his face blank. Gaverek was probably testing him.

"Sir," a soldier said as he approached. "The prisoner is strapped to the table." The warden and injured soldiers stalked up behind him. The warden shoved the soldier out of the way and came at Darmik, swinging his fist. Darmik ducked.

"Enough," Gaverek ordered. He pointed at the men Darmik had managed to overpower earlier. "You are all demoted for your incompetence." Turning to Darmik, he said, "Come with me."

They walked in silence. Once they were out of sight from everyone, Gaverek abruptly stopped. "Why are you here?"

"I'm not at liberty to discuss that with you."

"You're not going before the emperor until I know."

Darmik stared at his former mentor. Was he testing him? "Have you forgotten that I outrank you? You're out of line."

Gaverek leaned forward. "No one knows you're here. I can make you disappear."

"An entire platoon of soldiers saw me arrive," Darmik said. "And I sincerely doubt you want to be the reason our kingdoms go to war. If you injure me, I will personally see you destroyed."

His former mentor's eyes flashed with fury. He quickly turned and resumed walking. Two soldiers stood on either side of the door to Savenek's cell. Gaverek said, "Restrain Darmik. I want him held by the both of you."

"Sir, do you want him in a cell?"

"No. I want him with me. He's going to watch as I play with his companions." He smiled, turning to Darmik. "You're easy to read and predictable."

～

Darmik stood in a cell, his arms bound in front of him. Vesha lay strapped to the table. He'd already witnessed Savenek and Audek's interrogations. Since he'd been privy to many such events in the past, he knew how to emotionally shield himself from what was happening.

But Vesha was different.

He hadn't seen a female interrogated since his time in Emperion. Although Vesha was a trained soldier and knew how to fight, she didn't know what she was about to face. Hopefully, she was mentally strong enough to survive.

"Let's begin," Gaverek said.

Darmik tried to look at the situation objectively—once this was over, Neco and Ellie were the only two remaining. Then he would see his uncle and save Rema.

Two soldiers released the levers, flipping the top of the table upside down. Much to Vesha's credit, she didn't scream. Still strapped to the table, she was now parallel to the floor, about three feet above it. A soldier slid a bucket under her and released a different lever, tipping the table forward. Vesha's head was submerged in the bucket.

He'd been in her situation before. He knew the water in the bucket was ice-cold. The trick was to remain calm. He found it most effective to hold his breath, slowly releasing it in gradual intervals. If he panicked and breathed in water, it was quite painful.

Vesha's hands balled into fists, her legs twitching. She wasn't going to last much longer, and it had only been ten seconds. Emperion soldiers were trained to dunk a person's head under water for thirty seconds at a time. Her entire body jerked, but she had nowhere to go.

The soldiers lifted the table, raising Vesha's head out of the bucket. Sill facing the floor, she turned her head, looking at Darmik, her eyes wide with horror. Her body heaved and then she vomited, most of it splashing into the bucket still below her.

Gaverek knelt near her head. "Tell me why you're here."

Heaving in deep breaths, she said, "I . . . I'm accompanying Prince Darmik." Her hair dripped water onto the floor.

During their etiquette lessons aboard the ship, Darmik had made them rehearse these answers. He assumed the emperor would be the one asking, not an interrogator. Regardless, at least everyone gave consistent responses.

"Why is Prince Darmik here?" Gaverek asked.

"He . . . he . . . has a message for the emperor."

"What is the message?"

"I . . . I don't know. He ordered me . . . to accompany him, and I did."

"How did you acquire one of our military ships?"

Darmik wondered if there was a record of Captain leaving with the ship. Vesha glanced at him.

"Dunk her."

"No!" she screamed as the table tilted again, submerging her head in the filthy water.

Knowing she wouldn't last long, Gaverek raised his hand, giving the command to right the table. "Flip her face up."

The soldiers twisted the levers, flipping the table so Vesha lay face up. Her chest heaved up and down. Vomit covered her face and hair. "Why are you doing this?" she cried, her eyes wide with fear. "I don't know anything of importance."

"I'll be the judge of that." Gaverek stood before Darmik. "What do you suggest?" he asked. "The cane? Or the knife?"

Both weapons were painful. He'd witnessed Savenek and Audek's canings and had no desire to see Vesha abused. "I don't care. I'm here as a witness—not a participant—to your barbaric behavior. I had forgotten how . . . unrefined your kingdom is."

Gaverek studied him for several moments. "You're from Emperion. We put you in power. We are the strongest and largest empire in the world. Do not forget that."

Darmik took a step toward his old mentor. "The strongest empire?" He cocked his head to the side. "You're beating up a young woman simply to prove your power. That doesn't make you strong. It makes you pathetic."

Gaverek punched him in the stomach. Darmik hunched forward, grunting. "I'm pathetic?" His knee flew up, slamming into Darmik's jaw and making him fall to the floor. "You're the soft prince who's locked in a dungeon. You're the pathetic one, not me."

Darmik sucked in a deep breath, trying to work through the pain.

"I knew you had a soft spot for your companions. You're so predictable."

Darmik pushed himself up on his knees. "Has it ever occurred to you that my uncle might actually want to hear what I have to say? That you are jeopardizing your position by keeping me here?" He was running out of time.

"Move him to his own cell," Gaverek ordered the soldiers present.

As Darmik stood, Neco's scream pierced the air. He'd never heard his friend scream before. Something was terribly wrong.

Gaverek smiled. "I think I'll join that interrogation. It's always fun to watch lovers being tortured in front of one another."

Darmik wanted to tear him apart, but he maintained his position knowing his old mentor was goading him. If he showed any emotion or attempted to fight back, whatever horrors Neco and Ellie faced would be multiplied tenfold.

~

Darmik woke up in a cold, damp room. He was lying on the floor, his arms still bound in front of him.

The door opened and a small amount of light pierced the darkness. "Get up you filthy piece of trash," a soldier said. "The emperor is ready to see you."

While he'd managed to not be interrogated, watching his friends endure torture had been far worse. He stood, stretching his stiff limbs. The soldier took him to another room where his companions were gathered.

"Put these uniforms on," a soldier said. "Once everyone is dressed, I'll escort you out of the dungeon. If anyone makes a move against me or any other soldier, you'll be killed. Understood?" Everyone nodded.

The soldier removed Darmik's bindings and left, slamming the door on his way out.

They turned and faced the walls while they changed. "These are Emperion uniforms," Darmik said. "These are what the cadets wear. As in, the lowest-ranking uniform possible." He pulled off his pants and tunic, putting on the Emperion clothing. It made his skin crawl—he never thought he'd wear this uniform again. "In other words," he said, still facing the wall, "even though we're being taken out of the dungeon and to the emperor, they want us, and anyone who sees us, to know we're insignificant and have no rights."

Once everyone changed, Darmik surveyed his friends. He'd witnessed Audek and Savenek's interrogations. Both men had been dunked underwater and caned. "Did anything else happen to either of you after I left?"

"Nope," Audek said. "After they were done playing with me, they left me there."

"Same here," Savenek said, his voice harsh.

"What about you, Vesha? Are you okay?" Darmik asked.

She nodded. "I'd really like to find Rema and get out of here." Her face was pale.

He had no idea what Neco and Ellie had gone through. He looked at his friend, afraid to ask.

Neco wrapped Ellie in his arms, hugging her. "They did exactly what you said they would," he whispered. "They figured out what matters most to me, and they used it against me."

Ellie glanced up into Neco's eyes. "I'm sorry you had to see that. I don't want to be your weakness."

"You're not. You are my strength." He kissed the top of her head.

"Are either of you injured?" Darmik asked. "Savenek and Audek were both caned."

"We're fine," Neco answered. "They were mentally toying with us, trying to drive me mad. They hit Ellie a few times but that's all." Ellie's eyes glossed over with tears.

"Good," Darmik said. "I want everyone to remember what we discussed on the ship about how to behave. And no matter what happens, do not fight back. They won't hesitate to kill us."

The door opened and they entered the hallway now lined with soldiers. They were escorted along several hallways and up a steep flight of stairs. They exited into a small courtyard surrounded by a wall.

Gaverek was standing in the middle of the courtyard, waiting for them. "I see no need to take such a large party of barbarians to the palace."

This was what Darmik had feared—being separated from his friends. "Like you said, I'm soft. You don't expect me to see the emperor alone? Who will assist me when I'm tired or need help?"

His old mentor smiled. "You may take one person to attend you. That way if you do something I don't like, I have leverage."

Darmik wanted to keep Neco with Ellie. Vesha could barely stand on her feet. That left Audek and Savenek. Of the two, Savenek was the stronger fighter. Would it be more beneficial to leave Savenek here or bring him along?

Gaverek raised his eyebrows, waiting for his answer.

"It makes no difference," Darmik said. "Audek, why don't you accompany me?"

"Uh, yeah, sure," Audek said. Darmik glared at him, and he snapped his mouth shut. Maybe choosing him wasn't the best move.

"Excellent," Gaverek said. "You two come with me."

"Where will the rest of my companions be?"

Gaverek walked toward the door, not bothering to answer.

"He's quite friendly," Audek said sarcastically. "This should be loads of fun."

Darmik grabbed his elbow, dragging him along after Gaverek, a dozen soldiers following. "What part of *keep your mouth shut* are you not understanding?"

"It's shut! I'll be quiet now, I promise."

They exited and went down a short hallway. At the end, they stepped out into the bright sunlight.

"Oh man, how do you people stand this heat?" Audek asked the soldiers surrounding them.

Shaking his head, Darmik hurried after Gaverek, ignoring Audek completely.

"I can see you are an effective leader and commander. Your subjects are quite obedient," Gaverek said.

Instead of responding, he glanced around, trying to get his bearings. They were on the outskirts of the city near the military compound, which was directly north of the palace. To the east was the training facility nestled among the hills in the distance.

"Where's the color?" Audek asked, jogging to catch up. "This place is so . . . blah."

He should've brought Savenek instead.

Gaverek looked at Audek. "Everything is functional and serves a purpose. It obviously works, seeing as how we're the largest known empire in the world."

"No, that's not what I meant," Audek said.

Gaverek stopped and turned to face him.

"I . . . uh . . . meant that the place," Audek frantically waved his arms, pointing at the dry, brown hills and the garrison, "is . . . uh . . . rather limited in color."

Gaverek cocked his head to the side, studying him.

"You know . . . cause everything is brown."

"If you don't shut your mouth and refrain from speaking," Gaverek said, "I'll chop off your tongue. Understood?"

Audek nodded.

"Good. Let's continue—in silence."

Darmik balled his hands into fists, wanting to punch Audek. What was the point of teaching him how to behave in Emperion if he was going to ignore everything he'd learned?

They passed the garrison and headed toward the emperor's palace. When they reached the twenty-foot wall surrounding it, they were searched and granted entrance. Once inside, Darmik had a clear view of the pristine palace. The walls were made of shiny white stone tiles and the roof was covered in gold. Several round towers stood throughout the massive structure. Even more intriguing were the vibrant, colorful gardens surrounding the entire place, a stark contrast to the land outside the wall.

Audek huffed, about to say something, but Darmik covered his friend's mouth to prevent him from speaking. Audek's eyes widened when he realized what he'd almost done. They walked along a cobblestone pathway. Darmik had been here once before— when he first arrived at the mainland for military training and his uncle had wanted to meet him. After that one time, he'd never stepped foot in the palace or seen his uncle again.

They went through a golden doorway at least fifteen feet tall. Inlaid on each door was the royal crest of Emperion, along with a key. Audek grabbed Darmik's arm, pointing at the doors. He doubted it was a mere coincidence that Rema's key necklace matched the shape of the key on each door. "Permission to speak?" Darmik asked. "I'd like to make sure my man behaves properly."

Gaverek gave a curt nod. "Fine. Just keep your voices low since we are inside the palace."

Leaning toward Audek, Darmik whispered, "This building has been here for centuries. It was constructed when Emperion was formed over six hundred and fifty years ago." Rema's key was no simple heirloom passed down through the rulers of each generation on Greenwood Island—it had ties all the way back here, to Emperion. It would, beyond a doubt, prove her to be the true heir to the Emperion throne.

The hallway before them was adorned with gold-framed pictures, richly colored rugs atop marble floors, and ceramic vases filled with fragrant flowers. The ceiling was covered with intricate paintings.

"This is . . . it's . . ." Audek mumbled.

"Yes," Darmik agreed. "Please remember to show the utmost respect before the emperor. Do you remember how to bow and properly greet him?"

Audek nodded, his focus on the ceiling. Darmik followed his line of sight. The ceiling had a painting of a beautiful woman with long, dark hair. She held a key on the palm of her hand—an exact replica of Rema's.

"Try not to gawk. It makes us look like simpletons." He hoped no one noticed them observing all the keys. He thought back to his studies when he had been here before. He didn't recall anything about keys being a symbol or having any special meaning. Yet they obviously did, seeing as how they were everywhere.

Gaverek stopped before a large door with a key-shaped handle. "The emperor is in his receiving room. When we enter, keep your head down, wait to be presented, and then bow. Once he acknowledges you, you may rise. If you do anything disrespectful, I'll run my sword through you."

"But then there would be blood everywhere. Would the emperor want you ruining his room?" Audek asked in mock horror.

Gaverek's gaze darkened. "You wouldn't last a day under my command."

"Then I guess it's a good thing I'm not under your command. Now, are we going to do this? I'm ready to meet the all-powerful emperor." He clasped his hands together.

Darmik was on the verge of running his own sword through Audek just to get him to shut up. "Excuse me," he said, addressing the servant passing by. "May I please have the sash around your waist?" The woman looked confused but complied. Darmik took the fabric and tied it around Audek's head, covering his mouth. "You're going to get us both killed. Keep your mouth shut."

Gaverek chuckled and opened the door. Darmik stepped into the receiving room, quickly scanning it for potential threats. Not seeing anyone else present, he walked down the center aisle. There were several velvet-covered sofas and goldwood chairs throughout the room. In one corner stood a tall, stringed instrument. The walls were adorned with framed portraits of all the emperors who had ruled through the years. At the end of the aisle was a raised, marble dais with two intricately designed golden chairs. Looking closer at them, he saw keys were engraved in the gold—keys that also matched Rema's necklace.

Gaverek instructed Darmik and Audek to wait by the dais while he went over and knocked on a door off to the side. A moment later it swung open and he announced, "His Majesty, Emperor Hamen."

A regal man with fair skin and black hair entered the room. He wore a green tunic embroidered with the Emperion crest. A gold crown embedded with emeralds sat atop his head.

Darmik dropped to his knee, bowing his head in submission.

"Rise," the emperor commanded in a deep, authoritative voice.

Darmik stood and looked at the man before him.

"I didn't think I'd see you back here in Emperion," Emperor Hamen said.

"Neither did I expect to come back, Uncle."

The emperor smiled at Darmik's use of the word *uncle*.

"I assumed I'd receive a . . ." Darmik searched for the right word—not *warm* exactly. "A more hospitable greeting—one befitting my station."

Emperor Hamen crossed his arms, his tunic pulling tightly across his broad shoulders. "Everyone out."

Darmik felt Audek's questioning stare but refused to take his focus away from his uncle.

When the two of them were alone, the emperor asked, "Why are you here?"

He needed to word his answers carefully since he didn't know if Rema was in Emperion yet. "You sent an assassin to my kingdom."

"Greenwood Island is not *your* kingdom." The emperor took a deep breath and moved to the window, gazing outside. "What have you done with my man?"

"Nothing. But he has stolen something of mine."

"Oh?" The emperor kept his back to Darmik.

He wished he could see his uncle's face to ascertain his thoughts. "Yes. And I'm here to get it back."

Emperor Hamen turned and faced him, his eyes cold and hard. "And what is the item you *think* my man stole?"

"The woman I am going to marry."

The emperor's eyes narrowed. "You're a hard one to read." He rubbed his chin. "I have you and your companions thrown in the dungeon, you watch your friends' interrogations, and you don't fight back. Why? Simply to be granted a meeting with me?" He turned and faced outside again. "I thought it had something to do with a piece of important information you may have accidentally stumbled upon. But that's not the case. You're here because of my assassin." He strolled over to a velvet chair and sat, tapping his fingers on the armrest. His eyes scanned Darmik as if dissecting him. "Stop standing there and sit."

Darmik did as requested, taking a seat on the sofa opposite the emperor. He kept his mouth shut, waiting for his uncle to continue.

"Tell me what you know of the assassin's mission."

His uncle was testing him. He needed to tell a story infused with enough truth to be believable. "The assassin was looking for Lennek's fiancée, Rema, who had been sentenced to execution."

The emperor nodded, knowing all of this already. "Continue."

"Greenwood Island has a small band of rebels who try to undermine the king whenever an opportunity presents itself. In an attempt to flush out these men, I put a decoy on the gallows. The real woman was privately executed while the decoy was rescued by the rebels. I then secretly followed the rebels to their base camp. Your assassin took my decoy."

"And this decoy, as you call her, is your fiancée?"

"She is."

The emperor leaned back on his chair, a hint of a smile across his face. "Why so careless with the ones we love?"

Darmik didn't know how to respond to his uncle, but he got the distinct impression he was missing a vital piece of information.

"I'm going to be honest with you," Emperor Hamen said. "I find it hard to believe my assassin made a mistake."

"I tried explaining the situation to him, but he wasn't interested in reason."

"It seems we have a problem, don't we?"

Darmik's heartbeat quickened. Was Rema already dead? Was he too late to save her?

"My assassin hasn't returned yet."

Relief coursed through him and he could breathe more easily. If he was smart about it, he could save her.

"You will stay here until he does," the emperor said. "When my man arrives, I will verify the woman's identity. If you are lying to me, I'll have your companions executed." He stood.

Interesting that the emperor would threaten the lives of Darmik's friends, but not Darmik himself. Why couldn't he have a normal, decent relationship with a single one of his family members? Why did everyone treat him like dirt? Go out of his way to degrade him?

Emperor Hamen turned to go.

"Uncle, why is my word not good enough? Do you think so little of me?"

"No." He paused before the door. "But let me ask you this: do you think so little of *me*? Do you actually think I would sit back and allow *you* to marry her? You know what I do to anyone who poses a threat to or challenges my authority. Don't disrespect me by claiming something so trivial as love. This has nothing to do with love—and everything to do with power."

Did the emperor think Darmik only cared for Rema because of her lineage? Did he fear Darmik would try to overthrow him? "I just want to take my fiancée and return to Greenwood Island where we can be married and live in peace."

"You're not as good a liar as you think you are." His eyes locked on Darmik's, sending a cold jolt through him. "Let's not forget, I personally oversaw your training when you were here. I know everything about you." And with that, he turned and left.

CHAPTER SEVEN

Rema

*R*ema had been sitting on the cold, stone floor with the burlap bag over her head, her hands tied before her, for what felt like hours when she finally heard a man say, "Emperor Hamen is ready for the prisoner."

The rope attached to her bindings tugged her forward. She scrambled to her feet and was led through various twists and turns. Not being able to see only added to the panic swelling within her. Someone squeezed her elbow, bringing her to a stop.

"Your Majesty," a man said, his voice echoing. "Captain Nathenek of the Elimination Squad and his prisoner."

Someone pulled her forward. It sounded like two heavy doors closed behind her. "Your Majesty," Nathenek said.

"Rise," a dignified voice commanded.

"May I present to you Amer of Greenwood Island."

"I'd like to see the face of the woman who's been causing so much trouble."

Nathenek untied the rope around her neck, pulling off the

burlap bag in one swift motion. Rema squinted against the bright light, blinking several times as she took in the sight before her.

A handsome man in his early fifties stood in front of her with a look of curiosity on his face. He wore black pants and a simple tunic. She never would have known he was the emperor had it not been for the emerald crown atop his head.

She scanned the ornately decorated room. Gaudy gold covered the walls along with pictures of the emperor, his wife, and daughter. One of the portraits must have been painted recently because the emperor looked as he did in person. In the portrait, his wife stood next to him. She had beautiful chestnut hair, fair skin, and appeared to be of similar age to the emperor. Between them sat a girl of about fifteen years. Her skin was unusually white and her eyes were sunken in, giving her a sickly look.

Peeling her eyes away from the picture, she noticed large windows situated behind the emperor. Beyond the windows were lush green gardens, a stark contrast to what she'd observed in the city. The sun had just started to rise, casting the gardens in an eerie gray light.

The emperor tilted his head to the side and his eyes narrowed, assessing her. Rema tried to decide the best course of action. Play dumb and innocent? Or claim her birthright? She glanced at Nathenek, trying to ascertain the situation. He had his chin pointed toward the floor, meek and obedient. She focused back on Emperor Hamen. He had black hair, chocolate-brown eyes, and a jawline that distinctly reminded her of Darmik. She knew he was Darmik's uncle, but the similarities in their appearance them were uncanny.

"She doesn't look like much. Just a filthy commoner with her blonde hair and blue eyes."

She cleared her throat and raised her chin in the air. "I am Queen Amer Rema of Greenwood Island."

"Excuse me?"

"My name is Queen Amer, and you will address me as such."

He laughed, the sound echoing in the room. "I've heard a lot about you." He clapped his hands together. "You are a piece of work." Sitting on a chair, he crossed his legs, never taking his eyes off her. "The question is what to do with you," he mused, tapping his fingers on the armrests.

"Let me return to my island. I will keep trade open with you. We can peacefully co-exist."

"You're delusional. When I said, *what to do with you*, I simply meant do I have Nathenek kill you now? Or do I have you beheaded in front of the city for all to see?"

She suspected he would do the opposite of whatever she wanted. "I've been sentenced to a public execution before. It didn't go so well. I suggest you kill me now so you don't regret it."

The sound of steel rang through the air as Nathenek unsheathed his sword. Rema tried to appear calm even though her body shook uncontrollably. She stared at Emperor Hamen, daring him to order her death.

He stood and came directly in front of her. He had the same height and build as Darmik, and it unnerved her. "Are you positive you've captured the correct person?"

"I am," Nathenek replied. "She is the only one on Greenwood Island with that hair and eye color, and she bears the royal mark of which you spoke."

How did he know about her tattoo? Did he check her for it when he had drugged her and brought her down the mountain?

"Show me," the emperor demanded.

Rema shrank away from him. Nathenek sheathed his sword. Taking a hasty step toward her, he squeezed the back of her neck, causing a shooting pain to radiate down her spine. With his free hand, he tugged the neckline of her tunic off her shoulder, exposing the circular one-inch-wide mark. It was pale, almost a soft gray, with delicate lines of red interwoven into a complex symbol, looking like a unique piece of jewelry.

The emperor leaned in. "It's true," he whispered in disbelief. "Tell me, how did Barjon miss this one?"

Nathenek released her, and she quickly covered herself. "After the entire royal family was disposed of, King Barjon gathered his proof. He collected the head and tattoo of each one. At that time, he discovered that Princess Amer, who was only a few months old, didn't bear a royal mark. Barjon mistakenly assumed the island didn't tattoo their children until the age of one. Trell, whom I'm sure you remember as your previous chief battle strategist and King Barjon's father-in-law, tried to tell him that wasn't the case. Barjon refused to listen. Trell has been hiding in exile ever since."

Rema almost fell over. Trell was Darmik's grandfather? Neither Trell nor Darmik had hinted at any sort of relationship with one another.

Emperor Hamen crossed his arms. "I don't suppose you managed to locate Trell while you were on Greenwood Island?"

"I found him near her." Nathenek jerked his chin in Rema's direction. She kept her mouth shut, curious to hear what else he had to say. "Trell discovered Rema's true identity and was about to kill her."

Her legs wobbled. The old man had seemed so sincere when he said he wanted to join her cause and place her on the throne. Had he only done that to get close to her so he could murder her?

"Where's Trell now?" the emperor asked.

"I brought him with me."

"Excellent work, as always." Emperor Hamen went to the window, gazing outside. "Very well, she'll be publicly beheaded."

"Yes, Your Majesty. Next week with the others?"

"No. I want it done today. We'll hold a special execution. Now if you'll excuse me, I have duties to attend to." He turned and left.

"He's not what I expected," Rema said. She had assumed the emperor would be volatile like King Barjon.

"That's why he's so frightening. He is always calm and in control, yet lethal and unforgiving at the same time. He's not someone you ever cross while expecting to survive." Nathenek turned to leave. "Let's go."

She started to follow him when she noticed the handles on the doors were the shape of keys. She froze, studying them in greater detail. They were the exact shape and had the same features as her key necklace. She felt an overwhelming sense that she belonged here. Her key necklace was more than a family heirloom—it tied her to this strange land. She'd never cared about Emperion before now. However, these keys unlocked the secrets of her past, revealing a destiny she'd never imagined. It wasn't a choice but rather a duty to her people.

Emperion was hers.

She hurried from the room. "Are you going to cover my head again?" she asked, wondering where the burlap bag had disappeared to.

"No. I'm taking you directly to the Execution Tower where we keep those who are sentenced to die." He grabbed the rope, leading her along like an animal. "Hopefully there will be an empty cell for you," he mumbled under his breath.

Walking down the hallway of the palace, Rema became intrigued with the idea that her ancestors had walked down this very hallway. The rounded ceilings were covered with intricate paintings. She examined the beautiful artistry above her. Between two black horses was a picture of a key—an exact replica of her necklace. What did the key symbolize in the Emperion culture? There had to be a way to discover its true meaning.

Nathenek jerked the rope and Rema flew forward, almost losing her balance. He led her out of the palace and to a dirt path surrounded by vibrant green grass and lined with rose bushes. The path went to the wall encircling the grounds. Once they exited, a bleak landscape covered in sand greeted her. In the distance stood Emperor's City.

"I can't believe the sheer number of buildings," she said. "There have to be thousands of people living there." The idea of so many people crowded together, living on top of one another, was astounding. "There's open land over there." She pointed to the dry, brown hills outside the city wall, behind the palace. "Why don't people spread out?"

Nathenek chuckled. "You are young and naïve."

"But why is everyone so crammed together?" There was a lot of empty space surrounding the emperor's palace and the military compound.

"This entire area," Nathenek waved his hand at the open land surrounding them, "used to be covered with buildings as well. When Hamen married Empress Eliza and ascended to the throne, he ordered all the structures within one mile of the palace torn down and removed."

"What's on the other side of the wall surrounding Emperor's City?"

"Those hills are used exclusively by the army. Not only is the training facility located there, which houses all cadets and class-rooms, but the nearby land allows instructors to run various exercises and practice drills."

"What's beyond that?"

"There's nothing but dry, open land for several miles. There are small villages and towns scattered throughout the kingdom."

"Is all of Emperion so ugly?"

"You are full of questions today." He glanced sideways at her. "Why the sudden interest?"

"I'm curious. And talking helps pass the time."

Nathenek smiled. "Fine. I'll answer whatever you ask until we reach the buildings." Looking around, he shook his head and said, "No, the rest of Emperion is not like this. Emperor's City sits on the southernmost tip of the mainland. Farther north, the land becomes higher. The increased elevation brings cooler weather, more rain, and a lusher landscape. Granted, it's not like Green-wood Island, but it's not a desert either."

Rema scrunched her nose. "Why does the emperor live here instead of farther inland?"

He shrugged. "Security, I suppose. There are nine palaces throughout Emperion. The emperor spends time at each one, but he chose this one as his main residence because it's next to the empire's largest military garrison, it's near the ocean, and the city is well fortified."

Nine palaces? For what could he possibly need nine palaces? Were all of the emperor's homes as luxurious as this one? How could he afford to live in such luxury and maintain a large army?

"Enough questions," Nathenek said in a clipped tone, staring up ahead. His entire body went rigid.

She followed his line of sight. A squad of soldiers was jogging in their direction. As the soldiers neared, she moved to the side of the dirt road, giving them room to pass. Instead, the squad halted five feet before them.

"Captain," a man said, stepping forward, out of formation.

Nathenek slowly pulled the rope, bringing Rema closer to him. "Yes?" he said, his voice hard.

"We were sent to guard the prisoner. When we arrived at the Execution Tower, we were informed you hadn't delivered anyone yet."

The soldiers stood perfectly still, as if carved from stone. Not one looked at her. She inadvertently took a step back, away from them.

"We will escort you."

How did these men know she was being transported for execution? The emperor had only just sentenced her. It was as if they'd known she was here . . . but how was that possible?

"It's not necessary," Nathenek said. "I can take her to the Execution Tower alone more easily than with a squad of soldiers. The streets are crowded."

She prayed he outranked these soldiers and got his way. If the squad surrounded her, she would have no chance to escape.

"Of course, Captain," the man replied. He slid back into formation, and the squad resumed jogging toward the military compound. As they passed, Rema realized several of the soldiers were women.

"Come on." Nathenek pulled the hood of his cape over his head. Rema did the same, shielding herself from the harsh light and curious onlookers. They traveled in silence. When they reached the buildings, he turned down a narrow street. The tall buildings were built so close together that they touched. People were about, quickly walking with their heads down, paying no attention to Nathenek or Rema, even though he pulled her by a rope.

There were enough people around that if she could untie her bindings, she'd have a decent chance of disappearing among them. Very slowly, she slipped her hands under her cape, concealing them from sight. She walked a little closer to Nathenek so he wouldn't notice the rope wasn't as slack as it had been.

Turning a corner, something hooked around Rema's ankle and she fell. She hit the ground hard, unable to catch herself. Nathenek leaned down. She thought he was going to help her up; instead, he took a small piece of rolled paper out of his boot, placing it on the ground. Then he fixed the laces of his boots. Another man stopped and helped Rema to her feet. The man smiled and walked away, slipping the rolled paper up his sleeve.

Nathenek stood and jerked the rope, leading her down the street once again. She was about to ask him what had just happened when his head shook ever so slightly. There was someone watching them. She could feel it. Instinct told her to play the part of the prisoner, so she tried pulling away from her captor. When he yanked her back, she wiped her cheeks as if she'd been crying.

A few streets later, a man bumped into Rema's shoulder, throwing her off balance. Nathenek reached out, pushing the man away from her. She could have sworn she saw the guy take a small piece of paper from Nathenek.

"I want to know what's going on," she demanded.

"I'm a member of the emperor's Elimination Squad."

She nodded, listening carefully to what he said. "I took an oath and am dedicated to preserving the royal line."

Did that mean he was on another assignment right now? Were the men he'd exchanged something with also assassins? Once he delivered her to the Execution Tower, would he be on to his next kill? If he truly cared about the bloodline, then he should want to put her in power and not support Emperor Hamen. But he'd sworn an oath to the emperor, not her.

They turned onto another crowded street. Several food carts piled high with brightly colored fruits and vegetables lined one side, while carts filled with wares and goods lined the other. As people shopped, they hovered under canopies trying to avoid the scorching midday sun. Rema had never attended the market in her hometown of Jarko; yet, she suspected it was similar to this one. She observed people shopping for leather belts, candles, and utensils. Her stomach growled from the smell of smoked meat.

There was enough activity going on that she might be able to escape. Fumbling with the knots around her wrists, she loosened them. They approached four soldiers who were checking everyone's papers. Nathenek stepped to the left to pass by the soldiers. She hurried and moved behind him so he wouldn't suspect she'd untied her bindings. Sliding the rope from her wrists, she held onto it, waiting for the right opportunity to run. The soldiers nodded to Nathenek in acknowledgment, letting him pass without question.

There was a narrow space between two food carts that led to an alley. Dropping the rope, Rema casually stepped between the carts. When no one seemed to notice, she took off, sprinting down the alley. A ladder was attached to one of the buildings and she grabbed on, climbing as quickly as possible. She dared not look back to see if Nathenek followed. She sprang onto the rooftop and ran, removing her cape and tying it around her waist. At the edge of the roof, she jumped, flying through the air and landing on the adjacent rooftop three feet away.

"Stop!" Nathenek shouted. She heard footsteps quickly approaching.

When she reached the next ledge, she grabbed onto the ladder and descended, knowing Nathenek pursued her. Running to the main street, she spotted a man sitting on the ground with a gray fabric draped across his legs. She grabbed the man's cape, throwing hers back at him as she sprinted away. As soon as the cape was on her shoulders, she forced herself to walk so she'd blend in. Several people wore their hoods up, so she slid hers on and shielded her face as best she could. Unfortunately, the cape was a little long.

Stopping at a cart, she examined the various woven baskets as if interested in buying one. Holding a basket up, she pretended to inspect the bottom while secretly glancing down the street, searching for Nathenek. She didn't see him anywhere. Putting the basket down, she slowly walked away. Her best bet was to head toward the merchant port to try and board a ship unnoticed. She stopped at a cart selling leather boots. Examining a pair, she asked which direction the docks were.

The man selling the goods squinted, looking at her funny. "You're not from around here, are you?"

She'd forgotten about her accent. "No, I'm not." She couldn't afford to bring attention to herself. Savenek always told her to tell a believable lie. "I am with my father on a merchant vessel from the southern islands. We stopped to unload goods. I must get back before he notices I'm gone."

The man smiled. "The docks are that way." He pointed behind her.

She thanked him and hurried away, eager to distance herself from Nathenek. Looking at the position of the sun, she tried to get her bearings so she wouldn't get lost. Forcing herself to walk at a slow pace, she headed toward the ocean. After three blocks, there weren't any more vendors and the crowd thinned. She felt exposed so she kept her hood on, her head down, and pretended to walk with purpose.

Up ahead, five soldiers were headed her way. Since there weren't any side streets, she kept on course, desperately praying they wouldn't ask for her papers. She recalled Nathenek passing on the left, so she moved over to pass them on the correct side. The men talked and laughed, not appearing to be on duty.

Her heartbeat quickened as she neared the group. Forcing herself to walk at a slow, steady pace, she kept her eyes averted as she passed them. Once they were behind her, she tried to relax although her hands were shaking.

"Rema!" a male voice called out.

She automatically looked up to see who had said her name. Not seeing anyone, she turned around. The five soldiers stood staring at her, smiling. It felt as if a cold bucket of water had been tossed on her head. They knew who she was. Taking a step back, she wondered if she could outrun them in an unfamiliar city.

"Someone's looking for you," one taunted. The men spread out, blocking the entire street, leaving her no choice but to go the other way. She unclasped her cape, needing her legs free and uninhibited. Her only option was to run and hide.

"Why don't you make this easy on yourself and come here," the taller man in the middle suggested.

"Fine," she said, making her voice quiver as if she were weak and scared. "Just don't hurt me." Her shoulders slumped in defeat. When the soldiers laughed, she dropped her cape, spun around, and took off running.

Several shouts rang out behind her, but she ignored them and turned down a side street. Tan buildings lined the street, offering no opportunities to hide. She continued running, her lungs burning, but she dared not slow down. Boots pounded on the street behind her as the soldiers drew nearer. A few people loitered up ahead. She ran around them and spotted a dark alley on the left. Rounding the corner, she sprinted down the alley. When she came to the end, she was back on a main street and people were everywhere. She dodged around a group, almost losing her footing. Glancing back, she saw that all five soldiers were gaining on her. As she ran past a cart piled high with apples, she shoved it, causing the fruit to topple to the ground.

Turning down the next street, she hoped to find a place to hide. There were several doors, but she didn't have the time to stop and check to see if any were unlocked. There had to be a heap of trash or a feed barn somewhere to hide in. The soldiers were almost upon her. Unable to maintain this pace much longer, she ran to a crowded street, hoping to hide under a merchant's cart. She kept close to people, shoving a few, wanting them to get in the soldiers' way and slow them down. Glancing back, she saw they still pursued her. She couldn't gain enough of a distance to buy herself time to hide.

Someone grabbed her arm. Without thinking, she swung, punching her assailant in the stomach. He doubled over and she brought her knee up, slamming it into his face. He released her. The remaining four soldiers formed a circle around her. She looked at the merchants and citizens for help, but they avoided eye contact and moved away from her.

Four soldiers. How could she fight four men at the same time? Savenek always told her to hit and run away. Darmik had taught her to use her size and femininity to her advantage. Nathenek had expressed the importance of being confident and believing in herself. Taking a deep breath, she squared her shoulders and prepared to fight. The soldiers closed in, tightening the circle. Keeping her hands at her side, she tried to appear small and harmless. All four of them were at least a head taller than she was, with two times as much muscle. While she was nowhere near as strong as they were, she was flexible and fast.

The first soldier went to grab her wrist. She pulled her arm back and broke away, adrenaline rushing through her body. Aiming for his knee, she threw a powerful kick. The soldier yelled as his knee buckled beneath him and he fell to the ground, clutching his injured leg. The soldier standing behind Rema didn't hesitate to reach for her. She spun around to face him. Using her momentum and strength, she landed a punch right to his nose. He stood there, stunned, as blood poured from his face and his vision blurred from the hard hit.

The two remaining men rushed to seize her. She dodged one but the other grabbed her from behind, trapping her arms at her sides. She shifted her weight backward, lifted both legs as high as she could, and kicked the other soldier's stomach and head repeatedly until he fell to the ground. The soldier who held her tightened his grasp, but she quickly elbowed his stomach and groin using both arms. He loosened his grip. She faced him, pulled him down, and kneed his groin until she broke free.

She ran. One of the soldiers had already recovered and he sprinted after her, tackling her to the ground, smashing her face into the dirt. She rolled over to escape, but he was on top of her, punching her stomach and ribs to weaken her. Rema lay there in pain, gasping for air. Filled with anger and frustration, she used every ounce of strength she had left and punched him. He rolled her onto her stomach, forcing her hands behind her back.

"Go tell Captain we've got her!" the man said, wrapping a rope around her wrists while his knee dug into her lower back. She turned her head to the side, spitting out dirt. Two soldiers hurried away.

Even though they were on a busy market street, all the citizens studiously ignored them. Rema wondered if this sort of thing was a normal occurrence.

The soldier lifted her to her feet. "I was wondering how Captain lost you. Now I know. You're a squirmy one."

She glanced at a woman passing by, but the woman refused to

acknowledge her. The soldier dragged Rema down the street, the remaining two soldiers following close behind. People quickly moved out of their way, going about their business.

She tried wrenching free, but his grip on her arm was too tight. "Release me," she demanded. "How dare you treat me in such an undignified manner?" She spit out more dirt.

"This isn't undignified," the soldier said, chuckling. He grabbed her by her tunic and slammed her body against a nearby building, her head smacking against the stone, sending a sharp pain through her. The soldier lifted her, her feet dangling two feet above the ground. "Now this is undignified."

Since her hands were tied behind her back, she couldn't fight him. Tears filled her eyes as his lips slammed down on hers. Revulsion consumed her and she bit his lip, drawing blood. The soldier screamed and dropped her to the ground. She rolled to her stomach. As she started to stand, he kicked her side, knocking the wind from her body. She couldn't breathe. It reminded her of when she'd been thrown from her horse, Snow, and he'd accidentally stepped on her ribs. The soldier yanked her hair, forcing her to stand. Her vision swam.

"You're lucky I have orders to capture you alive." He held his free hand to his mouth where blood trickled from her bite. He released her hair and stepped away.

Nathenek strode past the soldier, coming to stand before her. His eyes narrowed, making him appear furious. "Let's go. Two of you will escort her, two of you behind her. And you," he said to the soldier who had assaulted her, "walk next to me."

The men fell into formation around Rema and started walking. Something wet and sticky dripped down the back of her neck. Breathing became laborious and her vision blurred. The soldiers on either side of her held her up.

"I . . . I . . . don't think . . . I . . ." Her voice trailed off.

Nathenek spun around, his eyes scanning her body. "Is that blood?" He pointed at her head.

"Yes," one of the soldiers answered.

"She can't die before her scheduled execution." Nathenek walked over and released the bindings around her wrists.

"Aren't you afraid she'll make a run for it?"

Maybe if she sat down, she'd feel better. She tried to sit, but Nathenek picked her up, cradling her in his arms. "Let's go," he commanded.

She turned her head toward him. If only she had managed to get away. Instead, here she was, captured and her body broken. Resting her cheek against Nathenek's torso, she felt something hard under his clothing. It was her key necklace—she was sure of it. Why did he have it on? She was about to ask when darkness consumed her.

Rema woke up as they entered a three-story structure.

"I have a prisoner for execution," Nathenek said, his voice rumbling in his chest.

She closed her eyes, hoping the overwhelming pain would go away if she fell back asleep.

"Put her with the others, down the hall."

"No," Nathenek responded. "She is injured and I need to ensure her survival until her scheduled execution. The emperor would be upset if he didn't have the pleasure of watching her die."

"Very well," the man answered. "Second level, third door."

She felt Nathenek climb a flight of stairs. She heard a door open and then she was placed on a hard, cold surface.

"Are you awake?" he asked, his voice soft.

"Yes," she croaked.

"Tell me what's wrong."

"Everything."

He sighed. "Let me see the back of your head."

She rolled onto her side, allowing him to investigate the wound on her head.

"What happened?"

"The one soldier threw me against a wall, and I banged my head. That's all."

His fingers moved her hair aside, examining the wound. "There's blood, but it doesn't look that bad."

"My stomach. I was kicked. It hurts to breathe."

"Why did you run?" Nathenek asked, lifting the bottom of her tunic to look at her wound. His fingers pushed on her ribs.

She hissed from the pain. "To get away from you so I wouldn't be executed."

He shook his head. "What were you thinking to take on five soldiers?"

"I wasn't."

"Obviously." He lowered her shirt. "Bruised but not broken."

"I just wanted to get away."

He sat cross-legged before her. "Those men have trained all their lives. You've trained for what? A few weeks?"

"I had to try." Tears filled her eyes. She would be hauled out to her execution broken. She'd never see Darmik again. She was unsuccessful as a queen and leader. She'd let everyone down. "I failed," she whispered.

"Wait here." Nathenek left and returned several minutes later with a basin of water and a small towel. He sat next to her. "I need to clean your wound to make sure it isn't serious." He gently moved her hair away from her neck. His fingers carefully felt around the back of her head. "It looks worse than it is," he said, immersing a cloth in the basin of water. "I'm going to wash the blood away." He began wiping the back of her neck.

She closed her eyes, having no energy to argue with him. What was the point in tending to her wounds when she was about to be killed? The cold water made her shiver.

"The cut on your head has already stopped bleeding."

The sound of angry voices drifted in from the window. "What's going on?"

Nathenek didn't answer. Instead, he pulled something out of his pocket. "Eat this."

"I'm not touching anything from you."

"It'll help control the pain."

She grabbed the small, brownish lump from his palm and ate it. It tasted bitter, but she immediately felt better. It sounded like a large crowd had gathered outside her window. "Are those people here to watch my execution?"

He shook his head. "No, your execution isn't until later." He stood and went over to the small window, looking outside.

"Then what is it?"

Nathenek rubbed his face and sat down, leaning against the stone wall of her cell. No longer feeling dizzy, she stood and went to the window. The large courtyard below was packed with people. Everyone stood facing a platform where a young boy of about ten years stood.

"What's going on?"

He didn't answer. He rested his head between his knees, placing his hands atop his head.

Focusing back at the courtyard, Rema watched two soldiers tie the boy's arms to a post. Then they ripped off his shirt, tossing it to the ground. Another man came out dressed all in black, carrying a long stick. The courtyard went silent.

"No!" Rema screamed, realizing what was about to happen. Several people looked in her direction. "He's only a child! Please don't hurt him!"

The cane went up, sliced through the air, and whacked the boy across his back. The sound of the cane tearing into the boy's flesh was utterly disgusting.

"Stop!" she cried. "Please! I'll take his place! He's only a child."

Strong arms wrapped around her body, pulling her away from the window.

"Don't watch," Nathenek whispered in her ear.

Tears streamed down her face. What kind of sick, twisted place was this? How could they harm a young boy? She buried her face against Nathenek's chest, sobbing.

CHAPTER EIGHT

Darmik

*T*he door closed behind the emperor. His words repeated in Darmik's head: *I personally oversaw your training when you were here. I know everything about you.* That seemed impossible. Darmik had only ever met his uncle that one time. Perhaps Hamen wanted to rattle him. After all, when he had said *You're not as good a liar as you think,* that certainly unnerved him. His uncle had to know he wasn't telling the truth about Rema.

Darmik needed to return to his friends so they could come up with another plan to rescue Rema. At least she hadn't arrived yet. Exiting the room, he found Audek, Gaverek, and the remaining soldiers standing in the hallway waiting for him.

"My orders are to escort you to the military compound where you will remain with your companions until the emperor decides your fate," Gaverek said.

"Interesting," Darmik mused, trying to figure out why they were being taken to the military compound instead of the dungeon.

"Yes," Gaverek sneered. "The emperor wants you locked up

but not mistreated. It seems he is acknowledging your title and family connection; otherwise, you wouldn't be handled so kindly." He turned and walked at a brisk pace down the pristine hallway, Darmik and everyone else hurrying to catch up.

With the sash still tied around Audek's mouth, he remained quiet as they exited the palace. If Darmik and his friends were sequestered at the military compound, he wasn't sure how they would intercept Rema. But he would find a way—no matter the cost.

They left the lush grounds of the emperor's palace and headed north to the stark, functional military compound. Since he wasn't cuffed, Darmik considered trying to escape. However, the area around the palace and compound was flat for a reason—so the guards on patrol could easily see. That meant if he started fighting with these soldiers, someone would see and come to their aid. His best bet was to go with them and be reunited with his friends. Then, together, they would figure out what to do.

Arriving at the military compound, Gaverek led Darmik and Audek between two buildings, through the empty courtyard, and inside a small two-story structure. There was a short hallway lined with iron doors. Gaverek unlocked one and motioned for them to enter.

Ellie, Savenek, Neco, and Vesha all sat inside, looking grim. The door slammed shut and Darmik held his hand up, indicating for everyone to remain silent. He scanned the room, noticing only one small window, high on a wall facing the courtyard. Since they hadn't climbed any stairs, their room was on the ground level and someone could stand outside the window, listening to their conversation. He pointed at the window and then at his ear, trying to convey his concern to his companions. They nodded in understanding.

Vesha started laughing. He glared at her and she mouthed, "Sorry," pointing at Audek.

Audek unknotted the fabric, throwing it at her.

Shaking his head, Darmik motioned for everyone to come toward him. When they were shoulder to shoulder in a tight circle, he whispered, "Rema isn't here yet. We need to find a way to escape."

"Any ideas?" Savenek asked.

"No, but be prepared. When an opportunity presents itself, we'll take it." He went over to the iron door and tried to open it. It was locked. Most likely, there were soldiers standing on the other side.

Neco squatted and Ellie climbed onto his shoulders. He carefully stood and moved to the window. She was high enough to see outside. She gave a thumbs-up signal, and Neco lowered her to the floor.

"How many?" Darmik whispered.

She held up two fingers.

He paced around the room, trying to figure out what to do.

Savenek came over to him. "What happened with the emperor?"

"Not much."

"Why are we here instead of the dungeon? Something is off."

He agreed—something didn't make sense. He went over everything that the emperor had said or implied. What was he missing?

"How do you know Rema isn't here?" Savenek asked.

"My uncle said his assassin hadn't returned yet."

"And you believe him?"

He replayed the encounter in his mind, searching for signs the emperor had been lying. When he said his assassin hadn't returned, he was sitting on a chair, his eyes focused on Darmik. In training, he'd been taught to always look a person in the eyes when lying to make the lie believable. "No," he said, "I don't."

"How can we discover the truth?"

They had to find a way out of here. What if Rema was sitting in the dungeon right now? The last time she'd been imprisoned, he had done nothing to save her. He couldn't fail her again.

Thinking logically, if she was in Emperion locked in the dungeon, then the emperor would likely order Darmik and his companions be held at the military compound to keep them from crossing paths.

"What time is it?" he asked.

"I'm not sure," Ellie said "If I had to guess, I'd say midday based on the position of the sun."

"Why?" Savenek asked.

"All executions are held at sunset."

"Uh," Audek whispered, "are we concerned that we're going to be executed? Or are we talking about Rema?" He glanced around at everyone, his face white.

"Both," Darmik said. "I have a feeling they're only keeping us alive until she's killed."

"We knew coming here was a long shot," Savenek said. "At least we tried."

"We haven't tried," Darmik said, his voice harsh. "We're only getting started."

They sat cross-legged in a circle, heads bent inward. "Our best bet is to get someone to open the door to check on us," Darmik whispered. "Then we can try to escape."

"How do you suggest we do that?" Neco asked.

"One of the women can scream," Savenek said. "Hopefully someone will open the door to see if she's okay."

It was a decent plan so long as the scream didn't draw too many guards. Getting into position, Darmik and Savenek stood on either side of the door. Neco and Audek waited by the window, ready to run forward and fight when necessary. Darmik nodded at Vesha sitting in the center of the room with Ellie.

Vesha screamed.

Nothing happened. Darmik held up his finger, wanting them to stay in position. He tensed, ready to spring into action. This plan had to work. He could hear voices coming from the other side of the iron door. He held up his fist—the signal for everyone to prepare to fight. Vesha grabbed her leg like she was hurt while Ellie sat by her side, comforting her.

The door swung outward and a soldier entered with his weapon drawn. Darmik tackled the man, knocking his sword from his hand. Ellie reached out, grabbing the sword. Darmik twisted, throwing the soldier to the floor and pinning him down. Several additional guards rushed into the room.

Savenek grabbed one, disarmed him, and held him in an arm lock. Neco managed to take another one down. However, soldiers stood behind Audek, Ellie, and Vesha, holding knives to their throats.

A man wearing a black cape glided into the room, his face concealed under his hood. "Release my men," he ordered.

Darmik contemplated his options. If he refused to comply, his friends would be killed. Would it be enough to give him an opportunity to escape? Were there additional soldiers in the hallway? Could he sacrifice the lives of his companions to save Rema? He glanced at Neco. His friend nodded, as if he understood what Darmik was deliberating, and he agreed. Sacrifice a few for the good of the many. This was what Emperion had taught him and what he'd practiced as commander. Yet, it was not how Rema operated. She would never sacrifice a few to save others. She would fight to save everyone.

Growling in frustration, he released the soldier, Savenek and Neco following suit. Six additional soldiers swarmed into the room. One held Darmik while another tied his hands and feet together.

Once Darmik, Neco, and Savenek were bound, they were tossed to the floor. The man in charge said, "Everyone out. I want six of you stationed outside the door. The rest of you are to report to the fifth sector for additional patrols. Dismissed." The soldiers exited and the iron door slammed shut, leaving the man in the cape alone with Darmik and his friends. "I want all of you lined up against this wall." The man pointed to his left.

Darmik shimmied his body over and used the wall as leverage to prop himself up to a sitting position. Everyone else did the same.

"I'm surprised you surrendered so easily," the man said, his cape still concealing his identity. "Why?"

There was something slightly familiar about his voice. "I saw no need," Darmik answered.

"No need to escape? Knowing full well you're going to die? Why not at least try?"

"I couldn't risk my friends' lives just to save my own."

"Is that all?"

Darmik sighed. He might as well be honest. "No, that's not the only reason."

The man bent down so he was eye level with Darmik. His face remained concealed in the shadow of his hood. "Tell me why."

"Rema wouldn't want me to," he admitted. "I also made a promise to a friend—no unnecessary killing." He let his head fall back against the wall. He'd failed. Not only was Rema going to die, but so were his companions.

"Excellent," the man said, pushing the hood off his head.

It was Trell.

"What are you doing here?" Darmik demanded, shocked to find Trell in Emperion. Was he working with Captain? Had he helped bring Rema here? If Darmik weren't tied up, he would strangle the old man.

Trell held a finger to his lips. "Keep your voice low," he whispered. "Rema is here."

Darmik's heart pulsed in his chest. He'd figured as much, but to have it confirmed was another matter. "Here in the compound?"

Trell shook his head. "I'm afraid not. She's at the Execution Tower. She is scheduled for execution."

Darmik sat there staring at the old man. "How are you even here? Did you kidnap Rema?"

Trell shook his head. "It's a long story. I'll tell you another day. For now, all you need to know is that I'm here to help."

That was good enough for Darmik. He didn't have time to sit there listening to explanations. He had to save Rema. "Let me go."

"It's not that simple," Trell responded. He slid a dagger from the sleeve of his cloak. "Turn around. I'll cut your bindings."

Darmik did as he asked, and Trell sliced the rope around Darmik's wrists and ankles.

"Stand next to the door," Trell ordered. Darmik did as instructed, wondering what the old man had planned.

Trell knocked on the door. When it swung open, he said, "I need two guards in here to help with something."

Two soldiers entered, not noticing Darmik standing silently against the wall. When the door slammed shut and locked into place, Trell took his sword and swung the hilt against the back of a soldier's head. He dropped to the floor.

Darmik used the same idea and hit the back of the other soldier's head with his elbow. Then he swiped at the guy's legs, sending him onto his stomach. Trell came over, whacking the back of the soldier's head with the sword as well, ensuring the man stayed down.

"You and Neco switch clothes with the guards," Trell ordered while slicing Neco's bindings.

Darmik quickly undressed one of the soldiers and exchanged his basic Emperion uniform for the soldier's elite one. Neco did the same with the other soldier.

"Put the cape on," Trell whispered. "Keep your head covered."

Once dressed, Darmik sheathed the soldier's sword in his belt and shoved the dagger in his boot.

"Done," Neco said. "Now what?"

"Tie them up, just the way you were."

Darmik took his cut bindings and wound them around the unconscious soldier. He propped him up against the wall, next to Neco's soldier.

"If there's anything with which to cover their mouths, use it," Trell said.

Darmik ripped off two pieces of his undershirt and shoved one into each unconscious soldier's mouth. Then Neco took the bottom of his undershirt and ripped two longer sections, tying them around the soldiers' mouths and heads.

Trell ordered Darmik and Neco to stand at attention with their backs facing the door. He went into the hallway. "I need the rest of you in here now." The remaining four soldiers entered the room. Trell slid his sword from its scabbard, flipped it around, and hit a soldier on the back of his head, rendering him unconscious. At the same time, Neco went after another soldier. Darmik realized he was responsible for the remaining two.

Savenek slid flat on the floor, ready to be of assistance. Darmik turned and tackled a soldier to the floor right next to Savenek, who lifted his bound legs and repeatedly kicked the guy until he no longer moved. Jumping to his feet, Darmik wrapped his arms around the remaining soldier, ramming his head into the wall until his body went limp.

"Quietly!" Trell insisted. "There are guards posted outside the window."

All the soldiers lay unconscious on the floor. Darmik started undressing the men, tossing their uniforms to his friends. Once everyone was free from their bindings and dressed in elite military uniforms, they tied the soldiers up, propping them against the wall.

"When we leave," Trell said, "I need two of you in front, two at my side, and two behind. You must walk in formation, in step, and not falter. Understood?"

Everyone agreed. Even though Vesha's hands were shaking and

Ellie remained close to Neco, both women were moving quickly and appeared to be holding it together.

"Where to?" Darmik asked. He wanted to go straight to the Execution Tower to rescue Rema.

"There's only one way for this to work," Trell said. "I'm expected at the palace. You will escort me to the entrance where I will then order you to the city for an additional patrol run. Once you're in the city, you can head to the Execution Tower." Trell pointed at the limp bodies. "With any luck, these men will remain unconscious a while longer. If they wake and make enough noise, they'll alert the soldiers on guard and we'll all be discovered."

One soldier moaned but his eyes remained shut. Darmik didn't want to hit him again and accidentally kill him. With the soldiers' mouths gagged and hands bound, he hoped they wouldn't be too loud when they regained consciousness.

"Let's not waste any more time," Neco said.

"Agreed." Since Darmik knew the way, he opened the door and led everyone from the room. He kept his shoulders back, head high, and walked with confidence. He made sure his hood was on, concealing his identity.

They made their way to the outer wall of the palace without incident. The afternoon sun beat down making Darmik light-headed. It had been over twenty-four hours since he'd last eaten. For once, Audek managed to keep his mouth shut.

When the palace soldiers opened the gate to admit Trell, he turned to face Darmik. "I'll be traveling with the emperor to the city for a public execution. Go and ensure the route is safe. Dismissed."

Again, Darmik took the lead. As they headed toward the city, he wanted to tear the hood off his head because he was hot and sweaty. However, the risk of sunburn was too great, and he didn't want to take the chance of someone recognizing him.

Traveling at a brisk pace, Audek finally broke the silence. "Do we have a plan?"

"I'm trying to figure one out right now," Darmik admitted.

"Do you know the layout of where the execution is being held?" Neco asked.

"Yes. It's a large courtyard surrounded on all four sides by tall buildings. There is only one entrance and exit for the public. I suspect there will be hundreds crammed in there to see the spectacle. Rema will be brought out onto a platform situated at the front."

"How many will be with her?" Neco asked.

"Usually it's just the person reading the charge and the executioner. Since Emperor Hamen is coming, I'm sure he'll want to be close enough to see the action. And where the emperor is, the royal guard is."

"I have one small dagger and a longsword," Savenek said.

Each of them had a sword and was dressed as an Emperion soldier. Could they enter the courtyard as soldiers on patrol and kill the executioner before he murdered Rema? Possibly. However, with the emperor's guard in attendance, if they made a move against the executioner, the guards would kill them. Then who would save Rema? Darmik balled his hands into fists, frustrated by his lack of options.

When they neared the city's edge, a man dressed in plain clothes ran out to greet them. "I have the items you requested," he said, waving them along.

"Thank you," Darmik replied, pretending to know what the man was referring to. "Lead the way." He noticed Audek scrunching his face, looking confused. Neco wrapped his arm around Audek's shoulders, whispering something in his ear.

The man took them to a building two blocks away. "I've been watching all day for you," he said, opening the door and ushering them inside a dimly lit fabric store. Spools of wool, silk, and cotton hung on the walls. "Here you go." He handed a pile of clothing to Darmik. "You and your companions can change in the back room." He pointed to an archway.

"Thank you." Darmik went down the dark hallway and entered a small room with one window serving as the only light. His friends crowded in behind him. "Keep your voices low," he whispered. "Quickly change and pretend you know what's going on." He handed everyone a set of clothing typically worn by civilians. When he put on the rough, brown trousers and tunic, he felt something hard against his hip. Fumbling inside the pants, he found a dagger. "Check for weapons," he told the others.

Ellie removed a small knife from her trousers.

"I have one, too," Vesha said.

Neco, Savenek, and Audek all found similar weapons.

Darmik's heart raced. Had Trell planned this? Once everyone had hidden their weapons, they exited the room and returned to the store.

"Hold on," the man said. He went behind a wooden counter and bent down, retrieving something. When he stood, he held fabric in his arms. "You must not forget the wraps for your face in case of a sandstorm." He smiled at them.

Darmik grabbed the top scarf and wrapped it around his head, mouth, and neck, everyone else doing the same.

"There isn't much time. Let's go." They exited the fabric store. Darmik waved them to the side of the street. "We're heading north-west to the tallest building in the center of the city. Does everyone see it?" Once everyone found it, he continued, "We need to split up. Head to that building. The execution site is at the base of it."

"What do we do once we get there?" Savenek asked.

"Wait," Darmik answered. "We'll see if Trell has anything planned. If nothing happens, then I'll kill the executioner before he kills Rema." He balled his hands into fists, determination taking over.

"And then what?" Neco asked.

Darmik had no idea how to get out of the courtyard alive with Rema.

119

"Once you take out the executioner, you'll be captured or killed," Neco said, folding his arms. "The only way to rescue Rema and make it out alive is to create a scene of utter chaos."

"Excellent idea. Audek and Vesha, you two will travel to the site together. Right when I kill the executioner, make a scene."

They agreed. "Where do we meet after?" Vesha asked.

"Head to the harbor and hide until I find you."

Vesha nodded. Audek grabbed her hand, and the pair took off toward the tower.

"Savenek, I want you to take Ellie."

Neco stiffened but didn't protest.

"You two are responsible for grabbing Rema and escaping with her. Go to the docks and hide down by the water. There are a lot of dark places near the pier."

"Very well," Ellie answered. She turned and faced Neco.

He wrapped her in his arms. "Be safe."

"You too."

Darmik glanced away, giving them a moment alone.

Savenek neared. "Thank you for your help and guidance. I will do my best to save Rema or die trying."

"Thank you." They shook hands. "You better get moving. You'll need to stand close to the front."

Neco released Ellie and she took a step back, still staring at him. "I love you," he said, his voice gruff.

Ellie smiled. "I know. And I love you."

"Let's go," Savenek said, pulling his wrap tighter around his face.

Ellie did the same and the two of them left, Neco watching their retreating backs. When they were no longer in sight, Neco asked, "What do you want of me?"

"I only have one dagger. If I fail, it's up to you."

Neco nodded. "I promise."

"I'm sorry to ask this of you."

"You're not asking. I offered. We're in this together."

Darmik was at a loss for words. All these years, through every-thing they'd been through, Neco had been like a brother to him.

"Stop," Neco said. "This isn't the end. Have a little faith." He smiled wryly.

During his time in Emperion, Darmik had witnessed several executions and beatings, not only at the military training facility, but here in the city as well. He knew from experience that there would be more soldiers in attendance than regular civilians, which led to the question—how would he kill the executioner and survive? He wouldn't. He was going to his death. As long as he saved Rema, it would be worth it.

They were one block from the Execution Tower. His hands trembled. Now was not the time to be afraid. He would need a steady hand to make the kill. There was honor in death, and saving Rema would be a noble act. She would bring peace and prosperity to Greenwood Island. In a land filled with evil and dark-ness, she was the bright, shining light.

"Is there usually this much activity going on?" Neco asked.

Darmik glanced at the people around him, hurrying to one place or another. "Yes. Because of the large port, this city attracts a good number of people. When you factor in the army, there are thousands who live and work here."

They arrived at the entrance to the courtyard and entered with everyone else, trying to blend in. Soldiers ushered people forward, cramming as many in as possible. Darmik and Neco found themselves in the center of the courtyard, surrounded by people.

Neco leaned in. "Do you have a clear shot?"

Darmik nodded. There was just enough room for him to throw the dagger. He focused on the platform. On the left side was a tall post with manacles attached to the top, stocks were situated on the right side, and in the center sat a large block of wood with chains hanging from each side.

Neco placed his hand on Darmik's shoulder, squeezing it. Their eyes met, and Neco nodded, giving him the support he needed to do this.

Nestled into the building behind the platform was a small area where the emperor sat so he could observe the spectacle before him. Darmik looked at the tower, wondering where Rema was. Commotion came from the left, near the door to the tower. A young woman was dragged out and placed in the stocks. A soldier announced that she was being punished because one of her children failed a class in military training. Another woman was brought out and chained to the post, her arms pulled tightly above her head. She was being punished for being out past curfew.

No other prisoners came out. "Where's the executioner?" Darmik mumbled.

"No executions are scheduled for today," the man next to him said. "There was an execution yesterday. A young woman, not from around here."

Darmik's vision swam, and he fell to his knees.

CHAPTER NINE

Rema

A knock sounded on the door. "It's time," someone called from the other side.

Rema pushed away from Nathenek. She must have cried herself to sleep in his arms. Her puffy eyes felt heavy and her head throbbed. She sat upright, staring at this man who'd brought her to her death. "How can you live with yourself?"

Without answering, he stood. "I'm supposed to escort you there." He reached down to help her up.

Ignoring his hand, she got to her feet on her own. "What is the official charge?" She adjusted her tunic and smoothed her hair down.

"Treason."

She laughed. This was the second time she'd been accused of and sentenced to death for treason. It was comical that King Barjon and Emperor Hamen feared her. After all, she was just a simple woman who'd never thought of ruling when all of this had started. Unfortunately, both unworthy leaders were on the verge of defeating her. This execution could not end as well as her previous one. She couldn't possibly be lucky enough to escape death a second time.

Nathenek gently took her arm, leading her from the room and down the winding stairs. Her wrists weren't bound. She had to try —she wouldn't die without a fight. Pretending to trip, she pulled her body down, hoping he'd let go. His grip only tightened. Twisting her arm, she rolled onto her stomach, kicking with her right foot. He easily blocked her kick, yanking her to her feet. The entire ordeal was awkward since they were on the stairwell.

"What are you doing?" he demanded.

"What do you think?"

Two guards appeared at the bottom of the stairs. "I've got this," Nathenek snapped. He half carried, half dragged her the rest of the way down.

At the bottom, she reached for the dagger in his pants, just like Darmik had taught her. The blow had to be fast, hard, and well placed. She managed to unsheathe his dagger. Lifting her arm, she plunged it down, aiming for Nathenek's side. The dagger caught on his tunic, missing his body. Strong hands grabbed her arm, pinning it behind her. In one swift motion, he flipped her so she landed flat on her back.

Nathenek straddled her, pulling her arms above her head. His angry eyes bore into hers. "You just tried to kill me."

She laughed, the sound half delirious. "You're taking me to my death." Her laugh transformed into sobs as she struggled to pull free. "Get off!" she screamed, thrashing her body. "I don't want to die!"

His grip tightened.

How could this be the end? Her entire family had been killed, her kingdom taken from her. For what? The emperor's quest for power? He'd destroyed her life, and now he was going to take it. The fight drained from her body. She wasn't strong enough.

Nathenek's eyes softened and he released her, helping her to her feet. Steady hands clutched her shoulders, pushing her forward. "Come on," he mumbled. "You can do this." He ushered her inside a room, the door slamming closed behind them.

The windowless room only had two torches hanging on the walls. Opposite from where she stood was another door. That had to be the exit to the courtyard—where she would die.

"Would you prefer to be blindfolded?"

She stared at Nathenek, completely dumbfounded by the question. "Does it matter?"

"I suppose not. I just thought it might be easier."

The door behind her opened and Nathenek stiffened. He dropped to a knee, bowing his head.

"Rise," a familiar voice commanded.

She turned and came face to face with the emperor.

"Ready?" he asked, raising his eyebrows, a smile tugging at the corner of his lips.

"To be slaughtered like a pig?"

He laughed. "Such a befitting end for you."

She balled her hands into fists, wanting to tear him apart. Instead, she said, "Please let me go." Tears pooled in her eyes. "I don't want anything to do with this nasty place. I just want to go home." *And I want to be with Darmik,* she thought.

"Your execution has nothing to do with what you do or do not want." He came closer to her, barely an arm's length away. "This entire empire is built on rules and structure. It may seem harsh at times, but it works. Your very existence threatens *my* empire. I have no choice but to have you executed."

Nathenek was right—the emperor's cold detachment was worse than King Barjon's mood swings. She quickly wiped her tears away.

"I don't know how your ancestor could have loved a commoner enough to not only marry her, but sire a child with her. Even though you have royal blood running through your veins, your blonde hair and blue eyes make you look like a commoner. No one would even know of your true lineage if it weren't for your tattoo."

He went to the door as if to leave when he paused and said, "I considered the possibility of marrying you to my son. It would have officially sealed the line." He shrugged. "But like I said, you look like a commoner and I can't ask my only son to marry you. I've spent far too much on his upbringing to throw it all away. There are far better choices for a wife, ones that will strengthen my empire. You are insignificant, and no one will ever know who you really are."

Rema thought of all the portraits she had seen in the palace. She recalled seeing one with a sickly girl about fifteen years old. There were no portraits of another child. "I didn't know you and the empress had a son."

His eyes narrowed, sending a chill through her because in that moment, he looked like Darmik. "We don't have a son together— only a daughter, Jana." He threw open the door and stepped outside into the bright light of day. Straight ahead was a raised platform covered with torture equipment.

She turned and ran. At the back door, she yanked on the handle but it wouldn't budge. Nathenek wrapped his arms around her, picking her up. "No!" she screamed, kicking and punching at him.

He threw her over his shoulder and exited the other door, stepping onto the platform. Pure rage filled her. She hated Nathenek for bringing her here, hated the emperor for killing her family and ordering her death, and hated life for being so cruel.

As he carried her, he pinned her legs against his chest so she used her fists to beat his back. "Let me go!" she screamed. "I've done nothing wrong!"

He slid her from his shoulder, dropping her on the ground. She landed on her bottom and frantically looked around to assess the situation. Behind the platform was an alcove where the emperor, Nathenek, Trell, and half a dozen guards sat. Hundreds and hundreds of people stood in the courtyard silently staring at her. She opened her mouth to tell them who she was when a soldier shoved a piece of fabric in her mouth, gagging her. Then he took a long strip of material and wrapped it around her mouth and head, rendering her speechless.

Two soldiers roughly jerked her arms forward, dragging her to the wooden block at the center of the platform. She kicked her legs, trying to get free. They wrapped her arms around the block, locking her wrists into metal cuffs. She was on her knees, her chest atop the block, unable to move. Someone gathered her hair, tossing it above her head, exposing her neck.

Fear like she'd never felt before took hold of her. Out of the corner of her eye, she saw someone dressed in solid black approach, carrying an axe. Another soldier stepped forward and spoke, "This woman is found guilty of treason. Her punishment is death by beheading." The executioner raised the axe with both arms.

This was it.

The executioner lifted the axe above his shoulders, preparing to chop off her head.

Rema squeezed her eyes shut.

CHAPTER TEN

Darmik

"*G*et up," Neco demanded.

Darmik couldn't imagine going on with his life now that he'd failed so miserably. He'd let the entire kingdom down, including the woman he loved. He had nothing left to live for, nothing left to give.

Neco reached down, pulling him to his feet. "Look."

He lifted his head. The two women were gone from the platform. Now Rema was chained to the block, her neck exposed, the executioner standing over her with his axe raised in the air.

Darmik grabbed his dagger and threw it, embedding it in the executioner's chest. As the executioner fell, the axe threatened to hurt Rema. Trell leapt forward and shoved him, sending the executioner tumbling from the platform along with his weapon, into a wide-eyed and stunned crowd.

While the crowd was focused on the executioner, Captain stepped away from the other soldiers and unsheathed his dagger. He reached up and slit Emperor Haman's throat. Blood shot out and the emperor fell to the ground. Lifeless. It took a moment before the soldiers in the alcove realized what one of their own had done. The soldiers ran for Captain. Captain raised his hand, holding onto something gold while yelling. The soldiers froze.

People in the courtyard started screaming, demanding to know what was going on. The emperor lay at Captain's feet, blood pooling around his boots. When Trell stepped forward, the courtyard fell utterly silent. Darmik peered at Neco standing as still as a tree with a dagger clutched in his hand.

"Release her," Trell ordered. One of the soldiers unlocked Rema's manacles. She stood on shaky legs, her face red and her eyes swollen from crying. The soldier untied the cloth from around her head and removed the gag from her mouth.

Nathenek handed something to Trell who took it and came to stand next to Rema at the front of the platform. He held up his hand and Rema's key necklace dangled from his fingers. The crowd gasped. Rema glanced at Trell, her eyebrows drawn together in confusion.

"The false emperor wanted this woman dead because of who she is. Rema," Trell pointed at her, "is the true heir to the Emperion throne. She is the direct descendant of Nero and is the bearer of the key." Trell placed the necklace around her neck. "I present to you, Empress Amer Rema, your true and rightful ruler."

Rema's eyes widened in shock as everyone dropped to their knees before her.

CHAPTER ELEVEN

Rema

*D*armik stood in the middle of the crowd, staring at Rema, as everyone around him knelt on the ground. She wanted to scream with joy, run to him, and throw her arms around his neck. More than anything, she wanted to kiss him.

Darmik smiled and knelt on the ground.

Rema was still trying to understand what had just happened. Apparently, she was now the empress of the largest empire known to man. And if she'd learned anything from her past experiences, it was to be confident and immediately take control. "You may rise," she told her subjects. Trell stood next to her smiling with an expression of awe and pride. "Do you have anything to say to the crowd?" she asked him, raising her head high.

Facing the people, he said, "Tell everyone Emperor Hamen is dead and the true heir now reigns. Notices will be posted. Dismissed." The old man turned and knelt before Rema. "I am yours to command."

"As am I," Nathenek said, kneeling next to Trell.

"Both of you have a lot of explaining to do. Rise."

"For now," Trell said, standing, "we need to get you to a secure location."

"Am I not safe here with you?" she asked, glancing at the crowd. A few had left, but many still remained.

Nathenek stood, claiming her attention. "You are safe with me, I promise. However, until news of you ascending to the throne is well known, it is best to be cautious."

She stared into his eyes, sensing something honest and sincere in them.

"Notices must go out to the commander and army immediately," Trell said.

The soldiers on the platform were staring at her with uncertainty. Although she didn't understand the key's significance, she made sure the necklace was clearly visible. Nathenek ushered her back into the Execution Tower where Trell started barking orders to the soldiers. The enormity of what had just taken place started to sink in. She was alive, Darmik was here, and she was the empress of Emperion.

"Where's Darmik?" she asked, eager to be reunited with him.

"He's here with a small group of people from your rebel army," Nathenek informed her.

"I want to see them. Now."

"Yes, Your Majesty," he said. "We're taking you to another location and will have them brought there."

"Let's go." Trell gingerly took Rema's arm, leading her to a locked door. A soldier opened it, revealing a long flight of stairs. Trell grabbed a torch and began descending into the cold darkness. She hurried after him, Nathenek right behind her. They walked through the narrow tunnel carved out of the earth.

To keep herself from thinking about the dungeon, she turned her thoughts to Nathenek. On the voyage here, he trained her, fed her, and didn't treat her like a prisoner. Since arriving at Emperion, he'd been hostile toward her only when others were around. When it was just the two of them, he'd been kind and considerate.

He'd given her hints to his allegiance, she just hadn't understood it at the time. She had never imagined that when he said he swore an oath to the true line that he meant her and not Emperor Hamen.

What was Trell's involvement in all of this? She wasn't sure how he and Nathenek were connected, but one thing was certain —she felt both men were trustworthy and had her best interests in mind.

After traveling through the dark tunnel for several minutes, they climbed a steep set of stairs and reached a locked door with a soldier standing guard. He unlocked the door and pushed it open. Rema stepped into a luxurious sitting room filled with plush velvet sofas and chairs. "Where are we?"

"One of the emperor's safe houses," Nathenek replied. "He has several throughout the city that he used for secret meetings or when under attack."

"Do you expect resistance? Will someone try to assassinate me?"

"We're not sure," Trell admitted. "This is simply a precautionary measure until we see where things stand."

"And Darmik and my friends?"

"Are being escorted here as we speak." He patted her shoulder.

Soldiers stood at the room's two visible doors. Rema paced back and forth, biting her thumbnail. A guard entered, going directly to Trell and whispering in his ear. She didn't like Trell having control over the situation, but she didn't see any alternative. The army knew and respected their former battle strategist. For now, he was the bridge between her and Emperion.

"How are you holding up?" Nathenek asked, coming to stand at her side.

It felt as if she was dangling over the edge of a cliff, clasping onto a thin rope that was about to snap. "I'm fine," she lied, forcing a smile on her lips.

He opened his mouth to respond when commotion sounded

outside one of the doors. He moved in front of her, shielding her with his own body.

The door flew open and Darmik burst inside. Rema shoved Nathenek aside and ran, jumping into Darmik's arms. She breathed in his familiar scent, felt his strong hands on her back, and knew everything would be okay.

Trell cleared his throat, and Darmik released her. The rest of her friends came into the room, all of them smiling at her. "Sorry to interrupt your reunion," Trell said, "but we need to move to another location. Word has reached us of civil unrest. People don't understand what's happening and they're afraid."

Darmik grabbed her hand, brought it to his lips, and kissed it. "It's good to see you alive and well." His eyes sparkled, sending a jolt of warmth through her.

"It's good to see you, too." Her cheeks hurt from smiling. She glanced at her dear friends, glad everyone was unharmed. They had all come for her; left the comfort of Greenwood Island and traveled across the sea for her.

"I'm sorry," Darmik said to Trell, "what were you saying?"

"Rema needs to be moved to one of the palaces outside the city. We will invite all the military leaders there and explain the situation. Then they can tell those under their command that Rema is the rightful empress. Announcements will be made to the civilians as well."

She tore her focus away from Darmik and put it to the task at hand. "Forgive me, but I need you to explain the *entire* situation to me, and I want you to start at the beginning. I'm not asking."

Trell removed his cloak and sat on one of the sofas, rubbing his face.

"Sir," Nathenek said, "we really should get Rema to another location in case anyone followed Darmik here."

"No," Darmik said with authority. "I want a quick explanation. Then *Rema* will decide how to proceed." He squeezed her hand, giving her strength and letting her know he was on her side.

Trell stared at Darmik, pride radiating from him. Rema suddenly remembered that Trell was Darmik's grandfather. She wanted to reveal their connection, but now was not the time.

"As you are aware," Trell said, "when Crown Prince Nero left with Atta for Greenwood Island over a hundred years ago, the line shifted. The true bloodline has always been Nero's first-born descendants. When Nero left Emperion, he wore the heir's necklace—a key with a ruby stone. The symbol can be seen everywhere around here. Just look at statues, paintings, or even buildings. Nero continued to pass the necklace down through the generations, as it had always been done in his family. He also carried on with the tradition of the secret royal tattoos. Our history and record books reveal both the key and the mark as the true line. If anyone from the true line wished to ascend to the throne, they could. Thus, the line would be returned to where it has truly belonged." He leaned back on the couch, crossing his legs.

"When the line shifted here in Emperion, so did the colors, symbols, and marks in order to reflect that change and to remind everyone that there had been a shift. When Hamen, a prince from a neighboring kingdom, married Empress Eliza and ascended to the throne, he was furious to learn he'd married into a false line. He was painstakingly aware that even his descendants would be part of the false line. He saw symbols every day that reminded him of this fact. After Empress Eliza's brother, Barjon, claimed he'd destroyed the true line, Hamen thought he finally carried the bloodline. He sent out a royal decree stating Nero's descendants were dead, and he was now the true heir."

Silence hung in the air as Rema mulled over everything Trell revealed. "How are you involved in this?"

"I'm getting there." Trell rubbed his face. "We Emperion people are all about rules. We adhere to them without question. Hamen told me to plan an invasion of a small, remote island and to kill the ruling monarchy. I did as he instructed. It wasn't until after I completed the task that I realized who I'd killed. I swore to protect the line in any way I could. I demanded all artifacts and artwork. I searched through everything trying to find the key necklace. When I couldn't find it, I knew someone had to be alive. Ever since I realized you were the heir, Rema, I have done everything in my power to keep you safe and bring you home to Emperion."

"What he says is true," Nathenek added. "I've been aiding him for the past two seasons. Although, I wasn't aware of your identity until I saw the necklace."

This information overwhelmed her. She sat on the sofa, pulling Darmik down with her, trying to wrap her brain around all that had been revealed. "What is the plan now that Hamen is dead?"

"We need to sort through those loyal to Hamen and eliminate them. We must establish your identity as the sovereign ruler and meet with the neighboring kingdoms to declare peace."

"What about Hamen's wife and children?" she asked.

"Empress Eliza lives with Princess Jana at the palace in Verek. The princess has been bedridden for months and no one has seen her. We can either execute them or have them sent to the dungeon for the remainder of their lives."

Neither option sounded appealing. "I want them exiled, not killed or imprisoned."

Darmik stiffened beside her. "I wouldn't recommend that."

"Why?" She couldn't fathom killing two women because of the blood running through their veins. After all, that was what Barjon and Hamen did to her family. She wouldn't stoop to their level.

"If they go to another kingdom, they could be used as political leverage. It's too dangerous to allow them out of Emperion."

"In that case, let's exile them here in Emperion. Find a suitable cottage in an unpopulated area. Have them guarded at all times."

"Very well," Trell said, nodding in approval.

"What about his son?" she asked. Perhaps he was here in the city, training to be a captain in the army.

"The emperor's wife only gave birth to a daughter," Trell said.

"Hamen told me he has a son."

"Excuse me," Nathenek said, stepping forward. "I was there when he said this to you. If you'll recall, he said he didn't have a son with the empress. Therefore, that implies he had a son with someone else."

"Who did he declare as his heir?" she asked.

"Princess Jana," Trell replied. "If she dies before she has children, then the line goes to the next living relative of the empress. That would be her younger brother, Barjon. Since he's the king of Greenwood Island, it would bypass him and go to his son, Lennek. However, since Lennek is the crown prince of Greenwood Island, it would go to Darmik."

Darmik stiffened. "Can anyone else lay claim to the Emperion throne?" he asked.

"Not that I'm aware of," Trell said. "Nonetheless, Rema's safety is our top priority. Until we learn where everyone's loyalties lie, I want every precaution taken."

"What about his son?" Rema asked. Could he claim the throne? Did he have any rights?

"That won't be an issue," Trell assured her.

"How do you know?" Darmik asked, folding his arms.

"Even if his son has no right to the throne, he could seek retribution for the death of his father," Nathenek added. "We must be cautious."

Trell shook his head. "There's nothing to worry about."

"Can we at least acknowledge the possibility?" Darmik asked.

Trell sighed. "Fine."

"There is one other issue I'd like to address," Darmik said. "What about Greenwood Island?"

No one said a word.

"I must do something to help *all* of my people," Rema said.

"Your duty is here now," Trell said.

"Yes," Rema acknowledged. "But the people of Greenwood Island also fall under my jurisdiction."

Savenek cleared his throat. Rema had forgotten her friends

were still in the room. "If I may," he said. "I'd like to offer a solution. What if, while you're waiting for the dust to settle here in Emperion, Rema returns to Greenwood Island?"

Trell shook his head.

"It's a great idea," Darmik agreed. "We need to get her to safety. What better way than on a ship to an island far away from here?"

"She needs to be here," Trell insisted.

"She also needs to return and eliminate Barjon and Lennek. Right now, they are her greatest threats," Darmik said. "A portion of the Emperion Army can accompany her to ensure her safety."

"You want me to send her to war?" Trell asked incredulously, his face turning red.

"No," Darmik said, twisting his body to face Rema. "I'm asking you, Rema, as empress, what do you command?"

Rema stood with her hands on her hips, looking at every single person in the room. She knew what she wanted—needed—to do. "I'm going to war."

CHAPTER TWELVE

Darmik

*D*armik stood alongside Rema at the bow of the ship, watching Emperion fade away in the early morning sun. He grabbed her warm hand, squeezing it tightly. This was their first moment alone since her almost execution yesterday. After she declared she was going to Greenwood Island, Trell immediately began preparations. They were now accompanied by a platoon of two hundred and fifty men on a total of six warships.

Rema squeezed his hand and then pulled away. He reluctantly let go. "Are you okay?"

She nodded, not looking at him. It had only been a little over a fortnight since he'd last seen her, but she looked different. The lines in her face were a little sharper, her muscles toned.

Neco approached. "I'm sorry to disturb you." He smiled at them. "But we need to go over a few things now that we're alone."

Darmik laughed—they weren't really *alone*. Granted, the other ships had approximately fifty soldiers each and this boat only had a dozen. He suspected Neco meant now that they were away from the overprotective and watchful eyes of Trell and Nathenek.

"Of course," Rema said. "Let's go below. It's too hot out here for my liking."

Neco led them inside to the galley.

"I thought we were going to the meeting room," Darmik said.

"No," Neco replied, taking a seat. "We all need to eat, so I figured we might as well talk here." He shrugged. "I already told everyone to meet us here."

There were several small round tables, each able to seat six people. Rema sat across from Neco, rubbing her eyes. Darmik sat next to her. Soon the rest of their friends joined them. Savenek grabbed an empty chair from another table and squeezed in between Audek and Vesha. Ellie found a large wicker basket filled with bread. She handed everyone a loaf before taking a seat next to Neco.

Vesha leaned over and hugged Rema. No one spoke, but Darmik suspected they were all thinking how lucky they were to be alive. He reached under the table and patted the top of Rema's thigh. She looked exhausted. They'd only got a couple hours of sleep last night while Trell had the ships loaded with goods and supplies for the voyage. Starving, he tore into his bread.

"I know Trell said the soldiers accompanying us are all trustworthy and loyal to Rema, but I think we should be extra vigilant," Neco said.

"I agree," Darmik mumbled. "Since Rema appointed me as head of her royal guard, I'd like to officially recruit each of you to serve during our journey to Greenwood Island."

Rema quietly picked at her food. It was unlike her to be so silent and not offer an opinion. He continued, "I want her guarded at all times." Everyone nodded their heads in agreement as they ate their bread.

Rema shoved away from the table. "I'm going to my room."

He grabbed his food and stood.

"No," she said placing her hand on his shoulder and pushing him back onto his chair. "Ellie and Vesha will accompany me."

Both women glanced at him as if seeking permission. He nodded. They rose and followed her out of the galley.

He wanted Audek to accompany them; however, Rema would take offense if he insisted on a male escorting her. He forced himself to keep his mouth shut.

"What's wrong with Rema?" Savenek asked around a mouthful of food.

"She's probably just tired," Neco offered. "She's been through a lot."

Darmik thought it was more than that. He'd have to speak to her privately when he had the chance.

"I asked you here for a reason," Neco said.

"I know," Darmik muttered. "Can we wait to plan the takeover until after we've adjusted to being at sea?" At least none of his companions were vomiting. Yet.

Neco laughed. "That's not why I asked you here." He stood and went over to a cupboard where he pulled out four wooden cups and a bottle of ale. "We need to celebrate." He set everything on the table.

"Here, here!" Audek cheered. "Lots to be thankful for! We got Rema back and we're not dead! I'll drink to that."

Savenek chuckled as Neco filled the cups to the rim and handed one to each of them.

"To Rema!" Darmik said. The four friends cheered and took a drink.

Darmik made his way to Rema's berth, concerned since he hadn't seen her all morning. Did she suffer from the motion sickness? Were the events from the past couple of days catching up to her? Outside her door, Ellie and Vesha sat quietly talking to one another.

"Rema's in there alone?" he asked.

Ellie nodded. "We've been out here the entire time."

"Do you know what's bothering her?"

"She hasn't said anything to us," Vesha said. "But she's been through a lot. Maybe she just wants some time to herself?"

"Or maybe she's sleeping?" Ellie suggested.

He squared his shoulders, suddenly nervous. He knocked on the door and waited for her to answer. Nothing happened. Perhaps she was asleep. Regardless, he wanted to make sure. Turning the knob, he opened the door a couple of inches and peered inside. Rema lay on the bed, facing the wall, her back to him.

He stepped inside, quietly closing the door behind him. She still wore the uniform of an Emperion soldier. Going over to the bed, he sat near the end by her feet. Her eyes were open, her face red and swollen as if she'd been crying. "Are you unwell?" Perhaps she was seasick.

She didn't respond.

"What's wrong?"

She closed her eyes, not responding.

"You're starting to scare me," he said gently. "Do you need some water to drink? Should I get Ellie or Vesha?"

Rema shook her head.

He scooted farther up the bed, near her back. Rubbing her shoulders, he said, "Please talk to me." Maybe something had happened that he was unaware of. Nathenek didn't mention anything, but Darmik didn't trust the guy—even if Rema did.

A thought suddenly occurred to him. "Is something going on between you and Nathenek?" Was she upset they parted ways? Did she have feelings for the man? He balled his hands into fists.

Rema sat up, staring at him. They were only inches apart. He wanted to reach out and caress her cheek, but he kept his hands to himself.

"I'm sorry," she said, her voice weak. She broke eye contact, looking anywhere but at him.

"Please tell me what's the matter."

"A lot has changed since we last saw one another." Her cheeks turned a rosy shade of red.

He smiled, thinking of their last encounter at the rebel fortress when they were kissing. He'd been about to propose. "Yes. A lot has changed." He felt a wall between them. He very much wanted to tear down that wall with his bare hands. "I'm worried about you."

"I'm fine," she insisted. "It's just a lot to take in. Not only am I responsible for the people of Greenwood Island—where we're about to wage war—but I'm now responsible for an entire empire. Do you have any idea how large Emperion is? It's a thousand times bigger than Greenwood Island."

He nodded, about to respond when she continued, "I'm only seventeen. I have no idea what I'm doing. Anyone else responsible for a kingdom would have spent his or her life preparing to rule. I'm being thrown into it. What if I fail?" She dropped her face to her hands, shaking her head.

He reached up, pulling her hands away so he could see her eyes. "Rema," he said tenderly. She peered at him. "You will fail."

Her glassy sapphire eyes widened and she jerked back. "If you know I'm going to fail, then what are you doing here?" Her voice had a hard edge to it.

"You misunderstand me." He put his hands on her shoulders, grounding her in place. "You will fail at some things. You can't possibly succeed in all you do." She tried to speak but he held a finger to her lips, silencing her. "Each time you fail, you will learn from your mistake. And it will make you stronger. You will be the strongest and most powerful woman in the world."

She sat perfectly still, processing all he'd said. "I'm scared," she admitted. "To have that kind of power. To know how to use it wisely."

"You have me and all your friends. We are here to help you in any capacity you need."

She leaned forward and gingerly kissed him on the lips. "Thank you."

CHAPTER THIRTEEN

Rema

*T*he past twenty-four hours had been so overwhelming that Rema wasn't sure what to do. Her heart quickened and her breathing became labored just remembering her almost execution. She thought she was going to die, having failed her people and never seeing Uncle Kar, Aunt Maya, or Darmik again. Now, not only was she alive, but Darmik was here with her and she was the empress of Emperion. Rema was now responsible for thousands of people and had an entire army at her disposal.

There was a tremendous amount of work to be done. While Trell and Nathenek stayed in Emperion to oversee the transition of power from Emperor Hamen to Rema, she was leading a platoon of soldiers to Greenwood Island to oust Barjon and Lennek. Once this war was over and won, she would return to Emperion and take her rightful place as empress. She planned to tour the entire kingdom to get to know and understand the people. Positive changes would be made to allow a more peaceful and fulfilling life. The army had to be restructured. Children would no longer be required to enlist, and the cruelty Darmik spoke of would end.

Rema hoped Darmik would return to Emperion with her. She could use his knowledge and expertise to fix the army, but she wasn't sure what his intentions were. She couldn't ask him to abandon his soldiers on Greenwood Island just to be with her. When they'd spoken earlier, he said he'd be by her side. She foolishly hoped that meant for the rest of their lives.

After being below deck all morning, she wanted to feel the sun on her face and the wind against her body. Darmik had mentioned training with everyone during the voyage to Greenwood Island in order to maintain their strength. It was time Rema pulled herself together and started acting like a leader.

Exiting her room, she found Vesha and Ellie sitting on the floor. Both women looked up at her with hopeful eyes. "I'd like to go to the top deck."

"It's about time," Vesha said, smiling.

"Yes, it is," Rema replied. She followed her two friends through the dark hallway of the ship and up a steep ladder. Stepping into the bright sunlight, she squinted.

"Her Royal Majesty," someone shouted. Everyone on the deck —crew, soldiers, and friends alike—bowed before her.

She had no idea what to do. Was the etiquette for an empress different from a queen? And why did everyone insist on being so formal around her? She was just Rema, a seventeen-year-old woman, standing before everyone in a used Emperion military outfit. She certainly didn't feel like an empress.

"As you were," she said, hoping people would go back to what they were doing before she came out. Darmik stood at the center of the deck holding a sword, a half smile on his beautiful lips. "Are you training?" she asked.

"We are." He looked at her through hooded eyes, making her heart skip a beat. She wanted to reach up and kiss him but decided against it with so many people watching.

Neco, Savenek, and Audek were sweaty and breathing hard. "All right," she said, turning to Ellie and Vesha. "Let's join them."

Audek dropped to his knees before her. "Rema, I mean . . . Your Highness . . . I mean, Your Majesty, right? Well, whatever your title is, I'm so glad you're here and safe." He hugged her legs.

"Audek!" Darmik shouted. "Get off!"

"Oh, uh, sorry," he stuttered, releasing her. "Aren't you glad she's here?" He scratched his head, standing.

Darmik grabbed Audek's tunic, pulling him in close so they were nose to nose. "Of course I'm glad she's here. But people are watching you. You will treat Rema like the empress she is—especially when others are around. Are we clear?"

Audek nodded and Darmik released him. Rema wanted to intervene and tell Audek that it was all right, that nothing had to change between them. However, things were different now. Darmik knew what he was doing and had her best interests at heart. If he said everyone needed to treat her like an empress even in an informal setting, then there was a legitimate reason.

"We were just running through some basic drills," Savenek said, diffusing the tension.

"Excellent." She faced her friends. "Before we resume training, I have something to say." She looked at each of them—at Vesha's warm smile, Ellie's bright and intelligent eyes, Neco's friendly disposition, Audek's wry grin, Savenek's intense gaze, and the love radiating from Darmik's entire body. "I want to thank you for traveling all the way to Emperion to rescue me. I'm honored by your steadfast loyalty and your courageous ability to put your lives on the line for what you believe in. Thank you."

"We're honored to serve you," Neco said.

Before she started crying, she said, "Let's get to work."

They spent the next hour running through various training exercises. It felt good to be using her body instead of worrying about her new title and position. Still, Darmik was careful around her, only pairing her with Vesha or Ellie. She suspected life would never be the same.

~

Rema sat on the bed while Ellie knelt behind her, combing her hair. "So, you and Neco." Glancing over her shoulder, she saw Ellie smiling. "How long have you two known each other? How did you meet?"

Ellie sighed, putting the comb down and sitting cross-legged before her. They'd never had a chance to talk about Ellie and Neco's relationship at the rebel fortress. "We've been together for about a year now."

What did that mean? Most people signed a marriage contract, courted, and then married shortly thereafter.

"The only time Neco came to King's City was with Darmik, so I didn't get to see him very often. But whenever he was in town, we managed to spend some time together."

"Why didn't you say anything while I was at the castle?"

"It never came up. And Neco and I weren't serious until recently." Her face turned a crimson shade of red.

"Serious? What does that mean? Are you two betrothed?"

Ellie chuckled, shaking her head. "While in the king's service, I was unable to marry."

"But you're no longer in the king's service."

Ellie buried her face in a pillow, laughing. When she glanced up, there was a twinkle of excitement in her eyes. "I know. What about you?" She lightly smacked Rema with the pillow.

"What do you mean?"

"You and Darmik," she said, exasperated. "Are you two . . . together?"

Although Rema didn't know what would become of their relationship, she nodded. She loved Darmik and wanted to be with him for the rest of her life.

"Do you plan to marry him?"

She'd undergone so many changes that she didn't have time to think about being married on top of everything else right now. "I need to focus on being empress over Emperion and Greenwood Island."

"Wouldn't you like to have someone by your side? Supporting you?"

She hadn't thought of having a partner before. Darmik would make the perfect husband—not only did she love him, but he would be someone who could share the burden of ruling.

"You're blushing!" Ellie teased her. Someone knocked on the door. "I bet that's him!" She jumped off the bed and answered.

Sure enough, Darmik stood in the doorway. He'd changed clothing since the last time she saw him. He now wore a solid black tunic and pants, matching his hair and setting off his brown eyes.

"I'll leave you two alone." Ellie smiled as she left the room, closing the door on her way out.

Rema stood. Before they set sail, Trell had given her a foot-locker filled with clothing. She suspected the clothes belonged to the previous empress. Since it was nighttime, she'd put on a soft white gown that appeared to be a fancy nightdress made of silk.

Darmik's eyes bore into hers, and she felt her body temperature rise. She fidgeted with her hands, unsure of what to say or do.

"Hi." He grinned and took a step toward her. "I, uh, volunteered for the night shift."

She ducked her head, her blonde hair cascading around her face. He planned to stay here all night? Why did things suddenly feel so awkward between them?

"So," he said, taking another step closer to her. "I assume you're tired?"

She nodded. It was rather late and she hadn't slept much over the course of the past two days.

He took another step toward her. "Audek is stationed outside."

"For the entire night?" Didn't Audek need to sleep? Did Darmik plan on sitting here all night watching her?

"No," he replied. "We're taking shifts." He ran his hands through his hair. "After my shift, Vesha will be in here with you."

She had no idea what to say or do. The room became stifling hot. During their time apart, she'd dreamed of being with him, of having the opportunity to kiss, a chance to tell him how much he meant to her and that she loved him. Now that he was here, alone with her, she had no idea how to do any of those things. She felt like an incompetent child.

"Since you're tired, why don't you go to sleep?" he suggested. His voice had a husky roughness to it, sending a wave of desire through her.

"Good idea." She avoided eye contact, hoping it would be easier to breathe if she didn't look at him. Even though this was the highest-ranking officer's berth and larger than the other ones, it was still rather small. Besides her bed and footlocker, there was a small desk and a rickety wooden chair. She wasn't sure where Darmik planned to sit during his shift.

"If you don't mind, and you're comfortable with it, I'll just lie on the floor."

During her voyage to Emperion, sleeping on the floor in Nathenek's room hadn't been very pleasant. Pulling off the top blanket from her bed, she handed it to him. "The floor is hard. Lie on this."

He took it, their hands briefly touching, sending a surge of warmth through her body. "Rema," he whispered. She glanced up into his warm brown eyes filled with desire. He tossed the blanket to the floor. "I love you." He took a step toward her. "When we were in Emperion, I thought you'd been executed." His eyes filled with tears. "I thought I'd lost you." He reached for her and she melted into his arms. He held onto her. "I don't ever want to lose you."

She leaned back, tilting her head to look up at him. "I love you, too," she whispered. "But I'm afraid of the future. I have to go back to Emperion."

"I know." He gently kissed her lips. "And I plan to be by your side for the rest of my life." He knelt on the floor, clasping both of her hands. "Rema, I know this is unconventional, that Kar and Maya haven't given their permission, but I want to marry you. Please be my wife."

He wanted to marry her? Tears slid down her cheeks. To be partners and to love one another for the rest of their lives was more than she ever dreamed of. "Yes, I will marry you."

Darmik smiled the biggest smile she'd ever seen. He jumped up, grabbing her and spinning her around. He gently set her back on her feet. They stood, staring at one another. Then he slowly lowered his head, kissing her. Rema intertwined her fingers in his hair, pulling him closer. His hands roamed over her back, leaving a trail of heat. She wanted to feel all of him but knew now was not the time or the place. His kisses moved from her ear to her neck.

"We should stop," she mumbled.

"I know," he admitted. "We should—but I don't want to."

"Neither do I."

He gently held her face, gazing into her eyes, love radiating from him. "We can announce our engagement after we win the war."

"Okay, but I'd like to marry soon."

He smiled, melting her heart. "Me too."

Rema hated being below decks because there weren't any windows. The air also smelled thick and musty. Since they needed to plan their arrival and how they'd connect with the rebels, she called a meeting to order on the top deck. Even though they'd only been at sea for two days, the sun had already decreased in intensity.

Everyone on board sat facing her. Darmik nodded encouragingly, giving her the strength she needed to take control. He told her the key to being an effective leader was to act decisively and with authority. Looking at everyone, she squared her shoulders, clasping her hands in front of her. She breathed in the cool, salty sea air and felt the wind against her body. She could do this.

"When we arrive at Greenwood Island, six warships and two hundred and fifty soldiers will be noticed immediately. Therefore, we must plan accordingly. Let me introduce you to two key people on our mission."

Darmik and Savenek stood and joined her. "This is Commander Darmik, from the King's Army. This is Savenek, a captain from the rebel army. I'm going to let each of them speak about the state of the island, what we can expect when we arrive, and their ideas on how to organize everyone once we're on the island. When they're done, I'm open to suggestions from all of you." The soldiers' eyes widened in shock. She doubted anyone had encouraged or valued their opinions before. She smiled, knowing things were already changing for the better.

Savenek cleared his throat. "Thank you, Your Majesty." Facing the group, he addressed them. "Commander Mako has been organizing the rebels and getting everyone down the mountain. They should be in various villages throughout the island by now, eagerly awaiting our arrival."

"The men from the King's Army who are loyal to me are amassing in Werden, a town a half-day's journey from King's City," Darmik added.

"Once word reaches Mako that we've arrived," Savenek said, "the rebels will travel to Werden and meet up with Darmik's men."

The ship lurched, and Rema widened her stance to maintain her balance. "What we need to figure out and communicate with the other ships is how to get to Werden. Does anyone have any ideas?"

The soldiers stared at her as if she'd sprouted the head of a horse, so she remained calm, patiently waiting.

Vesha raised her hand. "Maybe we can arrive at night? Then we can get off the ship quietly. The crew can stay behind. Once we're on land, they can set sail and hide the ships off the coast where no one will see them."

"I like the idea of hiding the boats," Darmik murmured. "I'm not crazy about getting everyone off the ships in the dark, though. I fear we'll still be noticed because there are so many of us. Even at night, people work at the docks."

"What if we split up?" Neco suggested. Each ship goes to a different port?"

"That might work," Savenek said. "We have a better chance of protecting the empress that way, too."

"Anyone else?" Rema asked. "I'd like a few more options to consider."

An Emperion soldier raised his hand. Rema nodded for him to speak. He stood. "If anyone is looking for us, they will have people watching the main ports. I think we should avoid the obvious and expected. Are there lesser known ports at which we can dock?"

Another soldier stood. "All of us are trained to swim. I do not see the need to dock."

Now they were getting somewhere. "What are the risks of swimming from the ship to the shore?" she asked.

"It depends on the water temperature, currents, and time of day," the soldier answered.

"I will not risk my soldiers' lives if there is another way," Rema stated. Several soldiers smiled. "As your leader, I will always put my soldiers and citizens first. Your safety and well-being are my priority. Thank you for your suggestions. I want some time to consider the best course of action. Dismissed."

~

Rema stood, staring at the night sky. The crescent moon's reflection glimmered on the water. Thousands of stars twinkled above. Leaning her arms against the railing, she breathed in the crisp, cool air.

She heard her guards questioning someone and hoped it was Darmik coming to join her. They'd been so busy strategizing that they'd barely had any time alone since his proposal. Glancing back, she saw Darmik dismiss her two guards. Her heartbeat sped up just seeing him.

"We should arrive tomorrow," he said by way of greeting. He stood beside her, wrapping a heavy, wool blanket around her shoulders.

"I'm nervous."

"So am I," he admitted. He leaned against the railing next to her, his lips pulled tight and his shoulders tense.

"I assumed you'd be used to this sort of thing," she said gently.

"I am—to an extent."

"Then what are you nervous about?"

He turned toward her, clasping her hands in his big, strong ones. "I'm worried about protecting you." His thumbs rubbed small circles against her palms.

"Once we land and join forces with the rebel army and your loyal soldiers, overthrowing Barjon will be easy. There's nothing to worry about."

"I hope that's the case," he responded. "But if there's one thing I've learned, it's to never underestimate my father or Lennek."

She understood Darmik's concern; however, who could possibly stand in their way or oppose their mission? The people of Greenwood Island were repressed, starving, and would welcome the removal of Barjon and Lennek. The King's Army was loyal to Darmik. There would be nothing to stop them from succeeding.

"There is one thing I'd like to ask you," he said. His hands stiffened around hers.

"What?" she whispered, suddenly nervous.

"Is there any chance I can convince you to hide somewhere until this is over?" He leaned back slightly, as if fearing her reaction.

Her eyes narrowed. He wanted her to hide while her people fought for her? Although it might seem like the safe route, she had no intention of being a leader who bid others to do her business. Her empire would not function that way. "No, there isn't."

She was about to explain why when Darmik smiled and said, "I didn't think so. Still, I thought I'd ask. If you hid, it would save me from worrying about you; although, the sort of person that would run and hide wouldn't be the one to have stolen my heart."

She reached up, tracing her finger along his cheek, down to his jaw, and then across his lips. His eyes darkened as he leaned down and kissed her. The blanket fell off her shoulders. She no longer felt the cold air as she leaned her body against his, craving his warmth.

CHAPTER FOURTEEN

Darmik

Since they were the lead ship, the other five vessels followed them as they sailed along the coast of Adder. Darmik stood on the top deck searching for the small fishing village. Neco said it would be hard to find and they needed to look carefully. These villagers lived a sheltered existence, trying to remain unnoticed to keep the King's Army away.

"We've been searching for over an hour," Rema said, squinting from the bright sunlight.

"Neco said there are fishermen here who can help. We will find them, I promise."

"I don't want to be spotted. Isn't that the whole point of this?" She fidgeted with her key necklace, searching the shoreline.

"Don't worry." Although he told her not to worry, he was concerned. This was her first act as empress and events needed to unfold smoothly for her to gain the army's respect and devotion.

"Drop anchor!" Neco shouted. He raised a horn to his mouth and blew, alerting the other warships to do the same.

Darmik wished they could sail closer to land; however, the

helmsman had informed him that if they sailed any closer, they would run aground. Crew members shouted commands to one another as they brought in the sails and lowered the anchor. Clutching onto Rema's hand, he took her port side so they could have a better view of the shoreline.

Neco ran over. "I have my five companions chosen. They are all strong swimmers."

"Excellent," Rema said. "You may proceed."

Neco smiled. "Will do!" He made his way over to where five soldiers were removing their boots, socks, and tunics. Ellie rushed over to him, jumping into his open arms. They kissed and her hair fluttered in the wind, wrapping around their heads, concealing the two of them. It was good to see Neco happy. He put Ellie down and gave Rema a curt nod before climbing onto the railing and leaping into the turbulent ocean below. The five soldiers did the same. The water had to be freezing. The six men all surfaced and began swimming toward shore.

Ellie came over and stood next to Rema, biting her lip and fidgeting with a strand of hair.

"This will work," Rema assured her.

"Of course it will," Darmik added. He peered over the side, watching the group swim toward land. The shoreline was a solid cliff made from dark gray and black rocks, extending as far as the eye could see. Vibrant green trees lined the top. Darmik followed Neco's path and saw a channel so narrow that he'd missed it when scanning the coastline. The fishing village must be through there.

After a good twenty minutes, all six men entered the channel. Shadows from the towering cliff made it impossible to see more than a dozen feet in.

"They made it," Rema said. She put her arm around Ellie, hugging her. "I didn't realize Neco was such a strong swimmer."

Ellie beamed. "I know. He has many hidden talents." She wiggled her eyebrows, and Rema laughed.

Darmik monitored the shoreline for potential threats. He

didn't see a single person at the top of the cliff; nevertheless, one could easily hide among the trees. All the ships had dropped anchor and were waiting. Seagulls flew overhead. After about an hour, a small fishing vessel exited the channel.

"I hope there's more than one," Rema mumbled. "Otherwise, this is going to take forever."

Looking at the size of the boat, Darmik estimated it could carry fifteen to twenty people. At that rate, the vessel would need to make thirteen round trips to get everyone to land. The fishing boat went to one of the other warships first, just as planned. Darmik watched it come up alongside the ship and hook several grapples to it, keeping the vessels together but preventing them from smashing into one another. A rope ladder was lowered over the railing and down to the boat. Once in place, soldiers began climbing down.

After twenty soldiers were on board, the grapples were withdrawn and the boat moved away from the warship, heading toward the channel. Another fishing vessel, similar in size and appearance, exited the channel and headed toward the warships.

Once the soldiers save a skeleton crew were off the first ship, it was to go to the Great Bay. They'd been told to dock at Plarek, the same port Nathenek used when he had come to Greenwood Island. Darmik suspected Barjon had men watching the ports. If so, the king would send what was left of the army there, far away from Rema's true location.

The second reason for sending the warship there was to serve as a signal to Mako. Mako had rebels watching the port. Once they spotted the ship, they would alert Mako and word would go out to the rebels to amass in Werden. Darmik hoped that everyone would arrive at Werden within a fortnight. Then, as one, they would march to King's City and overthrow Barjon and Lennek. Rema insisted on taking them alive. However, if either made a single threat against her, they would be killed. Even though Barjon and Lennek were his family, he felt no love toward them. All that truly mattered was ending their cruel and unjust reign, thus freeing the people of Greenwood Island.

Then the wrongs of his father and brother would finally be made right. Once that was done, he would be worthy of marrying Rema.

$\sim$

One of the fishing boats finally neared the warship on which Darmik waited. Men leaned over the railing, attaching metal grapples to the side of the boat. Once in place, Savenek tied the rope ladder to the railing and let it unwind down the side of the ship. Neco stood below, giving the thumbs-up sign.

Darmik wanted to go first. He climbed over the railing, his feet hitting the first rung of the rope ladder. He smiled at the anxious look on Rema's face, trying to reassure her, and then climbed down. The wind blew hard, causing the rope to sway. Luckily, the rungs were close together, making the descent easy. When he reached the bottom, a wooden plank was extended from the boat to the ladder. After his feet found the wood and he had his balance, he released the ladder. He slowly turned and made his way across the plank, jumping onto the deck of the fishing boat.

"About time!" Neco teased.

"How did getting everyone off the other ships go?"

"There were no issues. Everything is going according to plan."

Glancing back, he watched Rema climb down the ladder. "Is the village safe and secure?" he asked.

Neco nodded. "There is nothing to worry about." Neco had changed into dry clothing.

Darmik scanned the fishing boat, wanting to know who was aiding them. Two older men with white hair and gray beards stood near the helm of the vessel.

"They're good men," Neco said. "I've known them a long time."

He suspected there was more to the story, but Rema had just planted her feet on the plank. With outstretched arms, she made her way across with ease. Ellie followed close behind.

"Move to portside," Neco instructed them. "It's a tight fit." There were nets strewn all over the boat on various levers. The nets must be used to capture large quantities of fish.

Rema grabbed Darmik's hand and led him closer to the railing. They were soon joined by their friends. Once everyone was on board, the grapples were removed and the boat lurched away from the warship.

"Come on," Neco said. "Help me raise the mainsail."

Neco grabbed hold of a thick rope, pulling it with all his might. Darmik took hold behind him, and Savenek clasped it farther back. The three tugged until the rope went taut and the sail was raised. The boat cut through the rough water as it made its way toward the channel.

Darmik had never been on such a small vessel before. They bobbed up and down with the swell, and for the first time ever, his stomach felt as if it had dropped out of his body. He feared he would vomit. Refusing to show any sign of weakness in front of Rema, he took a deep breath and headed toward the bow. He hoped the position in front of the boat would ease his nausea.

As they neared the shoreline, the swell increased and the boat rocked so violently that water sprayed him in the face.

"This is absolutely fantastic!" Rema said, coming to stand next to him. "Have you ever experienced something so exhilarating?" Her enormous smile was contagious and he couldn't help but grin and bear the torture.

Even though the sun was shining brightly in the sky, the air was chilly since the winter season had not yet ended. The boat lurched to the side as the mainsail lowered and a smaller one rose in its place. The boat entered the narrow channel. Rocky cliffs towered on both sides, casting a shadow over the passageway. The boat slowed and the swell vanished. The channel was eerily quiet.

After a hundred yards, the passageway opened to a small harbor where one other boat sat docked.

"The smell is utterly atrocious," Rema whispered. "I guess it's from all the fish." She pointed at the landing where several piles of fish sat discarded.

Although his stomach felt immensely better, he was eager to be on solid ground. The boat pulled alongside the wooden pier and Neco jumped onto it with ease. He quickly tied the boat to the pier and attached a board its side.

When it was Darmik's turn to exit, he almost lost his balance because his legs weren't steady. Luckily, Savenek was right behind him and he grabbed the back of Darmik's tunic so he didn't fall into the water. Once on the pier, he turned to help Rema down the ramp, but she made it off with ease.

"Let's get everyone organized while we wait for the remaining soldiers to join us," she said. "So . . . how do we go about doing that?"

Darmik loved how she stood there with her hands on her hips, determined to accomplish her goals even though she didn't know what to do. "Would you like me to take charge?" he asked.

She nodded. There was only one problem with him taking charge—Rema's safety. He couldn't lead the platoon and watch out for her at the same time. Darmik waved Neco over. "We need to organize everyone."

"I agree," Neco replied.

Savenek stood off to the side laughing with Audek and Vesha. Money exchanged hands. They were probably betting again. "Rema," Darmik said, "if you want me to take control of this platoon while we travel to Werden, I will do it. But I'm going to place Neco in charge of your safety."

"That's fine. Just make sure Savenek has a job so he's occupied and not making mischief."

"Of course." Darmik chuckled. "Before I take command, I need to speak privately with Neco."

Rema kissed him on his cheek and left to join Audek, Savenek, and Vesha. Turning to his friend, he said, "I want Ellie and them," he nodded at Rema's group, "in her royal guard."

"I understand," Neco said. "But if you want me to watch over and protect Rema, I need someone watching your back. I think you should consider Savenek."

"I can handle these men."

"I know, but I'll only agree to be the head of Rema's guard if you have Savenek with you."

"Why Savenek?"

"He's not from Emperion and he's more qualified than Audek." The corners of Neco's mouth pulled up. He knew he'd backed Darmik into a corner.

"Fine," Darmik agreed, shaking his head.

He quickly got to work organizing the platoon. With two hundred and fifty men, he needed a scouting party so they could safely travel across the region of Adder to Werden unharmed. He surveyed his surroundings. There was only one wooden building at the end of the pier. Between the cliffs, there was a narrow valley. The area was rather exposed and he wanted to get them farther inland so they would be concealed amidst the dense vegetation.

The boat left to get another load of soldiers.

"Listen up!" Darmik shouted to the approximately seventy people standing around. "I need a scouting party. If you have this particular skillset, let me know."

Several dozen soldiers raised their hands. He randomly picked twenty men. "If you were chosen, come forward. The rest of you, wait patiently."

He leaned closer to Neco. "Assign twenty to serve as Rema's guard." Neco gave a curt nod knowing the type of person Darmik expected to have guarding their empress.

Darmik met with his scouting party, telling them his expectations: he wanted a report every thirty minutes—no matter what.

They were free to organize themselves however they saw fit. Scanning the ground, he found a small piece of driftwood. He wasn't sure of their precise location; but he had a general idea of where they were. Pulling out his dagger, he carved a simple map of Adder and Shano, marking the towns to avoid and the direction in which they needed to go to reach Werden. Once he was confident the men were ready, he sent them off to ensure the first leg of the journey was safe.

One major concern was that they didn't have the supplies necessary to travel so far. Luckily, the Emperion soldiers were not only trained to survive off the land, but they were used to it. Darmik appointed a squad of twenty men to act as the hunting party. They were responsible for gathering enough food to feed everyone.

Darmik planned to travel during the day and stop to sleep when the sun went down. He figured there would be approximately one hundred and ninety soldiers with him at any given time. Twenty were assigned to guard Rema. The rest would be hunting or scouting.

Almost all the soldiers had been transported from the warships to the harbor. Rema came up behind him, sliding her arms around his waist, hugging him. "How are things going?"

He turned around so he was facing her. "Excellent. We're almost ready to leave."

She looked up at him, her sapphire eyes practically shining. "Before we go, I want to meet and thank those who helped us today."

He wasn't keen on the idea of her interacting with the locals, but he understood her desire to do so.

"Fine." He kissed the top of her head. "But I'm going with you."

Her guard of twenty hovered nearby. Neco came forward and took her arm, escorting her toward the wooden shack. Instead of going inside as Darmik assumed they would, Neco took them around the shack toward the valley behind it. They climbed a small rise, all twenty of her guards in tow. At the top, it flattened out, revealing a village hidden from the harbor below. Two dozen wooden houses were situated in a horseshoe shape. A well was located at the end, along with a rickety-looking barn. About a dozen people of various ages milled about. Darmik stepped forward so he stood on Rema's other side.

Neco raised his arm in greeting. "We'd like to meet with the elders. Are they available?" He held onto Rema's right arm while her guard spread out around them. The people of the village stopped what they were doing and stared at them. "We mean you no harm."

Darmik realized that the presence of so many strangers must be intimidating. In addition, most of the soldiers had blond hair and blue eyes making it obvious they weren't from around here. "How about Rema's guard wait just below the rise, out of sight?" he suggested.

Neco agreed, ordering the others to go down the hill about twenty feet, still within earshot if called upon.

A middle-aged woman with tan skin and dark hair approached. "What do you want with us?" she asked.

"I want to thank you for your help," Rema answered in a clear, confident voice.

The woman looked her over. "Who are you?" she demanded.

"My father was King Revan, my mother Queen Kayln. I am the sole survivor." The woman took a step back, lowering her basket to the ground. "I mean you no harm," Rema said. "I am here with an army to remove Barjon and Lennek from power. I will restore peace to the island."

The woman fell to her knees, bowing her head. Other people took notice, whispering among themselves. Two men came forward. One had long white hair and a white beard. The other man, who was much younger, had black hair and brown eyes. Both wore simple brown pants and tunics.

Neco bowed. "Thank you for your help today," he said. "It is greatly appreciated. I would like to introduce Her Majesty, Queen Amer Rema."

Both men stared at her, not uttering a single word.

Rema stepped forward. "I am here to restore peace and prosperity to the island. I want to know how I can help you."

The younger man raised his eyebrows, skeptical of her claim. "How you can help us?" he asked. "We are the ones helping you. And you better not bring your war here."

"We will be leaving shortly and no one will ever know that we were here or that you helped us," Rema assured the man. "When I am in control of this island, you may come to me at any time for help, and I will give it."

Darmik suspected that Barjon had no idea this fishing village existed and these people wanted it to remain that way.

A small child ran up to Rema. "You look funny," the girl said.

Rema squatted down, coming eye level with the child. "My hair and eye color are very different from yours." The little girl nodded. "But I'm from here, just like you." Rema held up her arm, revealing her tattoo of a curved stock of wheat with a sword down the center.

"You're from Jarko?"

"I am."

The girl reached out and touched Rema's hair. "Why are you here?"

"To thank these kind men for helping me and my friends."

The little girl nodded, as if she knew what was going on. "Maybe I'll see you again." She turned and skipped away.

Rema stood. "Thank you for your assistance." She nodded her head to the two men in a show of respect before turning and walking away.

Darmik hurried after her. He glanced back in time to see Neco shake hands with the older gentleman. As they descended the hill,

Rema grabbed his hand, holding it tightly. She was shaking. "Are you okay?" He squeezed her hand.

"Yes," she replied without hesitation. "It's just that . . . well, I'm responsible for *all* these people. It is a huge obligation."

"It is," Darmik agreed. "But one that you are perfectly capable of handling."

She squeezed his hand back. "Thank you."

CHAPTER FIFTEEN

Rema

*W*alking to Werden was a long, tedious journey. Rema wore the army uniform everyone else did—sturdy boots, long pants, and a tunic. Unfortunately, the outfit was made for sandstorms and protecting the body from heat. It did little to protect her from the frigid temperatures of the island. However, it was better than traveling in a ridiculous dress.

She walked between Ellie and Vesha. Audek and Neco were in front of her, and the sixteen additional soldiers who'd been assigned as her royal guard walked behind her. Darmik asked that everyone refrain from speaking so they could travel unnoticed. Rema understood the need for discretion; yet, there were two hundred and fifty of them on a narrow dirt road. If the king had soldiers nearby, they'd be easily spotted simply by the sheer number of their group.

Neco dropped back and squeezed between Rema and Ellie. "I just want to check in with you," he whispered.

"I'm fine." He could have just turned back and asked her. Perhaps something was bothering him? Or maybe he wanted to be near Ellie for a few moments? She raised her eyebrows in a silent question.

He hesitated. "Audek is driving me nuts," he admitted. "The boy never shuts up." Ellie laughed, then quickly realized her error and closed her mouth. "I'm going to have him walk behind you, alone. I'll see if that keeps him quiet."

"I thought we weren't allowed to talk," Rema said. If she'd known she could speak quietly with Vesha and Ellie, she would have been doing so all along to help pass the time.

"We're not." Neco hurried forward, returning alongside Audek. He leaned his head in and spoke quietly to the man.

Audek glanced around like he was offended. Then he slowed, allowing Rema to pass him by. He fell into step behind her, mumbling the entire time. Before long, the sun began to set and the group stopped for the night. They left the dirt road and entered the forest.

"Are we going to sleep right here?" Rema asked Neco.

"We are. Darmik is setting up a perimeter. People will be on patrol throughout the evening. There is nothing to fear."

She chuckled. "I'm not afraid. I've never slept under the stars before. Other than it being quite cold, this is turning out to be an exciting adventure."

Neco stood staring at her. He blinked several times, his face not revealing any emotion. "You and Darmik are perfect for one another." He turned and started barking out orders to her guard.

Even though it was cold, Darmik refused to light any fires.

"He likes *you*," Vesha mumbled. "I thought he'd at least allow *you* to have a fire so you'd be warm."

Rema laughed. "He does care for me and my safety, and that's exactly why he won't allow any fires."

"It's so cold that my feet hurt. How many days until we're there?"

"At this pace, Neco thinks it will take us a little over a week," Ellie said.

The hunting group returned and started distributing food to everyone. A female soldier approached, giving Rema a handful of berries and nuts.

"Thank you." She took the food, sharing it with Ellie and Vesha.

"I'll be back, Your Majesty, with squirrel once it's cooked." The female soldier bowed and left.

"How are they cooking the squirrels if there's no fire?" Vesha asked. "Because if they're allowed to make a fire to cook, I'll volunteer to cook."

"Careful," Ellie teased, "you're starting to sound like Audek."

Vesha's face turned crimson and she shoved several berries in her mouth.

Neco came over, sitting down before Rema. He handed her a small leather pouch. "There's not a lot, but it should be enough until we find a water source."

She took a sip and handed it to Ellie. After a skimpy meal of squirrel meat, she fell fast asleep.

~

On the fifth day, Rema noticed a distinctive change in the atmosphere. The group condensed down to three wide, walking at a faster pace. Neco and Audek were on either side of her instead of Ellie and Vesha.

"What's going on?" she demanded.

"We're crossing the border from Adder into Shano," Neco whispered. "And the scouting party is late."

They continued in silence. For the first time, the hundreds of boots walking on the dirt path among the forest trees sounded loud, making Rema cringe.

Neco leaned down and whispered, "You have a weapon, don't you?"

She nodded, feeling the dagger strapped to her thigh. Thick

greenwood trees towered on either side of the path. Birds chirped overhead, the sound echoing in the forest. The soldiers in front of her suddenly froze. Neco grabbed her, pushing her against the trunk of a nearby tree, and shielding her body with his own. She couldn't see around him but she could feel the presence of her guard nearby. No shouts rang out indicating trouble. The birds still sang above. Neco moved away. Darmik was standing before her. "What's wrong?"

"The scouting party returned." He took a step closer to her. "I can't be sure, but something isn't right."

"What did they report?"

He ran his hands through his hair, a telltale sign he was worried. "There's a small city nearby, just south of us. I've passed through it several times before. It's a busy town with lots of activity. It has an excellent market for leather goods. Saddles and such."

"What's the problem? Are we too close? Do we need to go off course so we can pass by unnoticed?"

He shook his head. "The problem is the town of Ruven is completely deserted. The scouting party reported that not a single person was out in the streets. The windows are even boarded up."

"Did something happen there?"

"I have no idea."

Savenek appeared behind Darmik. "Everything is ready."

Darmik nodded. "Savenek and I are going to investigate."

Fear shot through her. "Why? You're in charge of everyone here. Shouldn't you send someone else?"

"Normally, that's what I'd do. However, since everyone here is from Emperion, they stand out and are unfamiliar with our customs."

She didn't want him putting himself in danger. Discovering what happened at the town wasn't a priority right now. They needed to reach Werden. She was about to overrule him when Neco stepped forward.

"Excellent decision, Commander."

Rema looked at the three men before her. They were all well-trained soldiers. If they saw the need to investigate, she had to trust their judgment. "Very well."

Darmik and Savenek turned and left. She wanted to scream but forced herself to maintain her composure. "Who is in charge while they're gone?"

"Technically, you are always in charge," Neco said. "However, I am the acting commander now that Darmik and Savenek are away."

She decided to focus on her soldiers instead of worrying about Darmik. "Are we going to remain here while they're gone?"

"I suggest we keep moving instead of sitting around. There could be undetected threats."

She agreed. Somehow remaining in one place gave her the sensation of being watched. "Send the scouting party out and let's go."

Neco gave the necessary orders, and the group started moving again. Rema kept reminding herself that Darmik was a competent soldier, and she had nothing to worry about. Her heart disagreed completely.

CHAPTER SIXTEEN

Darmik

*A*t the edge of the forest, Darmik and Savenek hid behind a large bush, surveying the area. Even though Savenek had proven capable of following orders and listening to Darmik, he didn't fully trust the guy. They hadn't been in battle together. They hadn't been responsible for one another's lives. All they shared was a desire to protect Rema—and even that irritated him. He saw how Savenek looked at her. He was still in love with her. And there was nothing Darmik could do to change that.

The only reason he agreed to bring Savenek along was because Rema was safest with Neco. If something happened while Darmik was gone, he knew his friend would protect her with his life.

"Smoke is coming from that chimney," Savenek observed. "The town can't be completely deserted." He stood.

"What are you doing? We can't just go walking in there. If someone's watching, we'll be spotted."

"I know. But we can't just sit here either. One of us needs to go and check things out. You're recognizable. That leaves me." He shrugged and started walking toward the deserted streets.

This was not what Darmik had in mind. He planned to observe the area for a couple of hours before entering. Savenek, as usual, was acting before thinking things through. He wanted to pummel him to the ground.

He watched Savenek make his way into Ruven, disappearing between the buildings. Scanning the area, he didn't see any movement. Nothing from the top of the buildings. Nothing from the edge of the forest. Where had all the people gone? What happened here? There weren't any signs of a scuffle or attack.

After two hours, he spotted Savenek walking along a street and exiting at the other end of the town. Savenek made his way into the forest—the farthest place from Darmik's position. Someone had to be watching him.

Darmik decided to climb a tree to get a better view of the area. He found a low branch and grabbed on, swinging up into the tree. He climbed the trunk until he could see most of the town. Not a single person was visible. He scanned the forest for Savenek. Several minutes later, he saw him slinking between the trees, frequently glancing back.

Darmik climbed down, careful not to jostle the tree and shake the leaves. When Savenek neared, he nodded his head away from the town and kept moving. Darmik hurried after him. They continued in silence for a good mile. "What's going on?"

"No idea," Savenek answered. "But something is scaring those people."

He stopped walking. "What do you mean?"

Savenek faced him. "Everyone is holed up in their homes with their windows boarded shut. I knocked on a few doors, but no one answered."

"How do you know people are inside?"

"I heard people walking around, plates hitting tables, people talking." Savenek shrugged. "I can't help someone who doesn't want my help."

Darmik started walking again. What could scare an entire town enough to make them hide inside their homes? He couldn't fathom a reason, but he had a horrible feeling he was going to find out. For now, they needed to catch up with their group. Maybe he could check another town along the way to see if they were in hiding too.

The pair continued in silence. Darmik's stomach growled and he wished he had a bow with him. Unsheathing his dagger, he held it at the ready while watching for small animals. Not far away, a rabbit munched on a patch of grass. With a flick of his wrist, the dagger embedded the animal.

"Next time, warn me," Savenek said, irritation clear in his voice. "I thought we were being followed."

Darmik chuckled.

"It's not funny."

After skinning the animal, Darmik made a small fire. He sat across from Savenek, each keeping watch for threats. As soon as the meat finished cooking, he kicked dirt on the fire, putting it out. He tore off a few pieces before passing the rabbit to Savenek.

"Can I ask you a question?" Savenek mumbled between bites.

Caught off guard, Darmik looked at him, trying to read his facial expressions and body language. Savenek's eyebrows were pulled tight, his body movements jerky. "You can ask," he finally answered, wondering what had irritated Savenek.

Savenek licked his fingers clean and then dried them on his pants. "What are your intentions?"

"Regarding what?"

"Rema."

"That is none of your business."

"She's my sovereign."

Darmik couldn't help but laugh. "So now you admit she's your sovereign?" It wasn't very long ago when Savenek constantly questioned her authority.

"I want to know if you plan on accompanying her back to Emperion."

"Of course I do. I'm going to be by her side for the rest of my life."

The corner of Savenek's mouth pulled up in a half smile. "Better ask her about that."

Why was Savenek being so cocky? "How do you know I haven't?"

The color drained from his face. "Have you made her an offer of marriage?"

Darmik and Rema didn't plan to announce their engagement until after Barjon and Lennek were dealt with, but Savenek needed to understand that he didn't have a chance with Rema. "I have," he admitted. "And she accepted."

Savenek blinked several times. "Oh." He looked away from Darmik.

"I'm sorry. I assumed you knew we were heading in that direction."

He nodded. "I did. Hearing it is still hard. I hoped you would stay here on Greenwood Island and lead the army. I thought if you two were apart, there'd be a chance for me." He picked up a short stick, twirling it between his fingers.

Darmik ate his last piece of meat, throwing the bone on the ground. "I assumed you would stay here on the island."

Savenek snapped the stick in half. "I'd like to be part of Rema's royal guard so I can protect her. Since she'll be returning to Emperion, I'd like to go."

Darmik didn't think that was a wise decision. "Hasn't Mako trained you to be a leader?"

"He has."

He wanted to suggest that Savenek remain here and command the army; however, that meant leaving him in control of Darmik's men. He wasn't sure he liked that idea either.

"I don't inspire men the way you do," Savenek said, tossing the stick behind him.

"Everyone at the rebel camp seemed to follow your authority."

"They did," he admitted. "But I've seen you with soldiers. Even the Emperion ones here with us, they'd follow you anywhere. I don't know how to gain that trust and respect."

"You can learn those things," Darmik said. "I can teach you." He couldn't believe he'd just offered to help Savenek.

"Rema inspires that same devotion." He leaned forward, resting his arms on his legs.

There was something Darmik needed to know before he considered Savenek's placement. "Knowing that we plan to marry, how can you want to be around her every day? Feeling the way you do about her?"

Savenek stood, brushing the leaves and dirt off his pants. "I don't know. Sometimes she drives me crazy, and all I want to do is run far away from her. Yet, at the same time, I want to make sure no one hurts her."

Darmik understood those feelings since he experienced them too. Looking around the area one last time, he scattered the firewood and bones, removing the footprints and any traces that someone had been there. "Let's go. We don't have to decide anything right now. Let's just focus on usurping Barjon and Lennek. Then we can sit down with Mako and talk. Rema might already know who she wants where. And you know her–what she wants, she gets. We won't be able to talk her out of it."

Savenek chuckled. "You're right. She's as stubborn as a mule."

A twig snapped and Darmik froze. Someone was watching them.

CHAPTER SEVENTEEN

Rema

It had been four days since Darmik and Savenek left to investigate the town. Four days and they still hadn't returned. Rema tried not thinking about it as she left the cover of the forest. She had wanted to stay and wait for Darmik, but Neco insisted they keep moving.

Traveling at a brisk pace across the open field, everyone vigilantly searched the surrounding area for potential threats. There wasn't much they could do to cover the trail two hundred and fifty soldiers left through the knee-high grass.

Neco fell in step beside her. "The scouting party just gave their update. We've entered Werden. Trell's place isn't far from here."

Rema nodded, unable to utter a single word.

Ellie wrapped her arm around Rema's shoulders. "Don't worry. They'll return. I'm sure of it."

"What if something happened to them?"

"Don't," Ellie chided her. "Darmik is skilled. He'll be fine. Besides, you can't let everyone see you sulking."

All she wanted to do was curl up in a ball and cry. Yet, that wouldn't do her or Darmik any good. She would be strong for everyone else. When she was alone, she'd allow herself to feel.

Up ahead, a massive gray structure stood out among the vibrant green grass surrounding it. The stone house appeared abandoned and lifeless.

"That's Trell's home," Neco said. "Most of the scouting party has already been admitted."

"Is anyone there?" she asked.

"Mako and a large portion of the rebels."

It seemed as if the soldiers started walking a little faster, eager to be safely inside with a roof over their heads.

"I suggest you order a couple of squads to patrol at all times," Neco added.

Rema nodded. "I trust your judgment. Do what is necessary."

He took hold of her arm, pulling her to a stop. "Do you trust me?"

"Absolutely."

"Then trust me when I say Darmik will return. Because he will."

She stared at Neco's intense gaze, wanting to believe him. But not a single word had been heard from Darmik. Even though he was a highly skilled soldier and an excellent strategist, if he ran into a portion of the army controlled by the king, he might be in trouble.

"Do you think Barjon would hurt his own son?" she asked, knowing Neco would tell her the truth.

His eyes darkened. "He would never hurt Lennek. However, Darmik is another matter entirely."

That was what she feared. Her chest tightened with panic.

Neco faced Trell's home, ignoring her piercing gaze. "Let's get you inside. Rain is coming."

The wind kicked up, making the tall grass sway like the ocean. The clouds darkened. By the time Rema reached the front door, a light rain started falling. She eagerly stepped inside.

A man she vaguely recognized from the rebel compound greeted her. "Welcome, Your Majesty." He bowed. "Everyone is being taken to a room and fed a hot meal."

"Thank you. What about my royal guard?"

"I will see they are taken care of and shifts are arranged," Neco informed her. "But for now, someone wants to see you." He smiled deviously as he led her from the room. He took her through several dimly lit hallways before entering a sitting room decorated with tapestries depicting constellations. An enormous, stone fireplace warmed the room.

Standing by the hearth, with his back to her, was a figure she recognized. "It's good to see you, Mako."

He turned and smiled. His gaze went to the sofa, and Rema followed his line of sight. Her aunt and uncle stood and rushed toward her. She threw her arms around them, and the three of them embraced.

"We never thought we'd see you again!" Maya cried.

Kar took hold of Rema's face. "My dear child, you're alive." Tears slid down his cheeks as he kissed her forehead.

Rema released her aunt and uncle. "We have much to discuss," she told them, not even knowing where to begin.

"All in due time, dear," Kar said. "I suspect there are a few things you need to take care of first since you just arrived. When you get a moment, come to our room. We can speak privately there."

Rema nodded and glanced over at the hearth where Mako and Neco spoke with hushed voices. Mako's smile dropped and his shoulders slumped forward. Neco must have told him about Darmik and Savenek. She suspected Neco was worried too, but for some reason didn't want her to fret over the situation.

Mako noticed her watching them. "Neco has given me a brief overview of what has taken place since your kidnapping. Apparently, events have not unfolded quite as we anticipated."

"What's wrong?" Kar asked, placing his hand on Rema's shoulder as if to protect her.

"Nothing," Mako responded. "Just that our dear Rema will not be with us much longer."

"Why not?" Kar demanded. "You said she would be restored to the throne!"

"She has been," Mako replied. "She's been restored to the Emperion throne. Rema is now the Empress of Emperion *and* Greenwood Island." He shook his head in disbelief, smiling. "Never in my wildest dreams did I think this would happen."

She was still getting used to the idea of being an empress. It sounded so strange and foreign to her.

Maya clasped Rema's hands, her face filled with concern. "You're going to Emperion?"

She nodded. "I have to. They need me. I have a lot of work to do to bring peace and change for the better."

"Are you ready for this responsibility?"

Kar patted Rema on the back. "It doesn't matter if she's ready or not. She is the true heir."

Neco cleared his throat, speaking for the first time. "I'm sorry to interrupt, but I must get Her Majesty situated and taken care of."

Maya hugged Rema again. "I can't believe it."

"Me neither," she mumbled. After saying goodnight to her aunt and uncle, Neco showed her to a large bedchamber where Vesha and Ellie sat waiting for her. A fire roared in the hearth and a tray of food had been brought for her.

After eating, she washed up and climbed into bed. She wasn't sure how she would manage to sleep when Darmik was out there. Why did something always come between them? At least he wasn't alone—he had Savenek. She fell asleep praying he would return safely to her.

～

The following morning, the sound of rain pounding against the rooftop startled Rema awake. Darmik was out there somewhere traveling through these treacherous conditions. Unease filled her. Something was wrong; she could feel it.

Sitting up in the canopy bed, she saw Ellie and Vesha still sleeping near the hearth. Not wanting to wake them, she slipped out of bed and put on her clothes from yesterday, eager to hear if any news of Darmik came during the night. She exited her room. Two soldiers from her royal guard stood in the hallway.

"Good morning, Your Majesty," they said in unison.

"I'd like to speak with Mako."

"Of course. Follow us."

The men led her down two flights of stairs, stopping before the door to the sitting room. "We'll wait here, Your Majesty."

Taking a deep breath, she squared her shoulders and entered the room. Mako sat at the desk, writing. No one else was there.

He glanced up. "Good morning. I trust you slept well."

"I did." She went over to the hearth, basking in the fire's warmth. "I'd like a report. How are things? Do we have a plan? Is everyone from the rebel camp here?"

"You definitely had a good night's sleep." Mako chuckled. "I will try to answer all of your questions. Everything is running smoothly. All rebels from the fortress, except for a few dozen, are here or on their way. I expect the remaining people to arrive in the next day or two. Everyone is eager to see you, although I have not yet explained that you are now the empress." He stood and came next to her. "How are you holding up?"

Steady rain pattered against the windows. Dark gray clouds loomed outside. Darmik was out there somewhere. Tears threatened, but she didn't want to show a sign of weakness. She squared her shoulders. "I'm fine, thank you." Darmik would advise her to be the empress she was born to be. "I'd like to address my people."

"Excellent idea. Not everyone has eaten breakfast yet, so I

suggest waiting an hour. I'll let them know you will be speaking in the hall downstairs."

"There's a level below the main floor?" Wouldn't that be underground? She'd never heard of such a thing before.

"Yes. There's a room filled with your family's artifacts—priceless heirlooms. Alongside that room is an empty gathering hall. It should be large enough for everyone to fit comfortably."

"My family's possessions are here?" She wanted to see the items, to hold a piece of her history. Would they make her feel connected to her family on a deeper level? She didn't know, but she was eager to find out.

"Yes. I will show you everything later. For now, Kar is in the stables waiting for you."

Why hadn't Mako said anything sooner? Rema hurried from the room, wanting to spend some time with her uncle.

Her two guards greeted her outside the room. "Are you going to escort me everywhere today?" she asked.

"No," one of them responded. "We're your guards for the first shift. We rotate throughout the day. There will always be two people guarding you inside, and twenty when you step foot outside."

She was never going to have a moment alone. Her life now belonged to her people and not to her. The men led her to a door at the east end of the house. When she stepped through the archway, she entered a small barn. Kar stood near a stall, brushing a white horse.

She ran, her guards chasing after her.

Kar glanced up. "I have an old friend here who misses you." He smiled and stepped aside.

Snow snickered, greeting her with his wet nose. Rema buried her face in her horse's mane. Snow was here. An immense sense of relief filled her.

~

After spending time with Kar and Snow in the barn, Rema felt rejuvenated. She found Ellie and Vesha playing cards and asked them to accompany her back to her room.

"I need both of you to help me," she said, leaning against the bed.

"Of course," Ellie responded. "What do you need?"

"I'd like to address the people here." She glanced down at her army uniform. She'd left her trunk filled with clothes on the ship. "Can you help me look like an empress?"

Ellie smiled. "I would love to."

Vesha went through Trell's closet and pulled out several tunics. Then she tore them at the seams. "I can make you something with this fabric."

Rema laughed. "I'd like to address everyone today."

"I can do it!" Vesha said. "Give me an hour and I'll have something magnificent for you."

"And while she's working on that," Ellie said, taking Rema by the shoulders and moving her in front of the mirror. "I'll do your hair." She opened a wooden box. "Look what Trell left for you." She carefully removed a gold crown. "This was your mother's." She handed it to her. "I'll arrange your hair around it."

Rema stood there, holding her mother's crown in her hands. It was solid gold with twelve keys etched into it. Beautiful red rubies were set in each one. She'd never seen anything so striking and unique—it was perfect. Placing it atop her head, Ellie carefully braided Rema's hair around it.

When Ellie finished, Vesha came forward holding a simple, yet stunning dress. Rema put it on and looked in the mirror. The heavy, black fabric clung to her body, making her appear thin and tall. The sleeves were green, matching the color of Emperion. A red sash was tied around her waist, complementing the rubies in her crown.

"Something fit for an empress," Vesha said.

She hugged both of her friends. "Thank you. I have one more favor."

"Anything," Ellie said.

"Come with me. I need you both there while I address everyone."

"You couldn't get rid of us even if you wanted to!" Vesha teased.

Feeling a sense of relief, she made her way to the hall downstairs, her friends at her side. When she entered, the room fell silent. Her stomach became queasy with the realization that she was going to speak before so many people without Darmik's silent, steady support beside her. Taking a deep breath, she smiled and tried to appear confident. She could do this on her own. She had to. Her guards helped her stand up on a table, overlooking everyone.

"Thank you for coming," Rema said in a loud, articulate voice. "I am grateful to have you by my side." She made eye contact with as many people as she could, wanting them to know how sincere she was. "As you know, I was kidnapped and taken to Emperion. What I want to share with everyone is that while I was there, I discovered that I am the true heir to the Emperion throne, and am now Empress of Emperion and Greenwood Island." Many of the rebels whispered to one another, surprised by the news. "I want you to know that I plan to bring peace to both great kingdoms."

Cheering arose. "However," she said, holding up her hands, "before I can begin to help you, we must remove Barjon and Lennek. With you by my side, we can rid the island of these tyrants. Justice will be served. Who's with me?"

A roar erupted in the room as everyone began clapping and cheering. Rema smiled, filled with a sense of pride.

~

Mako accompanied Rema to a small library. "I thought you said we were going to the archives room?" There was nothing here but books.

He smiled. "Watch." At one of the shelves, he jiggled a book. A loud groan erupted and the bookshelf swung open, like a door.

Her eyes widened. "A secret passageway?"

"It's not secret anymore. Trell left a letter detailing the location of the room and who is permitted to access it."

"I'm not sure Trell has a right to these items," she mumbled.

"He agrees. In his letter, he states that everything is yours to do with as you please."

Her heartbeat quickened. Her family's history was in there, only steps away.

Mako led her along a short hallway and down a narrow stairwell. At the bottom, he pushed on an oak door. The door they had entered through swung shut with a bang. "There are several torches. Wait here while I light them."

The room gradually lightened and Rema looked around, astonished at the sight before her. The large space was divided into sections. One contained statues and artifacts, another area was filled with books. To her right were shelves filled with boxes of various sizes. The last area was completely covered with white sheets, concealing the identity of what lay beneath.

"The room you spoke in is on the other side of that wall," Mako said, pointing to the left.

Rema meandered through the room, unsure of where to start. "Have you been in here before?"

Mako nodded. "After I read Trell's letter, I found this room. Although, I haven't investigated anything in here yet."

She went over to the boxes and pulled one down. Sliding an envelope out, she found a picture of a young man with a crown atop his head. She replaced it and glanced through the box, finding several similar pictures. Pushing the box back in place, she went to the area covered with sheets. She gently tugged on the white fabric and it slipped off a desk covered with papers. Sitting on the chair, she observed all the documents and maps, afraid to touch or move any of them.

"What have you found?"

"I'm not sure." The maps appeared to be the various regions of the island. Some of the paperwork had names written on it, others had dates with events.

Mako pulled one of the bottom pieces of paper out and set it on top. It had the layout of a large castle. He tapped the edge. "I'd like to study this one in greater detail."

"Here." She stood, offering him the chair. He sank down on the seat, staring at the paper.

She went over to the statues, observing the intricate detail. One was of a young woman wearing a crown. Engraved on the woman's outstretched hands was a key. Rema took off her necklace and held it next to a statue—the keys were identical. The room suddenly became overwhelming. So much of her past was hidden in here. She headed toward the door, needing some fresh air. Twisting the knob, it refused to budge.

"I didn't know there was another door," Mako murmured, coming up behind her. "Step aside and let me try. It's probably just stuck from lack of use." He turned the latch and banged on it. It flew open, revealing a solid black room. Mako grabbed one of the lit torches and went inside. He whistled in awe.

Rema stepped into the room. All the walls were covered with weapons. Swords, knives, daggers, longbows, crossbows, arrows, and spears. There were hundreds and hundreds of weapons— enough to equip a small army. How long had Trell been planning this?

CHAPTER EIGHTEEN

Darmik

*D*armik had no idea if the sound of a twig snapping was from an animal or a person, but they couldn't afford to stand there waiting to find out. He tapped Savenek's arm and pointed up. Savenek nodded. Darmik clasped his hands together and crouched down so Savenek could hoist himself onto the lowest branch. Once Savenek took hold, he climbed higher until he disappeared among the leaves.

A nearby tree had several broken limbs protruding from the trunk. Darmik grabbed one and pulled himself up. Then he clasped onto a branch, lifting himself higher up the trunk. He was about to take hold of another branch when he heard leaves crunching below. He froze.

Two soldiers wearing the King's Army uniform crept past. "Are you sure you heard something?" one asked.

"I thought I heard talking coming from this direction, but I must have been mistaken," the other one replied.

"Let's return to our squad."

Darmik didn't hear any more of their conversation. Just to be certain the soldiers were gone, he remained in the tree, unmoving, for several minutes. When his arms and legs could no longer hold his position, he lowered himself to the ground. Savenek joined him. Darmik nodded the direction the soldiers had gone, and the two of them silently headed that way, easily tracking the two men.

Darmik followed the trail as it circled dangerously close to where he and Savenek had been hidden in the trees. Then it veered back toward the town. He lost all traces of the men when he reached a dirt road. The road had several different footprints, and he guessed at least twenty people had recently passed through there. The two soldiers probably met up with their squad here. They must be part of a scouting party. He looked at Savenek who nodded in agreement—they needed to follow the soldiers to investigate. Perhaps they could shed some light on what was going on in the deserted town.

Darmik followed the dirt road in the direction of the footprints —heading away from the town. After a mile or so, he heard the sound of boots crunching on dirt. He went to signal Savenek to leave the path so they could get ahead of the soldiers, but Savenek didn't know the signals of the King's Army. They would have to stay together instead of splitting up. This would have been much easier with Neco.

He silently left the road and headed deeper into the forest, Savenek following close behind. When he was a good fifty feet from the path, he proceeded parallel to it, sprinting as fast as he could between the trees. Once he estimated he was far enough ahead of the soldiers, he slowed and cautiously made his way back toward the road. Thankfully, Savenek had enough skill to remain quiet as well. When the road came into view, Darmik pointed up, and Savenek nodded in understanding. He found a tree with a branch low enough on which to grab. He hoisted himself up the trunk, climbing until he found a solid branch to watch from. Savenek did the same from a nearby tree.

After a few moments, the squad of soldiers neared. Darmik

recognized several of the faces. This was a squad from the Third Company. Where were they heading? This company didn't normally patrol this area. Once the squad was far enough away, he climbed down, Savenek joining him.

"I want to follow them," Darmik said.

"Where does this road lead?"

"I don't know of any towns north of here." However, that didn't mean there weren't unmarked towns. The fishing village where they'd disembarked had been unknown to him. Feasibly, there could be others like that one.

"Then let's get moving," Savenek said, glancing at the nearby forest.

They headed away from the road about twenty feet and then walked parallel to the road, remaining silent so the soldiers wouldn't overhear them. Darmik thought back to when the squad passed by. They hadn't been carrying any supplies so they must be arriving at their destination soon.

After traveling about eight miles, the sun began to set. He expected the soldiers to stop for the night, but they gave no indication of doing so. Instead, several of the soldiers gathered large sticks, wrapping green ferns around the tops and lighting them on fire. Once the makeshift torches were lit, the soldiers continued walking on the road. Darmik couldn't light a torch or he'd be seen, and it was too dangerous to follow the squad in the dark. As much as he hated the idea of stopping, he had to for his own safety. He ran his hands through his hair, trying to figure out what was going on.

"Wise decision," Savenek whispered.

"Something's wrong. I can feel it."

"I'm sure you're right, but we need to focus on getting back to Rema. When we reach Werden, we can talk with Mako. Perhaps he knows what's going on."

"I agree. Let's find a place to rest for the night. I'll take the first watch."

~

They'd veered farther off course than Darmik realized. It took them an entire day to backtrack before they could head in the right direction toward Werden. He estimated they were now two days behind Rema. He was eager to reach Trell's house to ensure she'd made it there safely. Thankfully, with Neco watching over her, there was little to worry about.

Soaking wet from the torrential downpour, Darmik and Savenek climbed the last rise and descended into the valley, reaching Trell's land. Darmik's body shook and he could barely feel his fingers. The Emperion uniform he wore was ill suited to Greenwood Island's harsh winter conditions. About a mile from the house, a group of Emperion soldiers stopped them. Once they recognized Darmik, they let him and Savenek pass. He was glad to see the Emperions—that meant Rema was safely inside.

When he neared the front door, it flew open and Rema stormed out, Vesha and Ellie close behind. "Where have you been?" she demanded, standing in the pouring rain. "I've been worried sick about you." She pointed at him, the rain drenching her hair and clothes.

The sight of her—furious and scared—melted his heart. Not knowing what to say, he opened his arms and she fell into them, hugging him fiercely.

"I thought something happened to you," she said, not letting go. He could feel the warmth of her body against his. "You're not hurt, are you?"

Before he could respond, Savenek said, "No, we're fine. Thanks for your concern." He pushed past them and went inside.

Ignoring Savenek, she said, "I want a full report."

He loved it when she took control. She was going to make an excellent leader.

"Why are you looking at me that way?" she asked.

There were too many people watching so he shook his head,

giving her a devilish grin. Her cheeks turned a rosy shade of red. "Let's go inside," he said. "I'm freezing."

～

After changing into dry clothes, Darmik made his way to the sitting room. Savenek and Mako were talking in front of the fireplace while Rema sat on the sofa next to Neco. He stepped into the room, and Neco rushed over.

"It's good to see you." Neco patted him on the shoulder. "I'm not used to you being on a mission without me."

His friend's concern was touching. "Thank you for bringing Rema here safely."

Mako cleared his throat. "I'd like to thank you for doing the impossible and saving Rema from an Emperion assassin." He came over and shook hands with Darmik. "I never thought I'd say this, but I'm glad to see you."

Darmik chuckled. "Likewise."

Rema stood. "I'd like to know what you and Savenek discovered."

He quickly told them what was happening in the town. He also explained how they had run into the squad of soldiers and followed them. Mako wanted a group sent to investigate. Savenek offered to organize two dozen soldiers and show them where to go. Darmik insisted Savenek remain at the house; there was a lot of planning to do, and Savenek was a captain of the rebels. Savenek agreed and left the room.

Rema took hold of Darmik's hand, pulling him to the sofa. Mako and Neco sat on the sofa opposite them.

"Is everyone here at Trell's house?" Darmik asked.

Mako leaned back on the sofa, crossing his legs. "Not all my men are here. There are two-hundred fifty on patrol at any given time. Another ten groups of twenty are keeping watch from here to King's City. I don't want to be taken by surprise. That leaves approximately six hundred people here in the house. I also have a few hundred scattered throughout the kingdom. I didn't want to consolidate all my resources and have something happen that I didn't anticipate."

"And my men?" He'd sent his trusted soldier, Traco, here to Werden to organize the still soldiers loyal to him from the King's Army.

Mako shook his head. "There were only a couple of squads when we arrived."

That didn't make any sense. There were over ten thousand men in his army. He knew that some would have a hard time defecting, but he'd assumed most would pledge allegiance to him, not his father. He rubbed his face. How could they defeat Barjon and Lennek with less than a thousand men? "Where's Traco?"

"He's here," Neco replied. "I've spoken to him. Only a couple hundred men from the Fifth Company arrived. That's all."

"If Darmik's men aren't here, where are they?" Rema asked.

Mako shook his head.

"What about the deserted town?" Darmik asked. "Have you heard of any other towns or villages with people hiding indoors?"

"I haven't," Mako said. "But I haven't received any reports during the last week."

"What does that mean?" Was there nothing to report? Or had something happened to Mako's men that prevented them from returning?

"Something is amiss."

Hopefully, the two dozen men being sent to investigate those soldiers would uncover something.

To build morale, Darmik suggested they have a celebration in the large underground room Mako referred to as the gathering hall. Even though only a couple hundred men had arrived from the

King's Army, he still wanted to unify them with the rebels and the Emperions.

Looking in the mirror, he adjusted his tunic. This was an important event, and he wanted to look like a respectable soldier who knew what he was doing. Although he didn't recognize any members from the Emperion Army, he was sure most had heard of him as the *soft prince* who had come to train in Emperion.

It was strange to no longer be a prince or the commander of his own army. He was supposed to be in charge of Rema's royal guard but was temporarily serving as commander alongside Mako. While most of the rebels valued his opinions and held him in high regard, he found it difficult to give up the army he had worked so hard to build.

He ran his hands through his hair, pushing it away from his face. Since there wasn't enough room for everyone in Trell's house, Mako assigned four to five people per bedchamber. Darmik shared a space with Neco, Savenek, and Audek, all of whom stood at the door waiting for him.

"I'm ready," he mumbled.

Neco smiled and opened the door.

"Are you sure you're ready?" Audek asked. "Because we can all wait here while you run your hands through your hair and adjust your tunic a few more times. It's not like we have anything better to do than stand here watching you."

He grabbed Audek by the back of the neck as they headed down the hallway toward the stairs. "I am not one with whom you should joke," he said, his tone harsh. They came to a railing over-looking the floor below. He grabbed Audek's legs, hanging him over the railing, upside down.

Audek screamed. "I was only joking! You can take as long as you like to get ready! Please don't drop me!"

Darmik lowered him a bit. "You need to learn to keep your mouth shut."

"I'll try, I swear. I won't talk so much. Really, I promise. I think I can do that."

Neco snorted. Darmik tried to keep his face blank as he pulled Audek back up onto the floor.

Audek's face was bright red from having been inverted. "I'm truly sorry, sir. I—" He stopped, at a loss for words.

Darmik leaned toward him. "You're not the only one who knows how to make a joke." He burst out laughing, unable to hold it in any longer.

"What?" Audek asked, dumbfounded.

Darmik wrapped his arm around Audek's shoulders. "How does it feel to be on the receiving end for a change?"

"You really had me there," Audek replied, relief washing over his face. The four friends laughed. It was wonderful to be joking with one another instead of worrying about the upcoming battle.

A group of Emperion soldiers exited the room near them. Darmik asked, "Are you guys heading down to the celebration?" They nodded, standing stiff and awkward. "Walk with us. We're heading there too."

The Emperions exchanged looks with one another and joined Darmik's group. As they descended the stairs, one said, "It's cold here. It's a nice change."

After some more idle talk, they reached the gathering hall. Darmik couldn't believe the transformation that had taken place in a few short hours. Tables had been brought in and were filled with food and drinks. A group of rebels stood in the corner of the room, singing a fast-beat tune while dozens of couples danced.

Ellie ran over and grabbed Neco's hand. "If you don't mind," she said to Darmik. "I need some time with my man." The two of them melted into the crowd of dancers.

He searched for Rema, but she was nowhere to be seen. Vesha headed in their direction. She asked Savenek if he wanted to dance, but he gracefully declined.

"Do you know where Rema is?" Darmik asked her.

"She's with Mako. I'm off duty for the night." She turned to Audek. "Would you like to dance with me?"

He rubbed his hands together. "I would love to." The two of them joined the others dancing.

"Want a drink?" Savenek asked.

Darmik nodded. He could use a cup of ale to calm his nerves.

Savenek returned a few minutes later, carrying two pewter mugs. He handed one to Darmik. They clanked them together. "To Rema."

"To Rema." Darmik took a drink.

"The way I see it, if we could make it to Emperion, rescue Rema, and safely return, overthrowing Barjon and Lennek should be easy." He took a sip.

Darmik couldn't believe he stood there conversing with Savenek over drinks. He glanced sideways at him. "Nothing with my father is ever easy."

"I'm surprised you don't have any qualms about killing your own flesh and blood."

What bothered him was Savenek's lack of tact. He wanted to smack him. Instead, he finished his drink. "My father has never treated me well. Phellek was more of a father figure. As for Lennek, well, we've never been close." He recalled all the times Lennek had gotten him in trouble, lied, or even whipped him. No, their relationship was not a normal one, and he had no idea why. Until he'd met Rema, he hadn't felt loved by anyone. The music stopped, and all heads turned toward the entrance. Mako stood there, holding Rema's arm. She wore a simple dress and atop her head was the Greenwood Island crown. She was exquisite.

"Her Majesty, Amer Rema of Greenwood Island and Emperion," Mako said. Everyone bowed their heads and Rema entered the room, walking straight to Darmik.

"That's quite the title," he said.

She laughed. "I know. I can't make someone say that every time I enter a room."

194

The group of singers started another tune that Darmik didn't recognize. People all around them began dancing. Savenek said he needed to speak with Mako.

"Will you do me the honor?" Darmik asked, offering Rema his arm.

She took it and they moved closer to the singers. "I can't believe we're all here."

"I know." He squeezed her hand and swung her around so they faced each other. The couple next to them appeared to be doing a basic four-step dance. He smiled. The last time they danced together, she was engaged to Lennek. Now, she was his. "Ready?"

She nodded.

He lifted his hands, palms out, facing Rema. She placed her hands against his. Together, they raised their arms up and out. They stepped to the side and slowly turned around. Facing one another again, he stomped his feet to the beat of the music, Rema mirroring him step for step. The music sped up, and he moved his feet faster and faster, keeping to the rhythm.

Rema lifted her skirt a bit, allowing her feet to dance uninhibited. She tossed her head back, laughing. The song ended and everyone clapped and cheered. When the next song began, he slid his arm around Rema's waist, picking her up and spinning her around. When her feet touched the floor, everyone clapped four times and then stomped their feet four times. Sweat covered his brow.

Finally, the musicians decided to take a break and a woman replaced them, singing a slow tune. Darmik pulled Rema against his chest. He held her firmly, tucking her head under his chin. Her crown poked his skin, but he didn't care. It felt too good to have her in his arms. She hugged him, and he wished they could stay like this forever.

Neco and Ellie danced not far away, slowly moving to the music. Vesha and Audek also danced together, although they held one another at arm's length. Audek's mouth never stopped moving. At least Vesha was laughing. Maya and Kar stood off to the side watching Rema.

Darmik had been so wrapped up enjoying his time with Rema that he'd failed to see the obvious until now. While most people were dancing and having a good time, they were separated into three groups: the rebels, the Emperion soldiers, and the members from the King's Army. It was easy to tell each group apart. The Emperion people all had blond hair and fair skin, while everyone else had dark hair, eyes, and skin. Darmik's soldiers seemed hesitant of the rebels, and the rebels distrustful of the soldiers. These three groups would never be able to fight together in battle if they couldn't even mingle with one another.

"What are you thinking?" Rema asked.

"I'm wondering what I can do to unify everyone."

She gazed into his eyes. "I think that's a job for the both of us."

"Do you have an idea?"

"I do. I look like an Emperion but am from Greenwood Island. I think I should start to bridge the gap between the two. But you, my dear Darmik, can help merge your soldiers with everyone else. They need to know they can trust the rebels and foreigners."

He kissed her nose. "I have one suggestion for you."

"Yes?"

"Emperions enjoy strong ale. They celebrate with a drink."

"So you're saying I should offer them ale?"

Darmik smiled. "No, I'm not. You're the empress. You *suggest* they have a drink. Then make a toast. It's customary."

"Oh, right. Got it." She squared her shoulders and headed toward the Emperions, her guards close behind.

He went over to his soldiers from the King's Army. Since he didn't allow women to join, none of his men were dancing. Instead, they sat around talking and laughing with one another near the tables of food. When he approached, they lifted their cups in salute. He sat down among them.

One nudged his shoulder. "You and the new empress, eh?" Several laughed.

He waved them off, not wanting to talk about her with other people. "Why aren't more of you here?" He took a sip of ale and waited for someone to respond.

"We're wondering if word didn't reach the other companies," a soldier replied.

He'd already thought the same thing. Traco said he'd sent messages to all ten companies. Maybe something had happened to the messages? He decided not to push the matter right now. His objective was to unify everyone, not question the loyalty of his army. "Why are you over here? The Emperions won't bite."

"They look and talk funny," someone answered.

"Did you forget that I was born in and trained at Emperion?"

"But you don't look or talk like them."

"No, only the lower class has blond hair. Royalty have dark hair and eyes, like mine."

"Then why is the empress blonde?"

"Prince Nero fell in love with a commoner. When the emperor forbade the marriage, Nero came here with the woman—who had blonde hair and blue eyes. Rema is their descendant. And let's not forget, Nero brought other Emperions here. A lot were upper-class citizens with brown hair. A lot of you are likely descended from them. We are tied to the empire."

Neco came over and joined them. "I've been to Emperion," he said. "Let me tell you, we're a lot alike. They suffered from a cruel leader who ruled with an iron fist. Her Majesty is going to change all that. But for this to work, we need to help her by removing Barjon and Lennek." He finished off his drink.

Darmik glanced over at Rema speaking with the Emperion people. "Let's go toast our new empress." He walked over to her, not bothering to look back to see if his men followed.

"Thank you so much for your suggestions," Rema said. "I appreciate it." The Emperions she talked to smiled kindly at her.

"When we return to the mainland, I will be forming a committee of soldiers to help restructure the army. You are all welcome to join."

"Hello," Darmik said, interrupting her. He didn't want her making too many promises, especially ones regarding the army. Soldiers were used to following orders and needed the hierarchy of command. "I'd like to make a toast." He stood on a chair and whistled, getting everyone's attention. "Thank you for coming tonight to celebrate with our beloved Empress Amer Rema!" Cheering erupted throughout the room. He raised his cup. "May our conquest be swift, the punishment just, and victory sweet!"

"Here, here!" everyone yelled.

The door to the gathering hall burst open and a servant rushed in. "Commander Mako!" she shouted. "Someone is here to see you. It's urgent." Mako hurried forward and left with her.

Darmik jumped off the chair and took Rema's hand. "Something's wrong," he said. "Let's go find out what it is."

They dashed out of the room, Neco and Savenek right behind them.

"Wait," Rema said, coming to a halt. "Someone needs to stay behind and make sure people remain calm. I don't want anyone to panic unnecessarily."

She was right, but he wanted to stay with her and discover what was going on.

"I'll stay," Neco offered.

"As will I," Savenek said.

"Excellent," Rema replied. "Please make sure people continue to sing and dance. Darmik will inform you of the situation as soon as possible." She turned and hurried down the hallway.

When they reached the main floor, Darmik heard voices coming from near the entrance. He rushed that way and saw a man standing by the front door, dripping wet. Mako gave the servant orders for blankets and food.

"He has hundreds of them," the man said. "Hundreds."

"What's going on?" Rema demanded.

"Everyone to the sitting room," Mako said, ushering them down the hallway. "Quickly now."

Once inside the sitting room, Mako shut the door. "This is Parek, one of my scouts."

Parek removed his wet cape and went before the hearth. "I've been traveling for almost two days straight to reach you," he said, rubbing his hands together and holding them near the fire.

"Please tell our empress what news you have," Mako said.

A servant entered carrying a tray of food. She set it down and then excused herself.

"I infiltrated the King's Army and discovered what's going on," Parek said, his face grim. "Lennek has control of the army."

"Impossible," Darmik said. "There's no way my men would willingly take orders from him." Even though he'd renounced his position as prince and commander, he expected his men to follow him. He didn't think they would support a corrupt crown.

"They're not doing so willingly," Parek revealed, shaking his head.

"I don't understand what's going on," Rema said.

"Barjon and Lennek have kidnapped hundreds of the soldiers' children."

"What?" Rema said, jumping off the sofa and pacing the room. "He kidnapped children? He's using them to control the army?" She balled her hands into fists, fury radiating from her.

Darmik had always known his father and brother were ruthless, but this was excessive, even for them.

"Yes," Parek answered. "Lennek claims that once Rema and Darmik are dead, the children will be released." He rubbed his face. "There's more," he said. "For each person who defects and joins Darmik, a child is killed."

That accounted for the lack of men here from the King's Army. The few that had managed to join him must have done so before Lennek implemented his demented plan. "Where are the kids being held?" he asked. They had to be in a secure location, but he couldn't imagine the army guarding them since the children belonged to their fellow soldiers.

"No one knows. They haven't been seen."

"We'll just have to defeat Barjon and Lennek with the men we have," Rema said, seething with rage.

"I'm not sure we're fully equipped to go up against ten thousand soldiers," Darmik admitted. "I intended to have my men on our side. Now I'll have to fight them." He didn't think he could kill people he'd trained.

"We have weapons here," Rema said. "We will succeed." She stared into Darmik's eyes, a fierce determination taking over. "We will."

He wanted to believe her, but he'd been in battle before and knew what was ahead of them.

"Is there anything else, Parek?" Mako asked.

"Yes. Barjon has the army searching for the rebels."

"I suggest we organize ourselves and leave as soon as possible —before Barjon discovers we're here," Mako said.

Darmik rubbed his face. "I agree." This location was no longer secure.

Rema nodded. "Very well. Prepare for battle."

CHAPTER NINETEEN

Rema

*A*fter receiving the news from the scout, Rema climbed into bed, exhausted. How was she supposed to be responsible for all the people here? For the entire island? For Emperion? She couldn't do this. People's lives were at stake, and it was up to her to save them.

How could Barjon and Lennek take the army's children? They had to be frightened—taken away from their parents and locked up, not knowing if they'd be released. The only option she had was to quietly lead her army to King's City and defeat Barjon and Lennek before the King's Army stood against them. Then the soldiers could have their children back.

She tossed and turned, unable to sleep. Ellie breathed heavily while Vesha lightly snored. Throwing off her blankets, Rema slid out of bed and padded across the room to the window. The stars shone brightly overhead. Grabbing her robe, she left the room, quietly shutting the door behind her. Two Emperion guards stood in the hallway.

"Is something the matter, Your Majesty?" one asked in his thick accent.

"I can't sleep. I want to go outside to see the stars."

"We have orders to keep you inside the premises," he said. "It's for your own safety."

"I understand. What about the roof? Am I allowed to go up there?" She felt silly asking if she could do something since she was the empress and technically in charge of everyone. However, she knew Darmik and Neco set parameters with her guards for her own safety, and she would respect them.

The guards looked at each other. One shrugged and replied, "I don't see why not."

Rema had no idea how to reach the roof. She went up the stairs to the top level and began searching the hallways for a door that looked different from the others. She finally found an iron door. Shoving it open, she climbed a ladder and stepped onto the top of Trell's house. She pulled her robe closed and went to the edge, looking out at the land before her. Breathing in the fresh air, she gazed at the stars and thought about the task ahead of her.

This was *her* island. These were *her* people. It was *her* duty to make things right and help everyone live peacefully.

Someone cleared his throat and she spun around, coming face to face with Savenek. "What are you doing here?" She waved at her guards, indicating she would speak with him. They melted into the background, out of sight.

"I couldn't sleep," he said, his voice soft. "I was pacing in the hallway when I caught a glimpse of you going upstairs. It didn't take long to figure out where you were headed."

She leaned against the half-wall, not sure what to say to him.

He came and stood next to her. "Have you considered staying behind?"

She'd wondered when someone would suggest this.

"You won't even consider it, will you?" he asked.

Rema shook her head.

They stood side by side in silence. "After we get rid of Barjon and Lennek, are you going to Emperion?" he asked.

"Yes. They need me."

"We need you here, too."

"I know." It wasn't that she wanted to go to Emperion, but she had to. If she didn't return, someone else would steal the throne and that person could be even worse than Hamen. It was her responsibility to bring peace and stability to Emperion. She hoped Mako would agree to remain on Greenwood Island to oversee a smooth transition and to act on her behalf.

"I need you here," Savenek whispered.

Rema peered at him. He was staring into the night sky, not looking at her. "I agreed to marry Darmik."

He nodded, as if he already knew about her engagement. "I'd like to accompany you, to be a member of your royal guard, if you'll have me."

That wasn't the best idea, especially since he still had feelings for her. Plus, Savenek was reckless and unpredictable. However, she trusted him. "I would be honored." She didn't have the heart to turn him down again. "But you must understand that my heart belongs to Darmik. It always will."

"I know."

Rema reached out, placing her hand on Savenek's cheek. "Thank you for your friendship and loyalty." He closed his eyes, leaning in to her touch. She withdrew her hand and left.

Rema woke up to a flurry of activity. People had already started assembling outside. Once Rema, Vesha, and Ellie were dressed, they headed downstairs. People were running around, some carrying armfuls of weapons, others bags of food.

Maya and Kar rushed over to her. "You're not going with them, are you?" Maya demanded.

Rema sighed. "Of course I am. It's my army. I won't send them to do my bidding without me."

"You should," Maya said, crossing her arms.

"Your aunt is right," Kar said. "Now that you're in charge, you can send your army and servants to do jobs for you. You must ensure your safety."

"I know," she replied. "But just because I can, doesn't mean I should."

"I don't know if I should be proud of you, or slap you across the head to knock some sense into you," Kar said.

Rema laughed. "I'll take the first option."

Mako joined them. "I want everyone who's coming to go outside."

"Very well," Maya mumbled. "If Rema is going, so are we."

Her aunt and uncle were too old to participate in such a journey. However, she always hated when someone told her what to do.

"Are you reconsidering?" Maya asked, a smug look across her face.

"Absolutely not," she replied. "We should all head outside, since we're all going."

Kar chuckled. "That's my girl."

Stepping outside into the bright sunlight, she saw that Darmik had organized everyone into groups. He walked around giving instructions to various people. Someone came over and ushered Maya and Kar to one of the groups.

"I've been meaning to talk to you about the command situation," Mako said, recapturing her attention.

"What do you mean?"

"You need to make it clear who commands the army. Me? Darmik?"

Rema had asked Darmik to head her royal guard, but seeing him in charge made her realize it would be a waste of his talent.

"Darmik is the commander of my entire army, both here and in Emperion."

"Very well," he responded. "Then who is in charge of your personal safety?"

"I will speak with Darmik on the matter." Her inclination was to choose Neco as the permanent head of her royal guard; however, Darmik might need him in another position.

As if sensing her, Darmik glanced up and she waved him over. "I am officially appointing you as commander of my entire army."

His eyes widened. "It is my honor and privilege."

"As commander, who would you suggest head my royal guard?"

"Neco," he answered without hesitation.

"I think you may need Neco by your side," she countered.

He rubbed his chin, lost in thought. "I agree. If I'm to head the entire army, then I want someone I trust working as my second."

"So that leaves Mako, Audek, and Savenek."

Mako cleared his throat. "I would be honored to hold the position. However, I would like to stay here on Greenwood Island when this is over."

"I understand. And I would like you here, protecting my interests."

"I want Savenek in charge," Darmik said, surprising her. She didn't think he cared for Savenek. "Without a doubt, your safety is his priority."

"I will ask if he'll take the position." Mako bowed and left.

When they were alone, she said, "I didn't think you'd choose him, given his feelings toward me."

"That is precisely why I selected him." He kissed her forehead.

"I'd like to address the people before we go." Rema said.

"Of course."

Within five minutes, Darmik had everyone's attention. Rema ascended the steps leading up to the front door of Trell's house. She turned and faced everyone. She felt silly wearing the standard army uniform—pants and a tunic—since she also wore her crown. The weight of it atop her head reminded her of the responsibility she bore to these people.

"Thank you for being here," she said in a loud, clear voice. "Today, we begin our trek to King's City. Leading my army is Commander Darmik. He will be appointing some of you to the positions of captains and lieutenants for our mission. We have one goal—to quickly and efficiently storm into the castle and either capture or kill Barjon and Lennek, thus ending their tyranny." Cheering and applause erupted. "Let's move out!"

Darmik began shouting orders to his men.

Savenek joined her on the steps. "Thank you for the honor of allowing me to protect you. I swear, on my life, to serve you until the day I die." He knelt before her.

Rema touched his shoulder. "Thank you for your loyalty."

Mako approached. "Your horse is ready."

Snow pranced not far away. She didn't see any other horses. "Is anyone else going to be on horseback?"

"No. There aren't enough for everyone."

"Then I'll walk with my people."

Savenek rolled his eyes. "I'd forgotten how difficult you can be."

They traveled all morning before stopping for a quick meal. When they continued their trek, word came from one of the scouting units that the small village of Vara was deserted.

"Darmik has decided to pass through Vara in case anyone needs our help," Savenek informed her. "But he doesn't want you outside the village watching. He thinks you'd be too vulnerable. You're going to be somewhere in the middle of the army as we enter the village."

Word came down the line for everyone to prepare for battle.

Savenek unsheathed his sword. The men assigned to her guard carried either a sword or a bow. Rema removed her crown and hid it in one of the soldier's sacks so she wouldn't stand out among them.

The village came into view. It appeared as it should—no buildings were destroyed and there weren't any signs of a battle or struggle. However, there also weren't any people about, no smoke rising from chimneys, no dogs or animals roaming around. Rema removed her dagger, gripping the hilt.

"If a skirmish should arise," Savenek whispered in her ear, "stay at my side—no matter what." She nodded. "I want you to promise me."

"I give you my word, I'll stay at your side."

The first portion of the army reached the edge of the village. She tried to find Darmik among them.

"Let him do his job," Savenek said. "If you're worrying about him, and he's worrying about you, someone's going to get hurt."

"Perhaps if you kept me better informed, there would be no need to worry."

One of her guards snickered, and Savenek glared at him. A group of soldiers entered the village. The rest of the army waited for the signal to attack or retreat. No one uttered a single word. Rema held her breath, her heart pounding.

A soldier ran up to Rema. "Commander Darmik requests your presence," he said.

"What's going on?" Savenek demanded.

"I'm not at liberty to say," he replied.

The army started to move—half to the left, half to the right. Savenek told her they were going to form a circle around the village. While they did that, her guard surrounded her and made their way toward the village. When they reached the first building, she paused, listening. No signs of distress or indications of a scuffle.

"Let's go," she whispered. They entered the village of Vara.

Two-story structures stood on either side of the dirt road. "Where are all the people?"

"They could be hiding inside," Savenek said. "Maybe they're watching us." He looked at the nearby windows.

An eerie sensation came over her. She started walking faster, wanting to find Darmik. She spotted him up ahead standing with a squad of soldiers surrounding something. As she got closer, she saw they had a dozen men dressed in the King's Army uniform on their knees.

Savenek scanned the nearby buildings. "Stay close."

"Your Majesty." Darmik bowed. "We encountered these men who claim to be stationed here. We apprehended them with ease. With your permission, I'd like to interrogate them."

She stared into his intense gaze. He nodded ever so slightly. "Find out why they're here and where all the people have gone. Use whatever means necessary."

"Of course, Your Majesty."

"I'd like to stay," she added.

He stilled. "You want to witness the interrogation?"

"Yes."

He scrunched his forehead—an unusual gesture for him since he normally maintained a neutral expression. He had to be weighing his desire to shield her from anything unpleasant with her outranking him.

He gave a curt nod and turned to face his men. Neco stood above one of the prisoners, pointing a sword at the man's chest. Rema expected to see him near Darmik; however, she had not expected to see Mako and Kar there. Both men stood near the prisoners, also with their swords drawn.

"Bring that one here," Darmik said, indicating the captive on the end.

Neco grabbed the man's collar, yanking him forward. He threw the man on the ground, stepping on his neck and forcing him to remain down.

"Are you the only soldiers here?" Darmik demanded.

"Yes," the prisoner croaked.

Rema wondered if he was telling the truth. There were a dozen captives here. A squad usually consisted of twenty individuals.

Darmik knelt next to the man's head. "Pratok, we've known each other for quite some time."

Shock rolled through Rema. Darmik knew this man? Of course he did; Pratok was from the King's Army. It had to be difficult interrogating someone he knew. She squeezed her hands together, trying to remain calm and in control.

"We have," Pratok said, pursing his lips.

"So you know I can tell when you're lying." He flexed his fingers. "And you know what I do to people who don't provide worthy information during an interrogation." He cracked his knuckles, one at a time, the sound oddly loud in the quiet stillness of the afternoon.

Tears welled in the man's eyes. "I'm sorry, I have no choice." His arms started shaking.

"Tell me why you're here," Darmik demanded. "If you lie to me, I'll chop off your hand." Rema didn't think he'd actually do it, but she couldn't be sure.

"We were told to wait here," Pratok said. Neco lifted his foot, giving Pratok more room to speak.

"Who gave the order?" Darmik inquired.

"Prince Lennek."

"What are you waiting here for?"

"You," he cried, "but that's all I know."

Darmik cursed. Standing, he came over to Rema. "He's telling the truth. I'm not sure he knows anything else. I'll ask the others a few questions, but I don't think we'll get any more information."

"What makes you so sure?" Savenek asked.

"I know Pratok, and I know when people are lying." Darmik crossed his arms. "What I find more concerning is that Lennek specifically sent them here. Almost as if he knew we were coming."

Savenek chuckled. "Lennek is a moron. There's no way he knows we're here. He probably has soldiers all over the kingdom."

"No," Darmik responded. "He's smarter than you realize. And I fear we've walked into a trap."

Cold fear shot through Rema. Glancing at the nearby buildings, she felt people watching them. She wanted to leave this village.

"If we just walked into a trap," Savenek said snidely, "then why are we the ones standing here while they," he pointed at the prisoners, "are at sword point?"

"I don't know," he admitted.

Savenek laughed. "Who would have set it? Lennek?"

While Lennek might appear to be rash, careless, and a fool, he definitely wasn't. He was more intelligent than anyone realized.

"Never underestimate my brother or my father. Both are cunning and shrewd."

A thought occurred to her. Maybe the people in hiding knew something about the missing children.

"Tie the prisoners up," Darmik ordered. "They're coming with us."

She didn't want to take them as prisoners. However, they couldn't leave them here to report to the king and prince.

"We should kill them," Savenek mumbled.

"I promised Trell no unnecessary killing," Darmik said. "I intend to keep that promise." Reaching up, he took hold of Rema's key necklace. He traced the edges of it before slipping it under her tunic. "Let's get moving. I'd hoped to be in King's City by now."

CHAPTER TWENTY

Darmik

*D*armik hated that Savenek was always at Rema's side, pining over her.

"Stop staring," Neco said. "We're almost at King's City. You need to focus."

"Sorry." He knew Rema was safest with Savenek as her guard. Still, the guy irked him.

Greenwood Forest loomed to the right, open land lay to the left. There was only one more hill before King's City was in sight. Darmik estimated they would reach the outer wall in about two hours, right as the sun was setting. Attacking would be more effective in the early morning hours.

He raised his hand, signaling that everyone behind him should come to a halt. He told his runners to inform all captains and lieutenants to make camp for the night—they would attack at daybreak.

A horn blared in the distance. The ground rumbled, as if hundreds of horses were coming toward them. Darmik shouted,

"Weapons ready! Incoming!" Unsheathing his sword, he faced the open land before him.

At the crest of the hill, a lone man atop a horse pointed his sword directly at Darmik. "Attack!" echoed through the air.

A sea of horses, ridden by armor-clad soldiers, thundered down the hill toward them. Darmik had never gone into battle against men he knew. He shook his head; he needed to get into fighting mode.

Neco stood beside him. "Rema and Ellie are in the middle, surrounded by four squads of soldiers."

"Hopefully there's only one company." Any more than that, and they wouldn't stand a chance.

The horses stopped a hundred yards away. The riders pulled out longbows and aimed at Darmik and his men. He moved behind a tree, using it as a shield. Arrows sailed through the air all around him. A couple dozen men fell to the ground. The soldiers once again nocked arrows and aimed higher this time, which meant the arrows would be raining straight down. "Stay close to the trees!" he shouted. Arrows whistled through the air. A few dozen more men dropped to the ground.

"Should we attack?" Neco asked.

"We can't fight them while they're on horseback. We'll be slaughtered. Our best chance is to lure them into the forest."

The horses moved aside as another company of soldiers marched over the rise toward them. Panic shot through Darmik. Two thousand men from the King's Army were here. They were outnumbered two to one. There was no way to win this battle. Good men on both sides were about to die. He widened his stance, raised his sword, and mentally prepared to fight. He would not die today.

The armed soldiers drew near. "Ready?" Neco asked.

"I always am," Darmik replied, thankful to have his friend by his side.

"After you." Neco nodded his chin toward their attackers.

Darmik smiled and charged, the Emperions and rebels following him. The clash of steel rang through the air. He had to strike hard and fast. With Neco at his back, he raised his sword and sliced toward the first soldier he encountered. The man went down. He swung again, parrying a blow from another soldier. He countered with a wide swing, slicing his attacker across his stomach.

His movements became a routine—swing, parry, thrust. It felt like he fought for hours and yet, the enemy soldiers kept coming. Men littered the ground all around him.

"Commander!" Neco shouted. "They broke through our line. We need to assess the situation and locate our empress." There was a hint of panic to his voice that Darmik had never heard before.

He kicked the man in front of him, sending him to his knees. "Let's go!" He and Neco retreated, running deeper into the forest where the enemy soldiers had penetrated. He desperately searched for Rema, but she was nowhere to be seen. Everywhere he turned, he saw men from the King's Army.

"Neco, tell the Emperion soldiers to fight forward for ten and then back flank two back."

"What does that mean?" he asked, running behind Darmik.

"Just repeat the order, they'll understand. Then find Mako and tell the rebels to fight for another ten minutes. Then I want them to fall back the way we came, approximately two miles. We'll regroup there. Go quickly and relay the messages. I'm going after Rema."

His friend nodded and took off.

Chaos surrounded Darmik. He continued running, searching for her. Up ahead, a group of men stood shoulder to shoulder. Intuition told him it was her guard. He unsheathed his dagger, both hands now armed, ready to join in the fight. Two members of the royal guard went down, allowing the enemy to break through their line. Rushing forward, Darmik threw a dagger into the back of a soldier. He reached for his last dagger and hurled it into the neck of another. Several men turned to face him. He caught a glimpse of Savenek and Audek fighting, Rema still nowhere in sight.

The enemy came at him. Darmik swung his sword, blocking a blow and responding with a strike of his own. The sword he wielded was heavier than the one he typically used, and his arms grew tired. He had to force himself to be quick with his movements. He swung again, and the soldier blocked him. Darmik kicked him, sending him flat on his back.

Darmik ran toward Savenek and Audek. When he got closer, he saw Rema fighting with a soldier not far away. She stood with her feet shoulder-width apart, both hands on her sword, parrying each blow. He almost stumbled when he saw her. He'd never been prouder—or more frightened—in his entire life.

A sound rustled behind him. He spun and ducked as a sword flew over his head, narrowly missing him. Jabbing his sword forward, he sliced his opponent's leg. The man went down.

He righted himself just as another soldier's sword arced toward Audek's chest, cutting him open. Audek stumbled and fell to the ground. Savenek faltered. Darmik knew Savenek would be next. Without hesitating, he threw his heavy sword at Savenek's opponent, hitting his back. It didn't knock him down, but the distraction was enough for Savenek to refocus and stab the man.

Darmik grabbed his sword and ran toward Rema. She'd been disarmed. As she stood there, defenseless, the soldier she'd been fighting raised his sword to strike her.

"No!" Darmik hollered.

Savenek threw his knife, embedding it in the soldier's thigh. Rema pulled out a dagger, stepped forward, and thrust it into the man's stomach. His eyes widened as he lurched backward, dropping to the ground. Rema stood frozen in shock.

Darmik grabbed her shoulders. "Are you hurt?"

She looked at him with wide eyes, shaking her head.

"We need to get you out of here." He started to pull her farther into the forest.

"No. We aren't leaving without Audek."

He glanced back at Audek sprawled on the ground, Vesha and Savenek kneeling by his side. "Where's Ellie?"

"I don't know. I haven't seen her since the fighting broke out."

"Is he alive?" Darmik called to Savenek.

"Barely."

He sprinted back to them. "We must hurry." Enemy soldiers were fighting all around them. "I'll grab one arm, Savenek, you grab the other. Vesha and Rema, start running deeper into the forest."

The women did as instructed while he and Savenek lifted Audek between them. Audek moaned, blood soaking his tunic. They supported him while heading after the women. The trees thickened, blocking out the sunlight. Leaves crunched behind them. "We're being followed," Darmik whispered.

"Duck," Rema said. They dropped to the ground, and she threw a dagger at something behind them. She smiled.

Glancing back, he saw an enemy soldier lying on the ground, a knife protruding from his chest. "Where'd you learn to do that?" he asked, shocked by her accurate throw.

"Nathenek taught me."

"That was impressive."

"I know."

Once he was positive no one else had followed them, they headed north—the direction they'd come from earlier in the day. After they'd gone a solid two miles, he led them eastward to a dirt path. It was difficult to see now that night had descended and the moon was concealed behind thick clouds. Audek moaned and passed out. If they didn't tend to his wounds soon, he'd die.

"I hear something," Rema whispered.

"I told everyone to meet in this general area. The four of you wait here while I go and investigate." He removed his arm from around Audek. Vesha slid under Audek's arm, holding him up.

Darmik crouched low, staying close to the tree trunks as he moved through the forest. He heard a twig snap. Unsheathing a knife, he spun around and found Neco. "Am I glad to see you."

"Is Ellie with you?" His eyes were pulled tight with concern.

He shook his head. "Let everyone know I'm bringing in an injured man who needs medical attention."

Neco hurried away and Darmik returned to his friends. After switching places with Vesha, he and Savenek dragged Audek to where everyone else was.

When they arrived, an Emperion rushed forward to help. "We have a fire going over there." He pointed to the right. "That's where we're assessing the injured."

They lowered Audek to the ground next to the fire. A man rushed over, ripping open Audek's tunic and revealing a nasty gash across his chest.

Vesha gasped and fell to her knees next to him. "Audek, listen to me," she said, taking hold of his hand. "You're going to be all right." He remained unconscious.

"He's not going to make it, is he?" Rema asked, coming to stand alongside Darmik, tears dripping down her cheeks.

"I don't know."

Neco came over. "Ellie isn't here. I'm going back to the battle-field to search for her."

"It would be wise to wait until daybreak."

"If she's lying somewhere, bleeding, I have to find her before it's too late."

If the roles were reversed, and something happened to Rema, Darmik would do the same thing. "I'll go with you."

"No. You need to stay here. I'll take Savenek with me."

Darmik nodded. "Be careful."

Neco patted Darmik's shoulder and left.

Rema sat near Vesha, rubbing her friend's back.

"He needs stitches," one of the Emperion men stated. "But I am not very good at closing wounds."

"And medicine to fight infection," Vesha mumbled, her healer training kicking in.

Darmik watched the Emperion soldiers mix some herbs together and spread it over Audek's wound.

"I can do the stitches," Vesha said, wiping the tears from her eyes. "I'm good at it." She took the needle and thread. Two men helped hold Audek's skin in place while she sewed it shut.

"Rema," Darmik said, "can I speak with you?" She stood and came over to him. "We must find Mako and get the people organized. There's much to be done."

"Of course." She glanced back at Audek and Vesha. "There's nothing I can do to help him anyway. I might as well do my duty to my people."

They searched for Mako. Most people were either sleeping or tending to the wounded. If Darmik had to guess, he'd say there were a little less than half their people present. Did that mean the rest were dead? He finally spotted Mako sitting on the ground, his head between his legs. "How are you holding up?"

Mako sighed. "Better now that I know Rema is safe." He stood and joined them. "We . . . we lost so many." He rubbed his face with his hands. "It's like they knew we were coming. It was an ambush."

That was what Darmik had been thinking but didn't want to voice. "I saw Lennek there," he admitted. "He was wearing my commander's helmet."

"Lennek was there? Leading the King's Army?" Rema said, her eyes darkening. "I'm going to kill him."

"Your Majesty," a young soldier said, coming to kneel before her. "I'm so glad you're safe."

"Thank you," she replied, placing her hand upon the man's head. He smiled and left. "I suppose I should speak to my people."

"That would be most wise," Mako said.

"I don't want to address everyone as a group. I will go and speak to each person individually. I think that will help build morale. Plus, I need to thank everyone personally for their service and sacrifice here today."

Now that Savenek was gone with Neco, Darmik wanted to stay by Rema's side to ensure her safety until he returned. She went up to the first couple she saw sitting about ten feet away. She knelt, speaking in such a soft voice that he couldn't hear what she said. Standing a few feet away, he watched her. The two men she spoke to nodded, their faces haggard. She said a few more things and then both men smiled, their moods improving.

She stood and went to the next group, doing the same thing. Each group she spoke to smiled, their faces softening as if they truly appreciated her taking the time to talk to them and offer encouraging words.

After visiting a dozen groups, Rema came over to Darmik, kissing his cheek. "Have you seen my aunt and uncle?"

"No. I'm sure they're around here somewhere." He'd been looking for them for the past twenty minutes but hadn't spotted them anywhere.

She nodded and went to the next group. While she spoke, he continued to scan the area for Maya and Kar.

When she finished speaking to a few more groups, she stood next to Darmik, wiping her eyes.

"You can do this," he said encouragingly.

"I want to know where they are." She kissed his cheek and moved to the next group of people. Kneeling, she kindly smiled and began speaking to them.

He couldn't help but marvel at her beauty, strength, and compassion—he both admired and loved her.

"Commander, I'm glad you're back," one of his soldiers said.

"Thank you. I'm glad you were there today. Even though we didn't win, I'm honored to fight by your side."

"I didn't realize you and the empress were courting." He grinned.

Darmik laughed. "Yes, we plan to marry."

"She's a mighty fine woman. You're lucky to have someone so compassionate." He patted Darmik on the back and left.

He considered himself fortunate to have Rema in his life. As she spoke to the next group, she kept glancing back at him—panic in her eyes. He needed to find Kar and Maya.

Movement off to the side caught his attention. Neco and Savenek were walking toward him, Ellie limp in Neco's arms. Darmik rushed over, Rema immediately at his side.

"Is she alive?" Rema demanded, a sob escaping her.

"Yes," Neco said. "She's just exhausted and fell asleep in my arms." He gently nudged Ellie, and she opened her eyes.

Rema's shoulders relaxed. "Wait, is that blood?" She pointed at Ellie's chest. "Why is there blood on you if you're not injured?"

Ellie and Neco exchanged a brief look. Savenek stepped back as Neco carefully set Ellie on her feet. Then he, too, took a few steps away, giving Rema and Ellie privacy. Whatever Ellie was about to say, it must not be good. Darmik knew he should give the two of them space, but he wanted to be by Rema's side in case she needed him.

"I do have blood on me, but it's not mine." Ellie reached forward, hugging Rema.

"Whose blood is it?" she asked, her voice unnaturally high-pitched.

"Shh," Ellie said, rubbing her back.

"Whose?" Rema demanded, crying.

"I'm so sorry," Ellie said tenderly. "Kar and Maya are dead."

CHAPTER TWENTY-ONE

Rema

*R*ema's world swayed, everything going black as she collapsed to the ground. Strong hands grabbed her. It must be Darmik embracing her. Things became blurry, gradually coming back into focus. She could see again.

Darmik hovered above her. "Someone get her water."

She remembered what Ellie had said—Kar and Maya were dead. She wrapped her arms around Darmik's neck and squeezed, the tears coming. How could they be dead?

"Here." Ellie handed her a waterskin.

Rema shook her head. She just wanted to be left alone.

Darmik stood, pulling her up with him. "I'm going to find her a place to rest for the night. We'll regroup in the morning."

She caught a glimpse of Mako's stricken face, and she felt her heart squeeze in pain. "Ellie, please come with me. I need to know what happened."

"Of course."

Darmik led them about twenty feet away from the small crowd

that had gathered. Rema sat with her back against a tree trunk, Ellie on one side of her and Darmik on the other.

"Please tell me what happened," she whispered.

"I'm so sorry," Ellie said.

She leaned against Darmik's shoulder, taking comfort in his steadfast strength.

Ellie took a deep breath. "When the battle broke out, Savenek ordered us to form a protective circle around you. I was to your left. I saw Kar and Maya nearby, their panic clear. They were heading in your direction. They . . . they were so focused on you that they weren't watching behind them." Tears formed in Ellie's eyes. "The enemy came. I was fighting a man off. Out of the corner of my eye, I saw a soldier running toward Kar and Maya." She wiped her cheeks. "Savenek sent me to help them. As I ran over, a man shoved Maya out of the way. She fell, smashing her head on a rock." The words started coming quickly, and Ellie's eyes glazed over. "Kar turned and saw her. He screamed and engaged the soldier in a sword fight. More enemy soldiers came, and Savenek started condensing the line down, closer to you."

Ellie brought her legs up. She hugged them, resting her head on her knees. "While Kar fought the soldier, another one approached from behind him. I screamed, but it was too late. The soldier plunged a sword into his back. He tumbled forward, flat on his face. An Emperion came to my aid. We attacked the two men who killed Kar and Maya. After we took them down, I turned to see if you were all right, but you and Savenek were gone. Bodies were all over the place. Maya's body jerked and I ran to her. Maya tried talking, but I told her to be quiet. I grabbed her arms and pulled her out of the mess. I heard more soldiers coming. There was a large tree with huge roots that formed a small cave-like place to hide. I slid inside, pulling Maya down with me. I held her in my lap while listening to people run by."

Rema reached out, taking hold of Ellie's hand and squeezing it.

"Maya started mumbling. She begged me to watch out for you.

She asked me to promise her. I did. Then her body went limp—she was gone." Ellie buried her head between her knees.

Rema scooted closer to her friend, hugging her. "Thank you for what you did."

"I'm sorry I couldn't save them." Ellie's face was red and her eyes swollen.

"There was nothing else you could have done."

"I need to be with Neco right now." Ellie stood and left.

Rema couldn't believe her aunt and uncle were gone. The people who'd raised her, cared for her, and loved her. She buried her face in her hands, crying. She was a terrible leader. She couldn't even save her own family—how was she supposed to save a kingdom? An empire?

Darmik wrapped his arms around her.

"I want to be left alone," she cried. "I can't do this."

"Shh," he said.

"Go away." None of this would be happening if she'd never met Darmik in the forest that day. She'd be married to Bren, and Kar and Maya would be alive. Sure, she'd still be confined to her home in Jarko, but everyone she loved would be alive. She wouldn't be responsible for all these people. She wouldn't bear the weight of the crown.

"I'm not leaving you," he said. "I know how you feel."

"How could you possibly know?" she demanded. "You've haven't lost almost everyone you love."

He shook his head. "You're wrong." Releasing her, he sat across from her. She couldn't see his features very well in the dark.

"You know Barjon isn't kind and loving toward me. He doesn't act like a father. But there are others I love—and have lost. Phellek was the closest to a father figure I've ever had. Captain killed him right in front of me. Almost my *entire* personal squad died saving me from Lennek. Those were the men with whom I spent every day, with whom I fought, and to whom I trusted my life. *They* were my brothers. And you forget—my mother died delivering me into this world. How do you think that makes me feel? To know, and be reminded by Barjon, that I am the reason my mother is dead?" He scooted forward, taking her hands in his. "I know you're hurting right now. I know because I have felt your pain—I understand it. You are not alone because I'm here for you."

Staring into his eyes, at this beautiful man before her, she whispered, "I love you. I don't want to lose you, too."

He leaned forward, kissing her forehead. "I don't want to lose you either. When I heard the front line was broken, I was scared to death that the soldiers got to you. I don't know what I'd do if I lost you."

"Does it get easier? Does the pain go away?" It hurt just to breathe. It felt like her heart had been ripped from her chest.

"With time, it becomes manageable."

She wiped the tears from her cheeks.

Mako came over and sat down beside her. "I'm so sorry," he said. "Kar was like a brother to me. Losing someone is never easy."

"No, it's not," Darmik added, patting her hands. "Just remember, they spent their lives protecting you. You can honor them by finishing what they fought for. You can end Barjon and Lennek's tyrannical reign."

"We will end this," Mako promised.

"Thank you both," she said, glad to have these wonderful people in her life.

Darmik pulled a dagger from the sheath strapped to his thigh. "Phellek gave this to me." He handed it to her. She recognized it as his prized possession. "I want you to have it. I want you to use it to end this."

Mako stiffened beside her. "Let me see that," he said, his voice trembling.

Rema carefully handed it to him. He took it, his hands shaking. For several minutes, he just sat there, staring at it. The weapon was beautiful. There was a silver sun on the hilt, and the tip looked sharp and deadly.

He handed it back to Rema, his face white. "What's the matter?" she asked him.

"That is the knife that killed my daughter, Tabitha. I removed it from her chest, tossing it to the ground."

Rema stared at the weapon. "I want you to have it. Use it to kill the man responsible for this."

With trembling fingers, Mako delicately picked up the dagger, his eyes glassy. "I will kill Barjon and avenge my wife and daughter's deaths." His hands curled around the hilt, squeezing it tightly.

~

When Rema woke up the next morning, she immediately went to check on Audek. Vesha was sitting by his side. "How's he doing?" He was on the ground, covered with tunics that people had freely given to him.

Vesha glanced up at her. "Ask him yourself."

Rema knelt, not wanting to wake him up. Leaning in closer, she examined his face. His cheeks had some color to them. That was a good sign.

"Hey," he said, his eyes now open. "The all-mighty empress is here to see me!" She jerked back, and he laughed. "Ah, forgot I can't laugh. It hurts too much. Did you see they stitched me up?" He started to lift the tunics covering him.

"Stop," Vesha said. "She does *not* need to see that."

Rema couldn't believe he was awake and coherent. She'd expected him to die.

"He's been like this all morning," Vesha said. "He thinks it's funny." She reached out and took hold of Audek's hand.

"Is he going to make a full recovery?"

"I am," he answered. "You don't need to look so shocked. I

might not be the beauty I once was," he pointed at his torso, "but I will most definitely live." He looked at Vesha. "Thanks to you."

Vesha's face reddened as she stared at their joined hands.

"I need to speak with Darmik," Rema said, standing. "I'm glad you're well, Audek."

She spotted Darmik talking to Neco, Savenek, and Mako. She walked over and joined them. They were on their knees studying a map lying on the ground. "What's going on?" she asked. The map seemed familiar. Everyone looked at her, but no one spoke. "Someone needs to tell me." She looked pointedly at Darmik.

"We have an idea," he said, focusing back on the map.

"Which is?"

"The King's Army is taking orders from Lennek because he and Barjon have their children. If we rescue them, then my men can fight for me."

"Are you certain?"

"I'm positive."

"Regardless," Neco added, "we need to save the children. It's the right thing to do."

"What's this?" she asked, pointing at the map between them.

Mako cleared his throat. "This is a map of your parents' home. This is the castle into which Barjon stormed and slaughtered everyone."

"This is different from King Barjon's castle?" She knelt on the ground and studied the map in greater detail.

"Yes," Mako said. "After the massacre, the castle was abandoned. Since Barjon easily overtook it, he didn't want to live there. He chose a location farther inland, surrounded by flat land. That's where he built the castle in which he currently lives."

Rema still didn't understand why they were staring at the floor plan of her parents' home. What did this have to do with anything?

"Mako found this on Trell's desk," Darmik said. Rema remembered finding it there and Mako asking permission to study it.

"Mako has a theory." His intense gaze met hers. "He believes that the king is hiding the children there, and I agree with him."

She focused on the map of her parents' home. There were stables, courtyards, a great hall, towers, a kitchen, a throne room, bedchambers, and the royal nursery—*her* nursery.

Savenek pointed at the map. "It would be an excellent place to hide the children since no one knows of its existence."

"I'm not so sure," Neco mumbled. "I'd like to sneak into the enemy's camp and discover the location from a captain or Lennek himself."

"I doubt even a captain knows," Mako said. "The only way Barjon taking the children hostage works is if no one knows where they are."

"I agree," Rema said. "And it's too risky to have you sneak into enemy territory. I don't want anything to happen to you."

"He's more than qualified," Darmik said. She glared at him. "Well, he is."

Mako pulled out the dagger he'd received from Darmik. He sat there staring at it, lost in thought.

"This is what I propose," Rema said. "We go to this castle and see if the children are there. If they are, we rescue them. Then the men from the King's Army will join our side and we can overthrow Barjon and Lennek. If the children aren't there, then we've lost nothing by going there." She looked at Neco. "Then we return to Emperion and bring a larger army here. That way, we'll attack Barjon and Lennek with significantly less loss on our side." She grabbed her key necklace, holding onto it while waiting for their responses. Everyone started nodding in approval.

"I think it's a wise move," Darmik said, crossing his arms. "I'd rather get the King's Army on our side than fight against them."

"Very well." She let go of her necklace. "Tell everyone we're moving out. I want to be on our way as soon as possible." In the battle yesterday, more than half her army had been killed. She didn't want to sit there and make it any easier for Lennek to finish them off.

"What about those who are injured?" Neco asked.

"There is a rebel cave a few miles from here," Mako offered.

"Excellent," Rema said. "Assign one person to assist each injured individual to the cave. Tell them to stay there until they hear from us. Vesha should accompany them as well since she is a skilled healer."

"Yes, Your Majesty," they replied in unison.

They traveled to the northern section of Shano toward the Great Ocean, Rema's royal guard surrounding her at all times. She feared Lennek would be out searching for them, so she ordered Darmik to stay away from the roads.

When night came, everyone slept on the ground. Rema tossed and turned, imagining an army riding in and slaughtering them all while they slept. She knew Darmik had men guarding the perimeter; yet, it wasn't enough to keep the nightmares away.

Mako watched the queen tenderly kiss the princess before laying her on his bed. Queen Kayln removed the baby's blanket and slipped a red velvet pouch out of the bodice of her gown, tucking it under the collar of the princess's dress.

"I love you, my darling child. Keep this close to your heart. I'll always be watching over you."

With trembling hands, Mako picked up his dead baby and removed the knife, tossing it to the floor as if it was on fire. The queen handed Mako the princess's royal blanket. He wrapped Tabitha in it and kissed her forehead like she was still alive.

"Princess Amer is all that is left," the queen said, wiping her tears. "Even if she never fulfills her duty as ruler of our land, I want her to live." She pressed her lips to her daughter's cheek one last time.

Rema's eyes flew open. Everything around her was calm. She

felt her key necklace against her chest and rolled over, closing her eyes and trying to fall back to sleep.

Soft whispers drifted toward her and she strained her ears, listening.

"Please, I beg you, don't join the fight. You can stay back where it's safe." It sounded like Neco, but she wasn't sure.

"I understand your concern," Ellie answered. "But I promised Maya I would watch out for Rema."

"Neither one of you should be there when we go in."

She sighed. "I know you're worried, but I'm perfectly capable of taking care of myself. You know that."

"I do," he responded. "It's just that, I've never been in battle knowing the woman I loved was in it, too." There was a shuffling sound. "And I've never had anything to live for, until now. If I died, it was always for a good cause. Now I don't want to die. I want to live—with you by my side."

This was a conversation Rema should not be hearing. She rolled over, making as much noise as possible.

After traveling hard and fast for a week, Rema and her soldiers arrived at a twenty-foot high stone wall. They walked alongside it until they came to a section that was crumbled down, allowing them to easily climb over. On the other side of the wall, Rema froze, stunned by the sight before her. In the middle of the lush, green valley dotted with tall greenwood trees, stood an enormous castle. One side had collapsed in, another section was black as if it had been burned, and another section stood untouched by time. A stream wound its way around the place. Even though she didn't remember having been here before, she felt a connection to the castle, as if it called to her.

Mako came over. "There's a secret entrance. That's how I

escaped with you. I suggest we use it so no one knows we're here." He kept blinking.

She placed her hand on his forearm. "How are you doing?" This place held so many memories for him.

"I'm not going to lie. This will be one of the hardest things I've ever had to do." He stared into the distance, lost in thought.

Darmik approached. "We need to move to the bottom of the hill and hide before someone spots us."

Once they were hidden among the trees below, Rema asked, "Any suggestions on how to proceed?"

"It appears lifeless," Savenek said. "I don't see anything that indicates someone is inside." He kicked the toe of his boot into the moist soil.

She thought so too. Although, if Barjon had the children hidden there, he would make sure they were well concealed.

"A small group should be sent in to investigate," Mako said. "While that's happening, the rest of our army can surround the castle."

"Neco will go in with five men to locate the children," Darmik said.

"I'll show them the entrance," Mako said. "But I don't want to accompany them."

She turned to Darmik. "Are you going?" The idea of him going in there where her family had been murdered filled her with dread.

"I want to, but I need to stay here directing everyone."

Relief washed through her. Mako left to show Neco and his men the entrance to the secret tunnel. Darmik started organizing his soldiers into position. She leaned against a tree trunk, Ellie at her side. The sun rose high in the sky.

"What could possibly be taking so long?" Ellie asked, biting her thumbnail.

"There's a lot to investigate." The castle was huge. She had no idea where Neco would even start looking for the children.

"What's that noise?"

It sounded like horses' hooves. Savenek ran over, grabbing her arm. "People are coming!" He took her and Ellie deeper into the cover of the trees where they stood in silence.

After several minutes, Mako joined them. "A dozen soldiers were spotted riding their horses to the castle. Among them are Barjon and Lennek."

"Are you certain?" Rema asked, stunned. While she'd hoped to find the children here, she hadn't considered the possibility of running into the king and prince.

"Yes," Mako said. "Which can only mean one thing—the children are here."

Everyone looked to her for guidance. "We need to do something about Lennek and Barjon. Now may be our only chance."

"I agree," Mako said.

"Take us to the entrance. We're going in."

"I won't escort a large group inside," he said. "Otherwise Barjon will know we're here."

"Very well," she conceded. "Then take Savenek, Ellie, and me."

Mako led them to an area with several large boulders. Climbing over a group of mossy rocks, she recognized a boulder shaped like a bird—it was almost identical to the one near her home back in Jarko.

"Do you recognize this symbol?" Mako asked. She nodded and headed left, stopping before a cluster of rocks. Mako looked at her with his eyebrows raised.

"There," she said, pointing to an area where the rocks were piled high.

Mako smiled. "Kar taught you well." He went to the side of the mound and moved some vines aside, revealing a narrow entrance to a cave.

She was just about to step into it when Darmik ran up behind her. "Everyone is in position," he said. "They're spread around the castle. Neco found the children in the dungeon. He's going to start bringing them out."

"Barjon and Lennek are here," she said.

His eyes widened, clearly not expecting to run into his father and brother today. "Are you sure? We haven't encountered many soldiers. There's just a few inside with the kids."

"The army has to be nearby," Savenek said. "I bet Barjon and Lennek came here with only a couple of guards so they could keep this place a secret."

"That's plausible," Darmik mumbled. "Very well. Rema, wait out here with Savenek and Ellie. Mako and I will deal with them."

"No," she said, standing tall. "I'm going in." She pointed at the cave. "And the four of you will accompany me. We end this today." She pushed past him and entered. Blackness engulfed her. A dripping sound came from somewhere inside. Her heart pounded. Grabbing her key necklace, she whispered, "Mother, Father, Davan, and Jetan, please watch over me and give me strength. With your help and guidance, I will destroy the man responsible for ruining the kingdom and countless lives."

A hand slid around her arm. "This way," Mako whispered, pulling her forward. "Everyone keep a hand out to the side so you don't run into a wall."

They continued in darkness for a good thirty minutes before Mako stopped. "There are three ways in and out of the castle. I'm trying to decide the best approach."

Rema still couldn't see a single thing and was surprised when Darmik spoke right behind her. "Neco is bringing the children out through the west entrance, near the dungeon. I suggest we avoid that route."

"Good idea," Mako said. "Then we should enter on the east side of the castle."

They traveled in silence for a few more minutes. Mako came to a stop, the hand holding her arm shaking. "I'd always hoped to bring you here one day," he said. "I didn't think it would be under these circumstances." He released her.

She heard what sounded like wood sliding and then pale light illuminated the tunnel. Rema stepped past Mako and entered a small room. A bed was positioned against one wall, a bassinet in the corner, and a worn rug covered the stone floor. Looking closer, she noticed fabric on the floor. It appeared to be a dress—along with bones. She glanced at the bassinet, noticing the rusty brown on the frayed, ivory bedding. Covering her mouth with her hands, tears pooled in her eyes. She was standing in Mako's bedchamber where his wife and baby daughter had been murdered. Darmik, Savenek, and Ellie exited the room and entered the castle's corridor. Mako came to stand next to her.

"I'm so sorry," she said.

"So am I," he murmured before turning and entering the corridor.

She hurried after him. The stone flooring was covered with dried, bloody footprints. Part of the ceiling had collapsed, allowing sunlight to filter through and vines to climb down into the castle.

"This way," Mako whispered. He led them along the corridor. At an intersection, he peered around the corner and waved them forward.

As Rema walked up the steps covered with worn, red carpeting, she clutched the wooden banister, feeling the presence of so many lost. They climbed four flights of stairs and then Mako led them down an empty corridor. A tapestry hung on the wall, faded by time. It depicted a castle shrouded in clouds on a mountaintop —just like the rebel fortress. She reached out and traced the lines of the castle with her fingertip.

"Move it aside," Mako whispered.

She gently pushed the fabric aside, revealing a secret passageway.

Mako stepped inside. Rema followed him into the darkness. A

musty smell engulfed her. Mako counted to thirty and turned left. He counted to fifty and stopped.

"The royal wing is through this door," Mako said. "My guess is that's where Barjon and Lennek are. Ready yourselves. Ellie, I want you guarding this door so no one sneaks up behind us. No matter what happens, do not leave your position. The rest of you are inside with me. I'll count to three and then open the door."

Rema unsheathed her daggers, clasping one in each hand. She was ready to face the man responsible for murdering her family.

"One, two, three." Mako threw open the door and rushed inside.

She squinted against the bright light and hurried after him. Darmik, Savenek, and Mako quickly spread throughout the room. No one was there. Rema glanced around at the three sofas and two chairs. A large, empty fireplace was situated on one wall, several portraits hung on the others. It appeared someone had taken a knife and slashed them to pieces. Her chest tightened in pain. This was the sitting room her parents had used. An overwhelming sense of grief engulfed her.

She crept to the nearest doorway, peering inside. It was the nursery. *Her nursery.* Tears filled her eyes. She moved to the next doorway, but Mako shook his head. Slowly, she inched toward Darmik.

Voices came from the corridor to her right. Glancing that way, she saw four people walking directly toward her. One of them was Lennek. A cruel, vicious smile spread across the prince's face. "It's about time you showed up," he sneered as he stepped into the sitting room.

CHAPTER TWENTY-TWO

Darmik

*D*armik watched his brother saunter into the room, his royal blue cape billowing behind him and his circlet encased with sapphires upon his head. Barjon came in next, followed by the steward Arnek, and the captain of the Third Company.

Lennek chuckled. "I told you, Father, they would try and save the children. Kindhearted fools that they are." He folded his arms, standing before Rema. "I knew they would walk right into my trap."

"It's a good thing the Third Company is nearby," the king said, his eyes focused on Rema, hatred radiating from them.

"Yes," Rema said, squaring her shoulders and standing tall. "It is. I'm sure they're very interested in learning the whereabouts of their children."

Darmik smiled at her ability to see things clearly. "Yes," he added, "my men are escorting the children to their parents as we speak."

Lennek's cheek twitched, indicating he was nervous.

Rema said, "While you thought you'd lure us here to murder us, just like you did my parents and brothers, we thought we'd expose you for the fraud you are. You're under arrest."

Barjon laughed. "I'm under arrest? I beg to differ. You are the one under arrest, you churl." His face turned an angry shade of red.

Mako stepped forward. "I don't think you've been introduced to Her Majesty, Empress Amer Rema of Greenwood Island *and* Emperion."

The color drained from Barjon's face, and his beady eyes narrowed.

"That's right," Darmik said. "You probably haven't heard the news yet. Our dear Rema is the true heir to the Greenwood Island throne and the Emperion throne. She was named empress a month ago. Hamen is dead."

"Brother," Lennek sneered. "You always have to take what's mine." He unsheathed his sword, the sound of steel ringing through the room.

"I can't take something from you when you never had it in the first place," Darmik said calmly. He held the hilt of his sword, ready for his brother to attack.

"I hate you," Lennek said. "You think you'll gain power by supporting this harlot? Well, you won't." He unclasped his cape, tossing it off to the side, out of the way. "I'm going to kill you."

"Your own brother? You despise me so much, you'd kill me?"

"With pleasure." Lennek lifted his sword, holding it before him.

"And you, Father," Darmik said, turning to face Barjon while keeping an eye on his brother. "Why do you hate me? I've always done whatever you asked."

"I hardly think supporting the woman who's trying to overthrow me is doing as I've asked." Barjon removed his sword from its scabbard.

Although he'd always known it would come to this, it still hurt to see his father and brother prepared to fight against him. He'd hoped to arrest them, putting them in prison for the rest of their lives so they could learn the error of their ways. It seemed a just punishment for all they'd done.

"Is it because Mother died in childbirth?" Darmik asked, finally voicing the question he was afraid to ask. "Is that why you can't stand me?"

Barjon's face reddened, and he leaned forward. "You're not even my own flesh and blood," he spat. "When Hamen showed up after you were born, I knew you were his. Your mother didn't die in childbirth—I killed her for being the whore that she was."

It felt as if he'd been thrown from a cliff and was falling through air.

Lennek laughed, lunging at Darmik while he was momentarily distracted by what Barjon had revealed. Darmik swung his arm up and his sword clashed with Lennek's. Barjon thrust his sword toward him, but Mako parried the blow. The captain of the Third Company rushed forward, and Savenek stopped him. Arnek slunk against the wall, attempting to leave the room. He couldn't be allowed to go and get help. Rema stepped in front of Arnek, blocking the steward's path.

Darmik went on the attack, and Lennek met him strike for strike. He sped up his moves, maintaining his offensive position. Lennek still managed to keep up, deflecting his blows. Lennek had drastically improved. But Darmik had never lost to his brother, and he didn't intend to lose now. He swiped his leg out, tripping Lennek, who fell to the floor.

He glanced over to Rema. She swung her daggers at Arnek, causing him to turn and run. She pulled her arm back, flicked her wrist, and released a dagger. It embedded in Arnek's back, the mousy man tumbling forward onto his face.

Lennek stood and swung his sword toward Darmik's chest. Darmik stepped closer to avoid the strike, lifted his elbow, and slammed it into Lennek's ribs. Lennek wrapped his arm around Darmik's neck.

Mako and Barjon fought one another with swords, the clanking ringing out in the room and sparks flying.

Savenek lunged at the captain and swung the blade down, delivering a killing blow.

Mako's sword tumbled to the floor, his eyes widening in shock. Barjon smiled as he lifted his sword, pointing it at Mako's chest. Barjon pulled his arms back to gain momentum. When he thrust the sword forward, about to plunge it into Mako, Mako whipped out the dagger with a silver sun on the hilt. He flung it at Barjon's stomach where it embedded with a sickening squelch. Barjon stumbled as his sword came toward Mako. Mako stepped to the side, the sword missing him. Barjon stumbled forward, collapsing onto the floor. Blood pooled around his body like water.

Darmik faced his brother.

Lennek twisted and grabbed Rema, pulling her against his chest, a small dagger at her throat. "Drop your swords," he demanded. "All of you."

Darmik didn't trust his brother and knew he'd kill Rema the first chance he got. Seeing no other option at this point, Darmik lowered his sword to the floor, near his feet. Savenek followed suit. Mako was already without a weapon, and Ellie remained hidden in the corridor.

Lennek laughed. "You're all idiots, the entire lot of you." His arm tightened around Rema's shoulders and he dug the tip of the dagger into her skin, drawing blood. "I'm going to walk out of here, and no one is going to lay a finger on me. Is that clear?" He started moving toward the door, still facing everyone, dragging Rema along with him. Rema slid her hand down her leg, slipping it into the slit of her pants. Ever so slowly, she pulled out her last knife. Darmik nodded at her—she needed to kill Lennek before he noticed her weapon. Time was of the essence. Darmik's heart pounded as he watched the man he despised holding the woman he loved.

Rema leaned to the side and plunged the knife into Lennek's thigh. When he faltered, she bit his hand and ripped the dagger from him. He screamed. Rema twisted out of his embrace and thrust the dagger into his side, near his stomach. He hunched over, and she ran to Darmik as Lennek sunk to the floor.

Darmik wrapped his arms around her. "It's over," he whispered in her ear. "You did it." He'd never been so proud, or relieved, in his life.

Lennek screamed, pulling the dagger out of his side. With his hands covered in blood, he aimed the weapon at Rema's back and threw it. Darmik shoved her, hoping to move her out of the way, but it was too late. The dagger was aimed right at her torso.

Savenek leapt in front of Rema and the dagger embedded into him. He crashed to the floor.

"No!" Mako dropped to his knees.

Rema rushed over to Savenek, pulling his head onto her lap. With shaking hands, she removed the dagger. Blood trickled from the corner of his mouth.

Darmik grabbed the dagger and stalked toward Lennek, who retreated into the corridor.

"We're still half-brothers," Lennek wheezed.

"No, we're not." Darmik ran at him. He wrapped his arm around Lennek, holding him in place. "Now you'll never hurt anyone ever again." He slid the dagger across Lennek's throat, slicing it open and killing him. He shoved Lennek away from him and he tumbled to the floor, lifeless.

He removed his tunic and ran over to Savenek, pushing the material against his wound in an attempt to stop the profuse bleeding.

"You're going to be all right," Rema said, her eyes filling his tears.

"I . . . I'm dying," he choked out, a gurgling sound coming from his mouth.

Mako leaned down and kissed Savenek's forehead. "I'm honored to have filled the role of your father. You turned out to be a man who I'm proud of in every way." His shoulders shook as he hunched over, crying. "Thank you for being my family."

Rema put an arm around Mako, hugging him.

Savenek reached up, taking hold of Darmik's wrist. "Take . . . care . . . of . . . her."

Darmik nodded. "Thank you for saving Rema. I'll protect her with my life, just like you did."

Savenek's eyes rolled back and he stopped breathing, his hand falling from Darmik's arm.

This man, whom Darmik had started out hating, turned out to be more of a brother than Lennek ever was. And Savenek died with the greatest honor of all—saving someone he loved.

CHAPTER TWENTY-THREE

Rema

*R*ema couldn't believe Savenek lay lifeless before her—that he'd died saving her. She swore to live a life worthy of his sacrifice. Wiping the tears from her eyes, she stood and exited the room. She couldn't talk to Mako or Darmik right now. She needed space. Tracing her hand along the wooden railing, she walked down the corridor and descended four flights of stairs. She went through the crumbled great hall littered with weeds, hanging vines, and bones. The crooked front doors of the castle hung open. She walked out into the bright sunlight.

Neco stood on the steps, surrounded by dozens of haggard looking children. Behind them were hundreds of soldiers dressed in the King's Army uniform. The wind tossed Rema's hair as she stared at everyone before her. The soldiers removed their tunics, tossing them to the ground. Then, silently, they dropped to one knee, bowing their heads.

Darmik stepped next to her, slipping his hand around hers and squeezing it. Then he, Mako, and Ellie joined Neco, kneeling on the ground before her.

The next day, a ceremony was performed honoring Savenek and those killed in the battle. Rema also wanted to use this ceremony to honor those killed seventeen years ago. She'd never had the chance to say goodbye to her mother, father, and brothers. Mako had never had the opportunity to honor his wife and daughter. Rema also needed to thank Kar and Maya. This was for all of them.

Amid the tall greenwood trees just outside the castle, Savenek's body was placed on a large pile of wood. Mako positioned the dagger with a silver sun on the hilt between Savenek's hands. Darmik, Neco, and Ellie stood alongside the pile of wood. Rema and Mako approached the body, and Mako handed her a lit torch. She reached down toward the hay under the wood, lighting it on fire. The flames quickly grew, enveloping the wood and then Savenek's body. She stood back, holding Mako's hand.

"This is for the ones we've lost. May they find eternal peace." Rema closed her eyes. She was grateful for Kar and Maya's love, Savenek's steadfast devotion, her parents and brothers, and the friends here with her today. Reaching up, she touched her key necklace vowing never to forget those who died. She was the true heir and would reign with compassion and love for her people. She would be the greatest empress that ever lived.

She imagined her family watching over her, proud of the woman she'd become.

The following weeks passed in a blur. Notices were sent to the seven governors who all willingly chose to declare their allegiance to Rema. Darmik took full control of the army, ensuring a peaceful transition of power.

Rema chose to stay there at the castle, in her parents' rooms.

Darmik sent word to Trell, letting him know Barjon and Lennek were dead and asking if it was safe for Rema to return to Emperion. Most of the time, Rema was in meetings with governors and members of the army. She had to ensure strong leaders were in place here on the island before she left.

Early one morning, someone knocked on the door to her rooms. "Your Majesty, Mako is here to see you," Ellie said.

Rema glanced out the window; it was still gray outside. "Show him to the sitting room. I'll be there in a moment."

"Will do. And then I'll go and fetch your breakfast," she said with a smile. "That way, I can run into Neco before he heads out for his morning drills." She turned and left, practically skipping out of Rema's bedchamber.

Rema looked at herself in the mirror, imagining her mother doing this very thing seventeen years ago. She heard the deep timbre of Mako's voice. Taking a deep breath, she stood and went to the sitting room.

Mako was leaning against the hearth, his back to her. "Good morning."

He turned and faced her. "I'm sorry to disturb you so early in the morning."

"You may seek me out any time, day or night. What can I do for you?" She sat on the sofa.

"I've considered your offer to join you in Emperion. After much thought on the matter, I have decided to stay here on Greenwood Island." He sat next to her.

She'd figured he would want to stay. However, she felt obligated to at least offer him a position at her side. "Since you plan to remain here, I want to bestow the title of lord upon you and have you serve as the leader of Greenwood Island."

"I would be honored." He angled his body toward hers. "I don't want to sound grim, but we need to talk."

"About what?"

"Your parents were able to save you and preserve the royal line because they had the foresight to plan for an invasion. When you go to Emperion, I want you to take their advice."

Rema wasn't sure what he meant. "You mean to have a plan in case we're invaded?"

"It's more than that. Their ancestors built the rebel fortress decades ago knowing they needed a secret location in case anything ever happened. Only a handful of loyal subjects even knew it existed."

She took hold of her key necklace, fidgeting with it. "So I'm responsible for carrying on the line."

Mako smiled. "Exactly. You must make contingency plans to ensure the survival of your family."

She let go of the key. "I have a question for you. When was this necklace engraved?"

He shook his head. "The last time I saw your mother, she gave it to you. I assume Kar and Maya had the message engraved in case something happened to them before they had a chance to explain your lineage."

They sat in silence for several moments. "I'm sorry about Savenek. He was a good man."

Mako nodded. "He was." He patted her hand. "There has been too much death and destruction. I'm ready for your reign of peace."

One of her attendants cleared her throat. "Your Majesty, Neco is here to see you."

"Please show him in."

Mako stood. "I need to go. Just remember what we talked about."

"I will. Plans will be made to protect the line."

Neco was escorted into the royal sitting room just as Mako exited. "Is there something I can do for you?" Rema asked, curious as to why he'd come to see her so early in the morning.

He stood stiff and tall. "I wish to speak freely with you."

"Of course." Rema motioned to the sofa. "Please have a seat."

He sat and rubbed his face. Pursing his lips, he said, "I wish to marry Ellie."

She'd suspected as much.

"And I would like your consent."

She didn't feel it necessary for him to seek her approval. One of the laws she reinstated was that people could marry the person of their choice—there were no longer any contracts or governor approvals. "You do not need my blessing."

He leaned forward, resting his arms on his knees. "I believe I do," he mumbled. "Ellie is your lady-in-waiting, and I am Darmik's second in command. If you think our relationship would compromise your safety, then you have a right to refuse us."

She stood in front of him. "I am indebted to you. I want nothing more than to see you and Ellie happy." She took hold of his hands. "You're one of the most honorable men I have ever known. I trust, and believe, you will do your job." She wondered if Darmik felt the same way. She would need to speak with him on the matter.

"Thank you." He stood and hugged her.

"Your Majesty," her attendant said. "Darmik is here to see you."

Neco released her. "I'll leave you two alone." He turned and left just as Darmik entered the sitting room.

"You wanted to see me?" he asked.

"Yes." Rema felt silly for summoning him. However, she had been trying to speak privately with him for the past several weeks. It seemed every time they finally had a moment alone, someone interrupted with an urgent matter. She decided the best way to see him would be to summon him in the early morning hours before their work for the day began.

He kissed her cheek. She wanted to throw her arms around him but refrained from doing so. Before she got caught up in his eyes, the way he held her, or kissing him, she needed to tell him about Trell. "There is something you should know."

His eyes quickly scanned her body. "Are you all right?"

"I'm fine."

He wrapped his arms around her, pulling her against his chest.

"I learned something about you in Emperion."

He leaned back, looking at her with his eyebrows drawn together in confusion. "About me?"

"Yes. When I spoke with Hamen, he said that Trell is your grandfather." She waited for his reaction.

"Trell?" He released her and paced about the room. "The emperor . . . I mean, Hamen, told you Trell is my mother's father?"

She quickly explained the conversation she'd heard between Nathenek and Hamen.

He ran his hands through his hair, letting out a sigh. "Barjon would never talk about my mother or her family. Now I realize it's because he murdered her. No wonder Trell hates him so much. But why didn't he ever tell me?"

"You'll have to ask him. Maybe it was the only way he could be around you?"

He scratched his head. "It actually explains a lot, not only about my childhood, but about my father's relationship with Trell." He stopped pacing and came before Rema. "Did he say anything else?"

She remembered Hamen's sickly daughter, whom she'd exiled along with Hamen's wife. "You have a half-sister."

Darmik leaned his forehead against hers. "I think I've had enough half-siblings to last a lifetime. Are you sure you still want to marry me? I mean, I don't come from the best lineage."

"It doesn't matter who your parents are. What matters is who you are. And I love you."

He leaned down, and they kissed.

"Your Majesty," the attendant said. "There are two guests who seek an audience with you. Mako said they should be admitted directly."

Holding Darmik's hand, Rema instructed her attendant to escort the visitors in.

She heard them before she saw them.

"See, I told you," Audek said, "now that she's the all-mighty empress, we're horse hay."

"Will you please stop talking," Vesha responded.

"May I present Audek and Vesha," the attendant said.

Rema ran over and hugged her friends. She hadn't expected to see either of them. "Look at you!" she said to Audek. He was standing and walking on his own, although he was hunched over a little bit.

"As soon as he was well enough to travel, we began the journey here," Vesha said.

"I assume you've heard the news," Darmik said.

"We have," Audek muttered, blinking several times. "Savenek was a good man."

Vesha's eyes filled with tears and she looked away.

Ellie burst into the room, breathing heavily. "You won't believe who's here." She bent over, catching her breath. "Trell and Nathenek just arrived. Apparently, it's time for your coronation and wedding."

Rema clutched Mako's arm as he escorted her down the long aisle leading to the dais. On the dais were two throne chairs—the very ones on which her parents sat while presiding over court. Even though the castle was still being renovated, it seemed only fitting that her coronation and marriage take place here, where her family had lived.

In the front row on the left side, Ellie and Neco stood holding hands, Vesha and Audek next to them. Behind her friends were the governors, hundreds of commoners, and dozens of soldiers. In the front row on the right side, stood Nathenek and Trell. Behind them were hundreds of Emperions. At the end of the aisle, Darmik stood waiting for her. His eyes shone with love and admiration as she walked toward him. When she reached the dais, she turned and faced everyone.

"Welcome citizens of Emperion and Greenwood Island," Mako said. He stood before her holding her ruby ring. "I, Mako, Commander of King Revan's Army, do hereby grant and name Queen Amer Rema as Empress Amer Rema of Greenwood Island and Emperion, sole surviving heir of the royal family, to hereby lead, rule, and govern our great empire." He slid the ring on her finger.

Trell stepped forward carrying the items of regalia. He knelt before Rema, handing them to her. She took the ceremonial mace and family sword, holding them for all to see. Trell stood and returned to his spot.

Clutching the items, she faced Mako. He now held a red velvet pillow with her mother's crown sitting atop it, along with her key necklace. He lifted the crown and placed it on her head. Then he took the necklace and clasped it around her neck. Kneeling before her, he set his sword on the floor by her feet. "I, Commander Mako, do hereby pledge my life to you." He stood and sheathed his sword. "I give you Her Majesty, Empress Amer Rema!"

She stood tall as everyone in the throne room dropped to one knee, bowing their heads. "Rise," she commanded her subjects.

Mako took the items of regalia from her and set them aside. Darmik stepped forward, kneeling before Mako. Mako unsheathed his sword, placing the tip on Darmik's right shoulder. "I tap thee once, in the name of the empress, our protector. You have willingly and bravely come to this place today, hereby declaring that you are worthy to take Empress Amer Rema's hand in the marriage binding. Is this so?"

"Yes, My Lord."

"You may rise." Mako turned toward the crowd. "Citizens! We

are gathered here today to witness this man and this woman in a binding of life."

Rema and Darmik joined hands, facing one another.

"Commander Darmik, will you have this woman to be thy wedded wife? To love her, comfort her, honor and cherish her, in sickness and in health? Forsaking all others, keeping thee only unto her, so long as you both shall live?"

"I will."

"Empress Amer Rema, will you have this man to be thy wedded husband? Will you love, honor, and cherish him, forsaking all others, so long as you both shall live?"

"I will."

Mako handed each of them a solid gold ring. Darmik slid his onto Rema's finger, and she slid hers onto his.

"These rings symbolize your never-ending love for one another. May you be faithful to one another, live and grow old together, and may you be blessed with many children."

Darmik leaned forward and gently kissed Rema's lips. Warmth seeped through her body as she kissed him back. "Tonight," he whispered, sending shivers down her spine.

Cheers erupted as the happy couple faced the crowd. They smiled, joined hands, and walked down the aisle, exiting the throne room. Rema pulled him in to a hidden alcove where they embraced.

"Thank you," she murmured against his chest.

Darmik chuckled. "You're thanking me? For marrying you?"

"And saving me. Multiple times. We're going to make a great team."

"Yes, we are." He leaned down and kissed her. "We need to make an appearance at the celebration before people wonder where we are."

She took his hand and they went into the main hall where the celebration was in full swing. Food was served to everyone in attendance. For those unable to come, Rema insisted food be distributed to as many people as possible throughout Greenwood Island.

Thousands came to the castle to honor her—now that travel was no longer forbidden and people could move freely about the island.

After a week of celebrations, Rema and Darmik boarded an Emperion warship, ready for the journey ahead of them. They were accompanied by Trell, Nathenek, Neco, Ellie, Audek, Vesha, and hundreds of loyal soldiers.

The sails went up and the ship slowly moved away from the dock. In the distance, the sun was rising over the horizon, casting a warm light over them.

Although Rema was sad to leave Greenwood Island, she was eager to return to Emperion and face the challenges ahead—because where one story ends, another one was only beginning.

EPILOGUE

The nurse handed the baby boy to Rema. "I don't understand," she said, taking the baby in her arms. "I had twins?"

Darmik sat on the edge of the bed beside her, holding their daughter. "Can you believe it? A girl and a boy. We're truly blessed."

"You say that now, but can you imagine all the mischief they'll get into when they're older?" Rema glanced at the precious boy in her arms. "What should we name them?"

"How about we name the girl after my mother, Allyssa," Darmik suggested.

"And the boy?"

"I'm sorry to interrupt," the nurse said, "but I must inform Trell of the situation. He wants to make an announcement to the city."

Rema glanced at Darmik's beautiful brown eyes. "Tell Trell that the Crown Princess Allyssa is doing well. Her brother, Prince Savenek, is equally healthy."

The nurse bowed and left.

"Savenek?" Darmik questioned her. She nodded. He looked at the baby boy snuggly wrapped in her arms. "Savenek it is."

The End

REIGN OF SECRETS

Want more political intrigue? Read the spin-off series, Reign of Secrets, and find out what happens twenty years after *War*. Turn the page for a sneak peek of . . .

Sixteen-year-old Allyssa appears to be the ideal princess of Emperion—she's beautiful, elegant, and refined. She spends her days locked in a suffocating cage, otherwise known as the royal court. But at night, Allyssa uses her secret persona—that of a vigilante—to hunt down criminals and help her people firsthand.

Unfortunately, her nightly escapades will have to wait because the citizens of Emperion may need saving from something much bigger than common criminals. War is encroaching on their kingdom and in order to protect her people, Allyssa may have to sacrifice her heart. Forced to entertain an alliance through marriage with a handsome prince from a neighboring kingdom, she finds herself feeling even more stifled than before. To make matters worse, the prince has stuck his nosy squire, Jarvik, to watch her every move.

Jarvik is infuriating, bossy and unfortunately, the only person she can turn to when she unveils a heinous plot. Together, the unlikely pair will have to work together to stop an enemy that everyone thought was long gone, one with the power to destroy her family and the people of Emperion. Now the cage Allyssa so longed to break free from might just be the one thing she has to fight to keep intact. In order to save her kingdom, she will have to sacrifice her freedom, her heart, and maybe even her life.

CHAPTER ONE

*R*unning along the edge of the rooftop, Allyssa kept an eye on the man below. He was three blocks ahead of her as he sprinted down the street, clutching a bag of coins. Allyssa jumped the two-foot gap to the adjacent rooftop, not wanting to lose sight of the thief. He slowed and turned a corner into an alleyway. With any luck, he'd hide there and she could catch him by surprise.

Allyssa couldn't believe she was the one running on rooftops after him. Grevik had insisted only she could do such a thing because she was smaller, lighter, and more agile. She suspected her friend was just too much of a pansy to do it himself.

There was one more building to go. Unfortunately, the next one was much further away. If she had to guess, it was a good eight to ten feet. Keeping her breathing steady, she steeled her resolve and ran a bit quicker. She pumped her legs faster and faster, the edge of the rooftop rapidly approaching. Twenty feet to go. Why did she agree to this? *Focus,* she scolded herself. Now was not the time to think about it. Ten feet to go.

Her right boot hit the edge of the roof. Using all her strength, she pushed off, flying through the moonlit night. Her arms waved and her legs ran on air as she hurtled toward the adjacent rooftop, landing with a jolt. Starting to fall forward, she tucked her head, rolled onto her back, and somersaulted. Crouching low, her heart beat frantically. *Blimey.* A smile burst on her face. That was fun. Not that she was about to do it again, though.

Jumping to her feet, she glanced over the edge of the two-story building, searching for the thief. Sure enough, he was right below, hiding in the alley. Allyssa pulled out a dagger and slid onto her stomach. Peering over the side, she carefully aimed her weapon at him. As long as the thief stood still, striking him would be relatively simple. She counted to three and threw her dagger, watching it zoom down thirty feet and whack the man dead center in his right shoulder. He screamed, dropping the bag of coins as he looked frantically about for his attacker. The hilt was facing straight up and hopefully wouldn't give away her position.

If only Grevik would hurry and catch up. Shortly after they had started pursuing the thief, a rowdy crowd of about twenty men spilled out from a tavern, blocking the street as a fight broke out. Since Allyssa and Grevik didn't want to lose the thief, he told her to climb the building so she could follow him. She hoped Grevik had made it through the crowd without incident.

Standing, she scanned the adjacent streets, not finding her friend anywhere in sight. The thief still stood in the alleyway, not making an attempt to run. It was up to her then. She climbed down the ladder attached to the side of the building. Taking a deep breath, she stalked around the corner.

The man stood in the middle of the dark alley, clutching his shoulder. "Stay back or I'll gut you!" he screamed.

"Funny coming from an injured lowlife who steals," she answered, trying to use a deep voice.

The man laughed. "Go back home where you belong, little girl," he said, shaking his head.

"That's no way to speak to someone who's about to wallop you." She plucked her knives free and held them low. "Now give me the bag of coins you stole from the baker and maybe, just maybe, I won't kill you."

The man yanked the dagger out of his shoulder, stifling a scream. When his head tilted up, his eyes gleamed with malice. Based upon the way he held his body, prepared to fight, he had to have some skill. Nothing she couldn't handle, though. Not wanting to risk the weapon cutting her, she threw her knife at the dagger he held, hitting it hard enough that he dropped it, the metal clanging on the stone street.

"What are you waiting for? Scared?" the man taunted.

Allyssa meandered toward him as she tossed her cape behind her shoulders, freeing her arms and legs. "Yes," she whispered when she was only three feet away. "I am scared. Scared I'll kill you when you really deserve to be rotting in a jail cell." And with that, she spun and kicked his head, sending him to the ground. Much faster than she expected, he sprang to his feet and swung his fist at her. She stepped out of the way and was about to hit him when he punched her cheek. Stars exploded across her vision. *Blasted.* That would leave a mark.

"You did not just hit me," Allyssa said, seething with rage.

The man had the audacity to laugh at her. She flung her last knife into his thigh. He screamed. *Wimp.* Using a front kick, she struck his chest and he went flying to the ground. Just for good measure, and because he'd hit her face of all places, she went over and kicked his groin. He had the decency to curl into a ball and surrender.

A man ran into the alley behind her. She spun around and came face to face with her friend, Grevik. "It's about time you showed up." She smiled sweetly at him. "You missed all the fun."

He went over to the man lying on the ground, making sure he was knocked out cold. "While you were jumping over rooftops like a gazelle, I was stuck in that brawl outside the Snakeskin Tavern." He stood and turned to face her. "I can't believe you took this man on without me, Lilly."

The first time she met Grevik all those years ago, she'd told him her name was Lilly so he wouldn't suspect her true identity.

"I couldn't wait for you," she said with a shrug. Now that she could see Grevik in the moonlight, she noticed his knuckles were cut and bleeding. "Are you all right?" she asked, pointing to his hands, hoping he hadn't broken a bone.

He nodded. "It was easier to punch a few of the drunks to make my way through the brawl." Grevik scanned the rooftop. "I guess we can add jumping buildings to your ever-growing list of skills."

"It was bloody fun," she said, unable to suppress her smile.

Grevik shook his head. "You're unbelievable. Only you would think leaping through the air thirty feet off the ground over alleys is fun."

"You told me to do it so we wouldn't lose the thief." She picked up her knives and sheathed them.

"Blame it on me," he teased, wrapping his arm around her shoulder, tugging her closer to him. Allyssa stiffened before forcing herself to relax. This was the sort of thing friends did. "Come on," he said. "We need to drop this bloke off to my contact in the City Guard so I can go home. It's later than usual, and I don't want Mum to wake up and find me gone."

"I need to go home, too," Allyssa said. If she didn't arrive before daylight, she would be in severe trouble.

"Wake up," Mayra hissed. "Your mother is on her way. She'll be here any minute."

Allyssa groaned and snuggled further under the warm blankets. It was too early. She wasn't ready to wake up and face the day. Her body ached from running on the rooftops and fighting a grown man last night. Just a few more hours—that was all she needed. Mayra yanked the blankets off her. "You are cruel!"

Allyssa chided her friend. Grabbing her pillow, she smothered it over her face, shielding out the bright light.

"Didn't you hear me?" Mayra tried again. "Your mother will be here in less than five minutes. It is already mid-morning. If she arrives and finds you in bed, you know what will happen."

Mayra was right. Allyssa needed to climb out of bed and dress before her mother arrived. Otherwise, she'd never hear the end of it. She threw the pillow off her face and stretched.

Mayra's eyes widened at the sight of her, and she gasped. "What happened?"

"I'm tired is all." Allyssa yawned and sat up. "I want an easy dress to put on without a lot of frills."

Mayra shook her head, her eyes wide with horror.

"What is it?" Allyssa asked as she slid off the bed and moved to the tall mirror in the corner of her room. She expected to see a tired face looking back at her. Capturing thieves was no easy task. Staring at herself in the mirror, she hissed. "That son of a harlot!" she cursed. The entire side of her face was a deep, raging purple, the color of eggplant. She growled. She'd forgotten the thief had hit her last night.

"I'll get the dusting powder," Mayra said, running to the dresser. "Madelin," she called over her shoulder. "Find something purple for Allyssa to wear."

There was no way they were going to be able to hide this before her mother arrived. *Blimey.* Rushing into her dressing closet, she ran her hands over her long, brown hair, trying to tame it. She could feign an illness, but then she'd have to stay in bed all day with people fussing about her. The mere thought made her want to vomit.

Madelin plucked lavender fabric off a hanger and shoved it at her. Allyssa grabbed the material and yanked it over her head, shimmying into the outfit. Mayra rushed in, carrying the tray of powder. As Madelin cinched up the back of the dress, Mayra dusted Allyssa's face, trying to hide the nasty bruise.

Mayra shook her head. "If you had come to me right when this happened, I could have made a paste of herbs to lessen the swelling." She dabbed her brush into more powder and applied a thick second coat.

A knock resounded through her bedchamber. Her mother was there. Allyssa's hair wasn't even done.

"Keep your head slightly forward," Mayra instructed. "Try to hide the side of your face with your hair."

Allyssa nodded, looking at herself in the mirror. Even with the powder on, her face had a hint of purple to it. The sleeves and skirt of her lavender dress were adorned with thousands of small beads. With the color of the fabric and the shiny beading, it merely seemed as if the dress were reflecting on her face. *Brilliant.* She hugged Mayra and Madelin. "Thank you."

"No need to fuss," Madelin said, hugging her back.

"Now hurry," Mayra added, giving her a small shove. "It's not wise to keep your mother waiting."

Allyssa exited the dressing closet and entered the sitting area of her bedchamber. "Hello, Mother," she said, trying to keep her head angled so her hair covered her bruise.

Mayra and Madelin came up behind her. "Your Majesty," they said in unison, bowing before the empress.

Empress Rema quickly dismissed the royal guards and Allyssa's ladies-in-waiting. Once the door closed and they were alone, Rema's eyes narrowed. "Did you just awaken?" she asked, a hint of disbelief coloring her voice.

"No," Allyssa lied. "Why do you ask?" She prayed her mother didn't notice the bruise.

"I haven't seen you today. And you seem a bit...thrown together. Are you feeling all right?" Rema came over, gently clutching her daughter's arms as her eyes roamed over her body, inspecting her for some sign of distress or illness.

Allyssa stood there, knowing her mother was only concerned for her well-being. Since her twin brother died shortly after birth, and Rema hadn't been able to conceive another child, Allyssa was all she had. If her mother wanted to fuss, the least she could do was let her. She smiled, trying to reassure her, but had to stifle a yelp since her face was sore from being punched. "Yes, Mother. I'm all right," she forced herself to say, trying not to wince from the pain.

There was no way Allyssa could tell Rema that she snuck out of the castle at night to aid the City Guards in tracking down criminals. The empress would never understand or allow it, especially since Allyssa was the crown princess and the only heir to Emperion.

"Very well," Rema said, releasing her daughter. "I've come to tell you that a small ball will be thrown in honor of Prince Zek of Fia tonight." She moved to the window, gazing outside.

Allyssa wondered if the boring prince from the tiny kingdom of Fia was ever going home. He'd already been there a fortnight, and she'd been forced to sit alongside him at supper on more than one occasion. She couldn't take much more of his idle chatter.

"He's requested an audience with us tomorrow," her mother continued. "You will be there when he speaks."

Allyssa stood in front of the hearth, allowing the fire to warm her. She suspected Prince Zek would ask for her hand in marriage at the meeting. Although her parents had insisted she be present when such declarations were made, they hadn't pushed her into marrying. Yet.

So far, all the princes or high-ranking nobles who came hadn't interested her. Rema and Darmik told the gentlemen that their daughter was simply too young and in no hurry to marry. But she could only put off the inevitable for so long. She dreaded the day when she would have to choose who would live in this cage with her, who would rule by her side, and who would be her companion for life. Granted, it had worked out for her parents, but their story was far from usual. They were the lucky ones. Rema and Darmik had managed to choose each other and weren't forced into an awkward arranged marriage.

"Care to join me in the Throne Room for the weekly proceedings?" Rema gently asked as she turned to face her daughter with sympathy in her eyes.

Allyssa most certainly did not want to join her mother in that stifling place. However, she knew it really wasn't a question. "Of course."

Rema smiled and came over to her, linking their arms together as they exited the room. "Want to go riding with me later today?" she asked, kissing the top of Allyssa's head.

"I would love to," she answered. Riding with her mother was one of her favorite things to do. "But I'm going to have to decline. I'll need the time to prepare for the ball." In reality, she needed to rest. Her muscles were sore, and there was no way she could mount a horse—not after the events of last night.

"I understand," Rema said, patting her daughter's hand.

"Tomorrow?" Allyssa suggested, hoping she'd feel better by then.

"I look forward to it." The empress led them out of the Royal Chambers and to the corridor where their royal guards surrounded them.

"I forgot to tell you that the Legion of Emperion was thoroughly impressed with your handling of the meeting yesterday," Rema said, her eyes flickering with amusement.

Allyssa had to stifle her laugh. The Legion was made up of elderly gentleman. Her mother had told her to make sure she smiled but maintained control at all times by not letting anyone speak over her.

"Your father and I had a bet," Rema whispered. "He thought you'd lose your temper and yell at the lot of them."

Allyssa snorted. "And you didn't?" she asked, surprised.

"That's not to say I don't think you'll lose it in the future, but I knew you'd be able to remain composed the first time."

Allyssa laughed.

"Thanks to you, I won a new horse." Rema smiled.

"You bet a horse?"

"You know your father," Rema mused. "He jumped at the chance to acquire a new stallion. Too bad he lost."

Sitting in the Throne Room for hours, listening to the representatives from each of the five regions in Emperion drone on and on about the state of their land, nearly drove Allyssa to tears with boredom. She didn't know how her mother and father sat there listening to this once a week.

At least when she snuck out with Grevik, she was making changes for the better by helping citizens and ensuring criminals were put in jail. It felt like everyone who came to see the empress and emperor wanted or needed something from them. It was utterly exhausting, yet Rema managed to sit there with a kind smile, listening. Allyssa's father, Darmik, at least appeared a little antsy. He preferred managing the army to politics.

When it was finally over hours later, the royal family stood and strode down the aisle. Allyssa mimicked her mother and smiled at the representatives, who all bowed. The second she exited the room, she moaned.

Her father's eyes sliced over to her. "There are still courtiers lurking in the hallways," he mumbled so only she could hear. "Behave."

She rounded her shoulders and plastered the never-ending smile back on her face. "Of course," she said. "Forgive me."

He raised an eyebrow.

"I'm going riding," Rema announced. "I have a new horse I need to become acquainted with."

Allyssa knew her mother needed to break free from this place on occasion as well.

"I'll accompany you," Darmik said, taking his wife's arm and escorting her down the hallway.

Sighing, Allyssa headed toward the Royal Chambers, wanting nothing more than to crawl in bed for a few hours. She needed to have enough energy to not only make it through the ridiculous ball tonight, but also to meet Grevik afterwards. If she didn't have the chance to leave the castle for a bit, she'd go stark raving mad.

Marek, the head of her personal guard, stepped next to her. He wore his light armor with his gleaming sword strapped to his waist. "Care to spar for an hour before you dress for the ball?" he asked.

She fought a smile. He knew she loved to fight. After all, they'd grown up together sparring, especially since his father and hers were best friends. As tempting as his offer was, her body couldn't withstand the physical exertion right now.

"Are you sure you're ready for me to beat you again?" she teased.

He chuckled. "I let you win."

"As much as I would enjoy the opportunity to trounce you, I have too many things to do before the ball this evening," she said. "However, I do believe I will have some free time tomorrow?"

"I look forward to proving you wrong. Again," Marek said, smiling at her.

The head of her guard was rather handsome, she supposed. She'd grown up with him and his younger sister Mayra. Both of them had dark hair and eyes. Mayra was small and slim like her mother Ellie, whereas Marek was tall and lean just like his father Neco.

When Allyssa caught sight of a group of courtiers up ahead, she stiffened. She hoped the powder still concealed the nasty bruise on her cheek. Marek hadn't said anything to her about it, but then again, he knew better. Holding her chin high, she glided down the corridor. The pristine leaded glass windows allowed the sun to shine brightly through. As she approached the group, everyone bowed. Allyssa kindly smiled at her subjects. She was the heir to the throne, and they were supposedly beneath her. Yet...yet...she felt like a child playing at a game she knew nothing about. These people had been navigating court for years. They each had an agenda, wanted or needed something, and they were all here for a reason.

Allyssa kept walking, not wanting to give them the opportunity to talk to her. When she rounded the corner, she finally relaxed her shoulders.

A ball was nothing unusual since several were held each season. Rema insisted it was good policy to please the nobility. Allyssa had grown up attending these functions. At first, she'd been bedazzled by the glittering chandeliers, the fine clothing, and the ornate flowers. But after attending so many balls, they began to lose their appeal. However, at every single one, she made sure no one knew how she really felt. She smiled at, danced with, and listened to her subjects. Her parents had groomed her well.

Her father took her hand, leading her to the dais at the front of the room. That was when she caught sight of the decorations. "Are the flowers from the main courtyard?" she asked, stifling a laugh.

"I believe so. We didn't have time to have them brought in."

"Hopefully, no one will notice. We wouldn't want to offend the prince from Fia," she sardonically replied.

Darmik patted her hand. "Care to tell me what happened to your face?" he asked under his breath. Without a pause, he expertly led her through the throng of people who parted and bowed as they passed by.

Of course he'd notice. "It's silly," she replied, keeping a smile on her face. "An accident."

"Really?" he said, playfully pinching her arm. He knew she was lying. Being Commander for the army had taught him to notice such details and had made him far too observant.

"I assure you, it's nothing." She smiled at him. If she didn't convince her father, he'd send one of her guards to stand inside her bedchamber to watch her at all times. As it was now, having four guards posted outside was more than enough. Having someone actually inside her room would be beyond stifling. "It's embarrassing," she muttered.

"Sparring with Marek?" he asked, amused.

She allowed her face to redden, as if ashamed. Darmik chuckled, and Allyssa let him believe the lie. With any luck, he wouldn't question Marek about it. "Please, let it go," she begged.

Her father patted her hand again when they reached the dais. Allyssa stood at the front of the room while he left to escort Rema inside. When her parents made their entrance, the room went utterly silent. Everyone loved the empress. She had ascended to the throne at the age of eighteen and managed to take a kingdom devoted to war and turn it into the most prosperous and peaceful kingdom on the continent.

Allyssa hoped she could be half the ruler her mother was.

She peered down at her red gown. Rema had insisted she wear red—the color of Emperion. She didn't mind, actually. It set off her long, chestnut hair and blue eyes, which almost made her look pretty. Almost. She'd never be beautiful like her mother, though.

After her parents joined her on the dais, Prince Zek from Fia was announced. He was too tall and skinny for her liking. His face was pleasant enough—light brown hair with soft brown eyes. The prince bowed before her and asked for the first dance, as was custom. Of course, she smiled and obliged. His sweaty hand took hers, and they danced.

Surprisingly, he was a good dancer. The problem came when the prince opened his mouth. He never had anything interesting to say—he always discussed his kingdom's spice trade, or the weather, or the fact that he was in line to inherit the throne of Fia.

Thankfully, the song ended and a noble courtier immediately swept in and asked for a turn. She danced for about an hour with various partners, each conversing about his land, wealth, and what he could offer the crown. Once she'd had enough, she claimed she needed to rest. Allyssa slipped out the side door, hoping no one noticed.

Marek came up behind her. "Already retiring for the night?"

"Yes," she said, faking a yawn. "I'm exhausted."

He silently escorted her to the royal wing where Mayra and Madelin were dutifully waiting in her bedchamber.

"Did you even dance?" Madelin asked.

"Of course I did," Allyssa replied.

"If I were you," Madelin continued, "I'd dance with every available man." She spun around the room, dancing with an invisible partner.

Mayra shook her head. "It's a good thing she's not you, then. She's a princess, not a barmaid."

Madelin stopped in front of Mayra, placing her hands on her hips. "Excuse me?"

"Girls," Allyssa said, exasperated. She needed to hurry up or she would be late. "My gown."

Both immediately came over and helped her remove the dress. After Allyssa was in her nightclothes, her ladies-in-waiting left. Knowing her guards stood watch just outside her door, she quietly changed, pulling on wool pants and a tunic.

Grabbing her cape, she tied it on, making sure the hood concealed her hair and face. Satisfied with her disguise, she opened the laundry chute and climbed in. After closing the small, wooden door behind her, she slid down in complete darkness, landing in a pile of clothes and bed linens at the bottom. Carefully peering around, she made sure no one was about at this late hour. Certain it was clear, she climbed out and hurried from the room. Allyssa exited the castle via the servants' entrance.

She was free. Finally free.

ACKNOWLEDGMENTS

I want to thank my husband for putting up with me. Writing, editing, and publishing a book in a few short months is no easy undertaking. Thank you for watching the kids, running them to their activities, and taking care of everything so I could complete this book. I love you and cherish the support you give me.

Some very special people gave valuable feedback that helped shape War into what it is today. Thank you Elizabeth, Angelle, Stacie, Rebecca, Jan, Hope, and Jen. You girls are amazing and I'm honored to have your help and support. Thank you to my proofreaders Carol, Hannah, and Leah.

There are two talented people who read through the manuscript numerous times: Debi and Allyssa. I couldn't have written this book without the two of you. Not only did you offer insightful feedback, but you kept me going when I was exhausted and didn't think I'd ever finish. You put a smile on my face and remind me why I write. Your enthusiasm means the world to me.

I'd also like to thank Ashley Uribe at East West MMA for answering all of my silly questions and teaching me fighting maneuvers and techniques.

Thank you Kim and KimG-Design for the fantastic cover! You

did an amazing job capturing the essence of the book. You are a gifted artist.

Last, but not least, thank you for taking the time to read this series. Thank you for entering the worlds I create and falling in love with my characters. Your support and encouragement exceed my wildest dreams.

Jennifer Anne Davis graduated from the University of San Diego with a degree in English and a teaching credential. She is currently a full-time writer and mother of three highly energetic children. Her days are spent living in imaginary worlds and fueling her own kids' creativity.

She is the recipient of the San Diego Book Awards Best Published Young Adult Novel (2013), a finalist in the Next Generation Indie Book Awards (2014), and a finalist in the USA Best Book Awards (2014).

Visit Jennifer online at:
www.JenniferAnneDavis.com